LOVE IN THE WAGER

Also by Kasey Stockton

Women of Worth Series

Love for the Spinster

Love at the House Party

Love in the Wager

Love in the Ballroom

Ladies of Devon Series

The Jewels of Halstead Manor

The Lady of Larkspur Vale

The Widow of Falbrooke Court

The Recluse of Wolfeton House

The Smuggler of Camden Court

Stand Alone Regency Romance

His Amiable Bride

A Duke for Lady Eve

All is Mary and Bright

A Forgiving Heart

An Agreeable Alliance

Scottish Historical Romance

Journey to Bongary Spring

Through the Fairy Tree

Love in the Wager

WOMEN OF *Worth* BOOK FOUR

Kasey Stockton

GOLDEN OWL PRESS

This is a work of fiction. Names, characters, places, and incidents either are the product of the author's imagination or are used fictitiously. Any resemblance to actual persons, living or dead, events, or locales is entirely coincidental.

Copyright © 2019 by Kasey Stockton
Cover design by Once Upon a Cover

First print edition: August 2019
All rights reserved. No part of this book may be reproduced or used in any manner without written permission of the copyright owner except for the use of quotations for the purpose of a book review.

For my mom, the ultimate example of selflessness.

PROLOGUE

Edward

"Mr. Thornton, you've received a letter."

Sighing, I slapped the cards on the playing table, turning frustrated eyes on my butler, Melville. Could he not see that I was in the middle of an important game? One more hand in my favor and I would win enough to pay off my vowels to Mr. James. I took the letter, requesting Melville to bring more ale.

"My apologies," I said to Mr. James, flipping the letter to see who it was from. Lord Stallsbury. I could get to it later. I tossed it aside and turned my attention to the man across from me.

His eyes were sharp for a man so old, noteworthy when considering how much he'd had to drink that evening.

Melville returned with the requested ale and we waited for him to leave before playing once more. I filled my glass, downing half the contents quickly. We flipped our cards and the drink sank to the bottom of my stomach, souring. I clamped my mouth shut. How would I recover from this?

"One more game?" I asked, hoping to sound nonchalant.

Mr. James scoffed, tossing his cards to the table. "You've nothing left to wager, boy."

My eyes immediately sought the painting hanging on the opposite wall, over the older man's white head of hair. My country house, Thornville Place. My sister would be livid. But what else could I do? We couldn't very well pay all of my debts with the sale of the house anyway.

Either way, we were sunk.

"Perhaps I do."

I'd grabbed his attention. He glanced at me under bushy white eyebrows, his side whiskers twitching while he chewed on his cheek. "What is it?"

"Thornville."

He stilled, and I tried not to show my nerves.

"You serious, Thornton?"

I nodded.

"What's the wager?" he asked.

"The house, for all of my debts."

"Deal."

I shook my head. "*All* of my debts, James. If I win, you pay off everything. If you win, you get my house."

The older man tried to contain his smile and I knew I had him.

"Deal," he said, this time with more pleasure.

A warning rang through my body, but I paid it no heed. The ale had done nothing to blur my sensibilities, for I had drank a tenth of what I'd poured this evening for my friend. I could not find my practices unethical, for they were no worse than what I'd find in any gaming house in all of London.

The cards were shuffled and dealt, and there was a nervous energy about us as we played. My hopes rose with each new card and I found my heart beating in rapid succession in my chest. I'd dug this hole myself, but I was about to get Sarah and I out of this mess once and for all. It was time to quit the cards and focus on rebuilding my estate. Once my debts were paid, that is.

I watched James check his cards, a slight twitch to his mouth that I'd come to learn was his tell. I froze, unsure if he was eager or displeased by what he'd drawn. Swallowing, I laid my cards face up, my breath shallow and infused with equal parts fear and excitement.

James locked eyes with me, the whites of his own wide and energized. "Your life is about to change, Thornton."

He laid his cards and my world spun.

That was certainly an understatement. I let out a breath and closed my eyes. It was a done deal now, and there was no turning back.

"When shall I move in?" he questioned, sweeping the cards from the table and gathering them into a pile. Leaning back in his chair, he eyed me greedily and I itched to strike him with my clenched fist. But alas, it was not James's fault I had so stupidly wagered my home.

Thornville had been in my family for three hundred years. There was likely a line of Thornton ghosts surrounding our table and shaking their fists at me. 'Twas a good thing I could not see my ancestors.

"I must remove the heirlooms first, of course," I said. "But I can arrange to do so forthwith. It will not take long to vacate the grounds."

James nodded slowly, his hands coming to rest over his ample belly. He watched me intently and my skin crawled. He was plainly cooking something up in his mind, and I didn't think it was going to be good.

"Unless…"

I did not pay heed to the hope that rose within my chest. I

picked up my glass and took a sip as though whatever he was about to propose was of little consequence to me.

"Unless," he said again, "you would like to strike a deal?"

I lowered my glass, careful to guard my expression. "I'm listening."

"You've met my daughter, Lydia?"

I searched my brain for the face of Lydia James. She had been present at a ball recently and we'd been introduced—I was *fairly* positive for the name was quite familiar—but I couldn't bring a face to mind.

Nodding, I said, "We've been introduced."

James did not move, but smiled. "Yes, I recall. She is a meek little thing who cares more for her books than her own father. She wouldn't make any trouble. In fact, I think she would make a thoroughly respectable wife to any man. Quiet and obedient, what more could you want?"

My eyebrows screwed together. I'd lost control over my features, but I could not follow his line of thought. "What are you suggesting, sir?"

"Do you want your house back?"

Would agreeing be a violation of my pride? Of course I wanted my house back. I simply stared at him, waiting for him to continue.

"Well," James said calmly. "You can have it back—and I will relieve your debts to me—if you but marry my daughter."

I held my breath, watching the older man's side whiskers quivering as he waited. I'd gambled more than my share during my life, but never before had the stakes been so high. A woman's life, surrendered to me in exchange for a house?

But to be free of the debts I owed Mr. James, to be given the chance to restore my ancestral estate and perhaps have a new beginning?

The temptation was strong, drawing me in with the appeal of a second chance.

But, the woman.

I could not even recall what she looked like. I had met her recently, so if she was horse faced or covered in warts, surely I would remember. Though, in exchange for my house and relief of some of my debts, it was an enticing prospect regardless of her appearance.

"I will pay *all* of your debts," Mr. James said. Had I waited too long to speak? He appeared eager now. The cards were on my side.

Clearing my throat, I said, "*All* of my debts? My debts are numerous."

"And my fortune is sufficient. I will pay off all of your debts and you can keep your house if you will agree to marry my daughter."

What choice did I have? Marriage to Miss James, regardless of her appearance or demeanor, was worth what this man offered me. I was a weak man, a gambler, but I was willing to give it all up for the chance to redeem myself.

For my family and their future—for my sister, Sarah—I would sacrifice.

"Very well, Mr. James," I said. "You have yourself a deal."

CHAPTER 1
LYDIA

I checked my basket, but the books were hidden well and I was fairly positive Father would not request to look through it, anyway. Light poured through the windows of the breakfast room, bathing my aging father in an ethereal light and highlighting his wrinkled face.

"Did you have a pleasant evening?" I asked, swinging the basket beside my leg as I waited for Father to finish chewing his toasted bread. He picked up the goblet beside his breakfast plate and gulped his wine, before setting it back on the table with a loud thunk.

"I had a productive one," he said.

Oh, dear. I did not like the look he was training on me at present. It did not bode well for the busy day ahead of me. I must skirt this quickly if I was going to escape.

"Shall I tell Mrs. Humphrey about your recent acquisition, Father? I believe she would love to see the painting for herself. She once told me how she adores landscapes containing sheep."

I watched distraction take over his features. "You are to see Mrs. Humphrey today? A silly woman. Though, she is welcome to come see the painting."

I was not going to see Mrs. Humphrey, but that was irrelevant. "She shares our home county, you recall," I said softly.

He nodded, and I curtsied. It was done. And easily, at that. I turned for the door and nearly made it out when he called to me.

"One thing first, Lydia." He cleared his throat. "I have obtained a husband for you."

I stilled, my hands gripping the basket tightly. Glancing back over my shoulder, I considered his words.

He'd found me a husband? But how could he have done so? For at least two Seasons I'd had no suitor worth mentioning. And furthermore, I liked it that way.

"You remember Mr. Thornton?" he continued.

That man? Of course I remembered Mr. Thornton. How could one forget the man who requested a dance and failed to arrive at the start of the music? It had been mortifying, watching him dance with Miss Hannigan in my stead. Clearly, *I* was not memorable to *him*.

I turned to face my father fully. "I do not comprehend."

He gave me a condescending smile, tilting his head. "He has requested your hand and I agreed. The banns will be posted tomorrow and the wedding shall occur in three weeks' time." He took another bite of his toasted bread before continuing, "You will find him to be an amiable husband, I am sure."

My mouth hung slack. "Have I no say in the matter?"

"It is done, Lydia. There is no say to have."

Energy drained from my person. "All is not lost yet, Father. Perhaps we can come to another arrangement? Might we call on him and discuss this in person?"

"The notice went out this morning," he said crisply. "It is done."

My shoulders sank. If a notice was sent to the papers, it was, indeed, done. Unless... "Father," I said quietly, "what if I refuse?"

His hand paused just before his toast reached his mouth. Setting it down, he leveled me with a look. "You cannot refuse. We've come to an agreement and signed the papers. You will marry Thornton, and if you do not, you shall not be welcome here anymore."

My heart plummeted in my chest. I nodded, swallowing the bile which threatened to rise from my throat. Turning away, I walked from the room with my shoulders set and my back straight. Life had just altered for me in no small way, and I was prepared to adjust accordingly. If only I could *understand* the motives behind Mr. Thornton's offer. He'd ignored me at the ball only a fortnight prior after begging a dance. I had only been grateful no other person was present when he'd requested the dance, aside from my father, of course, or it would have been significantly more embarrassing.

'Twas a blessing, I supposed, that Society was light, at present.

Nodding to my maid, Christine, as she stood waiting in the hallway, I waited for Jacob to open the front door and stepped outside into the brisk Autumn air. Baring trees littered with gold, dying leaves set the backdrop for our quiet street, and I inhaled a lungful of the cool air, pulling my shawl tighter about my shoulders while clutching my basket closer to my chest.

Glancing over my shoulder to be sure my servants were trailing behind me, I set off for King Street. My steps carried me rapidly toward my destination as though my feet could outrun my thoughts. I walked a fair distance before glancing back to ensure my servants were close behind me, and instantly regretted my haste. While we walked about London a good deal, Christine was clearly not as eager to arrive at Mrs. Coulter's house as I was, and her red cheeks and rapid breathing were testament of her struggle. I halted at once.

"Jacob, please obtain a hackney for the remainder of our

journey. I find that my wish to arrive is greater than my desire for exercise this morning."

"At once," Jacob said, bowing. He turned for the road and I pretended to find an interest in the contents of my basket to give Christine a moment to catch her breath. One would think after our consistent forays to King Street my maid would be accustomed to the distance, though I could not fault her today for not being accustomed to the speed.

We arrived at Mrs. Coulter's home minutes later, and the kind, simply dressed matron ushered us into her parlor. My stomach sat uneasy from the short carriage ride, but a few deep breaths later, I was well enough.

I sat at the end of her blue brocade sofa and set the basket on the cushion between us. "I shall do my best to obtain funds in the future, but I was hopeful these books would be useful for now."

Mrs. Coulter reached for it, moving aside the cloth to reveal an array of children's books. "These are splendid," she said, moving them about and reading the titles. "The novels you brought me last week have already been well utilized by some of our more educated students, but I find them a bit advanced for the younger set."

I nodded. "I believe I am ready, Mrs. Coulter, if you can convince your husband to accept my assistance."

She opened her mouth to speak but I sensed another excuse and lifted my hands to stave her. "Please," I begged. "I know I have no experience, but I can read and I hold the desire to help. Are those qualifications not enough?"

Sighing, she gave me an endearing smile. "You know Thomas appreciates your desire to help. But he fears for your safety and age. Reasonable concerns, I allow."

"But I shall not volunteer in the Mint. And I bring my maid and footman with me anytime I leave the house. Surely they are sufficient protection?"

Hinges squealed as the door inched open and a pudgy little finger appeared around the edge. Sighing, Mrs. Coulter shot me an amused glance. "They might be, but I cannot speak for Thomas. Allow me to discuss the matter with him further and I shall have an answer for you by next week."

I swallowed, nodding. It was not a guarantee, but it was a good deal closer. "Thank you. What else are the children in need of? Might I produce something for the schools?"

"If only one percent of London were as charitable as you, Miss James, the entirety of its population would be well taken care of."

A blush warmed my cheeks as I cast my eyes down. I was not looking for praise. "I only wish to help."

A small boy snuck through the open door, darting behind the sofa. Mrs. Coulter reached forward and squeezed my hand. "And we are quite grateful, indeed. Now, what do you say to a treat? I shall ring cook right away and request a plate of the divine shortbread she baked only this morning. Of course, it is too bad my dear children are all busy at present or we could invite them to join us."

A small, blond head popped up behind us. "I am here, Mama! I am not busy at all!"

I could not help but laugh at the hopeful gleam in the child's eye. I glanced back at Mrs. Coulter and the delight reflected in her own caused my heart to squeeze. Her life was a balance of her own joyful family and helping poor London children learn a basic education. I could not imagine a more blissful existence than that.

"It shall work out for the best eventually," Mrs. Coulter said. "Do not imagine that Thomas will turn you away forever. He merely wishes to protect you."

"I understand." Which, I did. But I also knew how teachers were difficult to obtain and I was a willing, free participant.

Mrs. Coulter rang for tea and sent an excited little boy to

retrieve his siblings. "Might I inquire on something of a personal nature?" Mrs. Coulter asked after the tea arrived.

I nodded, accepting my cup and sipping the bitter liquid. It was not as strong as I was accustomed to, but it was a decent blend.

"Thomas read the announcement this morning in the newspaper before he gave it to our neighbors. I was unable to see it for myself, so tell me: is it true you are engaged?"

How odd to answer such a question before speaking to my betrothed. *Was* I engaged to be married if the man had merely signed an agreement with my father and not asked me himself? I supposed the announcement was more ironclad than any vocal agreement could be. I attempted to refrain from slumping my shoulders, pasting a smile on my face instead. "Yes, I am to marry Mr. Thornton."

She looked at me a moment, searching my face. Could she see through my false courage?

"I am not acquainted with the family," Mrs Coulter said. "But I wish you well."

I sipped my tea to avoid responding. It felt unreal. It likely would until Mr. Thornton approached me himself. If he could remember to.

Smiling to myself, I turned to the children sitting quietly at the table against the far window. "I've brought a few books with me," I told them. "They are for your father's schools, but I am sure he won't mind if we read a few of them now. If your mother could be persuaded to allow it."

"Allow it, Mama!" the children sang in unison.

Her endearing smile was broad. "Of course. But you must thank Miss James for reading to you."

I slid over on the cushion to allow space for the children to sit beside me. For one miniscule moment, I imagined myself in the role of mother and the idea warmed my soul. Perhaps marriage would not be so horrid, after all. Perhaps it would even be a blessing. Even if my husband had a habit of forgetting about me.

CHAPTER 2
EDWARD

He'd done it. He'd actually, truly done it.

I sat back against the cushions, letting my head fall against the top of the sofa. Sunlight streamed between the drapes and cascaded onto the carpet before me. I watched as particles floated within the bright sphere of light and danced about as if they, too, had been summarily relieved of a massive amount of debt.

I lifted the note to read the words again, allowing my gaze to drift slowly over the last few lines. *Everything has been taken care of, and my daughter has been informed of the arrangement. You no longer owe money to any man in London—but you shall owe me if the wedding does not occur forthwith.*

Freedom was sweet, and my shoulders were significantly lighter for it. I would now be able to focus my attentions on bettering my estate and building a life for myself at Thornville—with my new wife.

Swallowing the lump in my throat, I sat up tall.

Lydia James. It was my own fault for my distraction at the ball where we'd met, but I could hardly remember what she looked like.

Resting my elbows on my knees, I stared, mesmerized, by the dancing particles within the shaft of light once more. James's note had been abundantly clear. He'd relieved my debts, but I was not out of the woods completely until the wedding took place.

It would likely be in my best interest to call on Miss James and smooth any discomfort caused by our arrangement and the way it came about. James had indicated that he had already spoken to his daughter. I couldn't imagine her finding the agreement pleasing, but I could do my best to make the transition easier on both of us.

I folded the note from James and crossed the room to tuck it into the top drawer of the writing desk situated beside the window.

Pausing, I perused the painting hung on the wall, depicting Thornville in all of its glory. I felt a beat of trepidation at returning to the area, but shook my head to ease my discomfort. Surely I was not the only person involved who wished to keep quiet.

And regardless, the house was an absolute oasis away from Town, with seclusion and beauty found within the grounds and surrounding woods. Sarah and I had been orphaned many years ago, but had spent a good deal of our childhood within those walls. It was an idyllic place to run about and get into mischief.

Sarah. I would need to let her know about my impending nuptials. She would likely wish to meet my bride. And now that I'd pulled us from the dark claws of overwhelming debt, she could return to London in style.

She might even have a chance of obtaining a competent husband now.

Gazing at the oil painting of the house, I smiled to myself, allowing my fingers to trail along the hedge of Blackthorn which lined the perimeter of Thornville's garden. It was difficult to tell in the wintertime, but the grounds were lovely, and that hedge had once been my mother's pride and joy.

I would not mess this up. James had given me an opportunity to start anew, and I would not succumb to the distinct temptation which lay in a game of cards.

In fact, I would never, *ever* touch playing cards again. If I could refrain from such, I could retain what little fortune I had left and build a life for myself, my sister, and my future children.

Oh, and I supposed for my wife as well.

Shaking my head, I slung my hands in my pockets and left the room. It would take some getting used to, but I would not forget my wife again.

In fact, it would likely be easier once I recalled her face. I needed to call on her, and I would do so immediately.

My life had just turned around and I was not about to waste this opportunity.

CHAPTER 3
LYDIA

My emotional state felt a tad ragged, so I chose to have Jacob procure a hackney for the ride back home. With an empty basket swinging lightly from my fingertips, I climbed the stairs to our stately townhome in Mayfair and stepped through the open door, nodding at our butler, Harrington, before removing my shawl and gloves and delivering them into his waiting hands.

Voices trailed down the hallway, alerting me to the presence of another man in our home. The masculine timbre reached my ears, belonging to a voice far younger than my father's, and causing a wave of prickles to run down my neck. Could this be Mr. Thornton?

Hesitating before the looking glass in the hallway, I smoothed back tendrils of my rich dark hair and pinched my cheeks for color. Anticipation heightened my nerves as I pushed open the drawing room door and stepped inside.

Instantly, I deflated upon seeing the young Mr. Radmahl seated opposite Father in the high wingback chairs beside the fire.

"We were just speaking of you," Father said as Mr. Radmahl

got to his feet, bowing. "You've come at the most opportune moment, for Radmahl is determined to wish you well."

I curtsied before coming to sit on the couch across from the men.

"I only read the notice this morning," Mr. Radmahl said, his dark red hair falling forward in the Brutus style and nearly blocking his eyes. "I am well acquainted with Thornton, as we are neighbors in the north."

The north? I had not considered before how Mr. Thornton might own a home away from London. Surely it would not affect me, however. Ours was not a love match and Mr. Thornton would likely not mind where I spent my time.

A knock sounded on the door and Harrington stepped forward, delivering a card to Father. A wide smile spread on his round face and he nodded to our butler before turning to Mr. Radmahl. "You are in luck, young man. Thornton himself has decided to join us."

My heart pounded, color rising to my cheeks. I didn't know why I was so nervous when the man had sought *my* hand in marriage, and not the other way around. Surely he had his reasons. Though, I would not mind learning what they were.

"Good day, Thornton," Father's voice boomed, startling me. I forced my gaze to move slowly over my shoulder toward Mr. Thornton so I might not appear too eager; I was vastly displeased when I finally looked at the man.

Had I expected a sort of jolt within me at the sight?

He was very much the same as I recalled him appearing at the ball, possessed of light brown hair and a square jaw, only now he wore an expression of apprehension upon his brow. A light of recognition passed in his eyes. His hands clasped his gloves tightly and he seemed to hesitate before approaching us and bowing to me.

His boots, I noticed, were particularly shiny without a hint of dirt attached to them. Father would undoubtedly approve.

I stood, delivering a curtsy, fluid and meek. It should not have been a surprise when Mr. Thornton chose to sit beside me on the couch, but it *was*. I did my best to swallow my reaction, smiling at him pleasantly. Did he recall the moment from the ball as clearly as I did? Likely not.

If only I'd thought to grab my work basket, then I could mend that hole in my shawl and give my hands something to keep them busy. Instead, I clasped them, awaiting Father's direction.

Mr. Thornton spoke, his voice low and even. "Have you had a pleasant morning, Miss James?"

"Yes, I have. Thank you for inquiring."

"And thank you for choosing to visit when I might offer my well wishes," Mr. Radmahl said with amusement. "I had no idea you were looking to wed, Thornton. What an interesting surprise."

Silence sat in the room for two beats of the mantle clock. "Indeed," Mr. Thornton agreed.

I caught a trace of restraint in his tone. Or, perhaps I was imagining it.

There seemed to be a level of dislike between the men, but I could not put my finger on the precise cause.

Unaware of the unease in the room, Father began a discourse on the fine horse he'd bet on just last week, capturing the men's attention and leaving me to ponder. Would it be very inappropriate to request a private conference with Mr. Thornton, or would Father prefer I remained in his presence? Our engagement ought to allow us a moment together, but Father could be quite opinionated, and I didn't wish to displease him.

"How fortunate that your luck turned around," Mr. Radmahl said, "but gambling itself can be a slippery slope to ruin if one is not careful."

"Yes," Mr. Thornton agreed, his face tight. "It is frightfully dangerous." He turned to Father. "Mr. James, might I request an audience with Miss James? Perhaps a ride in my phaeton?"

"By all means," Father answered, gesturing us off with his arms. I caught Father's gaze dipping down toward Mr. Thornton's boots and the subsequent smile of approval. I had been correct.

Turning to Mr. Thornton to accept the invitation—though once again it was directed at my father and not to me—I found him watching me closely.

"Should you mind very much?" he asked.

Had he read my mind? Appreciation for his consideration won out and I almost accepted when hesitation halted me. Would now be the moment to inform Mr. Thornton of my aversion to carriages? But then, an open, slow phaeton should not be too bad. Bravely, I shook my head. "I must retrieve my bonnet, sir, but I should only be a moment."

He nodded and then I fled to my bedchamber. It was all happening so quickly.

Securing my bonnet under my chin, I sucked in a deep breath and went downstairs to meet my future husband for our ride.

Lydia

I was grateful Mr. Thornton chose to drive down lesser known streets and leave the highly occupied park for another day. I was not overly fond of extra regard and that morning's announcement, along with our close proximity on the seat of the phaeton, were likely to garner an unhealthy dose of attention.

"Your father tells me you like to read," Mr. Thornton said, after two city blocks of silence.

That made sense. Father knew *that* about me, if nothing else. "I do. It is a favorite pastime of mine."

Another street passed quietly, punctuated by the sound of horses' hooves and carriage wheels, until I asked, "Do you read, as well?"

"Not much, no. It is *not* a favorite pastime of mine."

What sort of person didn't enjoy reading? Stumped, I reverted to silence. When around children or people I knew well, conversation came easily. With strangers, however, I never quite knew how to proceed.

"I suppose your father spoke to you already?" he asked.

"Yes," I answered, shifting on the seat to face him better. He handled the reins with ease and maneuvered about the road smoothly. What did I say next? Should I thank him for an offer of marriage which I did not receive, but had been directed to my father without my knowledge?

No, I think probably not.

He cleared his throat. "I appreciate your cooperation in our unique situation. It must have come as quite a shock to you."

"Indeed, it did."

"I flatter myself that I am offering you the opportunity to venture outside of London. Something, I am told, you've seldom done."

Oh, dear. How did I phrase this the right way? "I am perfectly content in London."

"Yes, it is a wonderful metropolis. Yet, you will enjoy Thornville too, I vow. The estate is a positive oasis and the house itself is nothing to smirk at. A little away from society, but it is near Melton and shall make for a pleasant wedding trip."

A wedding trip was acceptable, but not a permanent residence. I wished to stay in London. I needed to stay in London. The Sunday schools were *here*. Mrs. Coulter and her husband were here. I glanced away, gathering the courage to speak, when I caught sight of the bridge which led to Vauxhall Gardens.

"Might we venture over the Thames?" I asked, surprised at myself. "I have a wish to see White Hart Street."

He regarded me curiously, before turning the horses toward the river. "I suppose so."

We crossed the wide waterway and drove through Vauxhall, the streets growing less reputable the further we ventured from the river. We continued, then turned right on White Hart Street, slowing the horses to a stop.

"It is nice," Mr. Thornton said, looking about us at the plain brick buildings.

There was nothing worthy of note, but Mr. Coulter's school resided on this street and it would become the place for my first teaching assignment…eventually. I looked at Mr. Thornton from under my lashes. Surely he would not forbid my volunteering efforts once Mr. Coulter accepted me. Perhaps I ought to err on the cautious side and not mention *precisely* how I was planning to volunteer.

"That is all," I said. "We can return now. Thank you for following my whim."

He smiled at me and my stomach constricted. Oh, dear. I had not considered that I would be marrying such a handsome man. I didn't know what to do with that information.

The drive back across the bridge was completed in quiet, though I found myself reflecting in a way that was far from comfortable.

"Thank you for allowing me the pleasure of driving you about," Mr. Thornton said.

I dipped my head, avoiding the familiar gaze of the women walking down the side of the road. Returning to Mayfair, there were any number of people who recognized us.

"It was my pleasure," I said. "Thank you, Mr. Thornton."

He opened his mouth to speak, but paused, searching my

eyes. Nodding concisely, he delivered a wide smile. "Shall we plan to meet again before the wedding?"

Would it change anything? Perhaps it would help us to know one another better, but the union had been announced and the agreement signed. What did it matter how well we knew one another?

"If you would like," I said finally.

Amusement played on his lips. He pulled the phaeton in front of my home and stopped, tossing his reins to his tiger and coming around to help me down. His large hand closed around my own and through the gloves, I felt his strength. I hazarded a glance at his face and found him watching me. His thick brows were pulled together in concentration and he lifted my knuckles to his lips, bestowing a soft kiss on the back of my gloved hand.

I mounted the steps and entered my home in a daze. Perhaps getting married wouldn't be the absolute worst thing in the world.

CHAPTER 4
EDWARD

She was more beautiful than I recalled.
 Since I had not remembered her before stepping into the James' drawing room, that was not such an odd thing. Still, I hadn't expected her to be beautiful.

I directed my phaeton toward my club, leaving the horses with my tiger while I climbed the stairs in a daze and admitted myself into the parlor. Claiming a table in the far corner of the room, undisturbed by the other patrons and secluded with my own thoughts for company, I ruminated.

Her dark hair would rival a raven in sheen and depth, and her intelligent eyes forced me to sit taller in my chair, aware that I likely would not get anything past her.

I ordered a drink from the waiter and leaned back in the leather armchair, fingering the supple, worn arm of the chair as I allowed my eyes to drift closed. I recalled meeting her at the ball, but she had been quiet and shy—not unlike her demeanor today—and conversation had been difficult.

I could only hope that would change as we came to better know one another. Her oddity in wishing to see White Hart Street, a plain, grungy road covered in bare brick buildings raised questions. Perhaps in time, she would answer them for me.

"Marriage, eh?"

I kept my eyes closed a moment longer. I knew that voice well, though I despised its owner with every fiber of my being. Swallowing my distaste, I allowed my gaze to fall upon the red-headed man who had nearly derailed my life.

"Radmahl."

His smile was snake-like as he spun an eyeglass around his finger. Nodding to the seat opposite me, he did not await my approval before lowering himself and stretching his long legs out before him.

"She's quite a gem," he continued. I could only assume he was referring to my betrothed. "Intelligent, but can't be bothered with any suitors, according to her father. It's odd that she went from having no interest in the beau monde, to suddenly being betrothed."

I would not allow him the satisfaction of speaking. He was suspicious, as anyone who knew either Miss James or myself had any right to be. But he was imprudent and needed to leave me be.

"Perhaps," Radmahl continued, "she was unaware of the arrangements as they were being made. Many men commit folly within the late hours of the night. Particularly after imbibing."

Did he know about the card game already? The waiter delivered my drink and I picked it up, gulping two large swallows in the face of Radmahl's judgement. His smile grew wider and I glanced away, uneasy.

He opened his mouth to speak again and I cut him with a look, downing the remainder of my drink in four large swallows and setting the glass on the table between us with a thunk.

Rising, I did not so much as acknowledge him with a nod or a glance before I took myself swiftly from the room. His chuckles, low and distinct, followed me from the parlor and into the stairwell.

Shivers ran down my arms and I shook them to release the tension gathering there. He was likely still bitter over the ordeal from last year, but I would not let that get to me. If anything, *I* was the one who could put him in his place. I'd thought that by ignoring the man he would simply receive the hint and let me be, but alas, his head was too thick to retain the message.

There were mere weeks left until the banns would be read to completion and I would marry Miss James. I needed to get my affairs in order so I might remove to Thornville and start anew.

Inhaling a deep breath of smoggy London air, I glanced to the sky. Filth like Radmahl had no place in my future. And I would soon be leaving that part of my life behind.

CHAPTER 5
LYDIA

Sunday's sermon was nothing like I had anticipated for such a momentous day in my life. I could not help but watch Mr. Thornton through it all, wondering if he felt as off-putted as I did when Mr. Ridley began to preach on the finer points of raising children to be good Christians.

He clearly knew of our wedding, as he would be performing it within the hour, but I hoped it was not a lesson directed at us. The looks the congregation sent our way said otherwise, however, and I was sure everyone assumed it was intentional.

The ceremony was quick, completed at the end of the church service. Mr. Thornton smiled at me as we stood before Mr. Ridley, though it was strained. Wrinkles formed around his eyes, and the spark I'd seen during the ball weeks before was missing. For a man who had sought out my hand in marriage, one might believe he would anticipate the occasion with greater joy. Not that the lack thereof was offensive in any way, but I couldn't help but wonder if he was not as prepared for this marriage as I had let myself believe.

The wedding breakfast held in my father's home after church was intimate. Mr. Thornton's own sister was unable to attend, and my father had not invited many people. My mother had been the social one of our lot, and though my father appreciated a night with men at his club or gambling in our parlor, he was not one for frivolous social activities, as he had always called them.

It was nice to know he considered my wedding frivolous.

Mrs. Coulter lowered herself into a chair beside me at the end of the table laid out with tea and desserts. She grinned at me, her tea cupped in both hands. "I have good news, Lydia. I'm thrilled to *finally* tell you that Thomas has found a place for you to help teach. He would have come to tell you himself, but he was needed at the new school on White Hart Street."

Anticipation filled me, mixed with a healthy dose of nerves. I'd wanted to teach these children to read since I'd met Mrs. Coulter and her husband at a soiree during the Season months before. That I had no actual experience in teaching was a minor thing, wasn't it?

I sighed. "I am finally approved to teach and yet I must put you off until I am back from my wedding trip."

"Do not worry yourself. The school will be here when you return," Mrs. Coulter said, swatting away the complaint with a flick of her wrist. "Where are you going for your trip?"

I took a sip of tea. "Northumberland."

"How very...north."

I grinned. "Mr. Thornton's ancestral home is there. We shall see the house and return forthwith. I am sure it will not be quick enough for me, though I am not completely certain when we are to return."

She watched me a moment before setting her empty cup on the edge of the table. "May I give you some advice?"

I nodded, mirroring her by setting my teacup on the table before us.

"Enjoy the time together. When you return to your life here, it will not be the same. Do not waste the wedding trip wishing you could be in London slums reading to poor children."

I could not hide my smile. "But I do wish that."

She chuckled. "You are singular, indeed, Miss James. But you take my meaning, I am sure."

Nodding, I said, "I believe I do." Though it would amount to nothing. Ours was not a typical marriage.

I did not know my husband at all. Despite his request during our drive to visit me again before the wedding, I'd seen Mr. Thornton only once more. The majority of our time together was taken up discussing the finer points of the wedding date and who would be invited to the wedding breakfast. He'd also inquired after the warmth of my wardrobe. Evidently, I was in need of a warmer cape—preferably one lined with fur.

Our trip could not take longer than a fortnight, I was sure, so I had not bothered obtaining the cape, but I did order a warmer pelisse. It would likely do the trick *and* would be more practical for when we returned to London. My clothing had gotten me through plenty of cold London winters; how much worse could Northumberland really be?

"Have you completed your trousseau?" Mrs. Coulter asked.

"Not quite. I've begun embroidering the linens, but it will take me awhile yet. I considered bringing it with me to occupy my time while Mr. Thornton pursues his own interests." I paused, considering Mrs. Coulter alone in her house, as she often was when I called on her. Her husband was gone frequently working for the schools, and I knew her children fulfilled her, but I also knew how deeply she loved her husband.

Even if the love was missing from my marriage, I could find a way to be content with my situation, just as Mrs. Coulter was infinitely satisfied with her own. Children to care for and a person to speak with over dinner—what more could one possibly want?

"Do not underestimate Mr. Thornton," Mrs. Coulter said,

pushing a blonde tendril away from her face. "He may appreciate spending time with you, as well. You are an excellent conversationalist."

When it came to books and children, yes, I was. But with a man I hardly knew who had already admitted a dislike for reading? The idea of making conversation with him was tedious. The journey to White Hart Street had contained very little talking, and most of it was on his end.

I hoped to have an easy, comfortable relationship with him *eventually*. But I did not expect it to occur overnight.

"Thank you, Mrs. Coulter, for opening your home to me. I have appreciated our chats."

"As have I," she agreed. Smoothing her hands down her pale blue skirts, she said, "You might have been accepted as a volunteer teacher now, but don't let that stop your visits to my home. I always look forward to them."

Warmth spread over me. "As do I."

Mrs. Coulter rose. "I am afraid I must return home. I wish you well, dear." I stood, allowing her to pull me in for an embrace. She was not much older than I but had taken me under her wing in such a way that made me feel like a younger sister to her. I almost felt like a daughter, but that was a little absurd. My mother had only been gone for three years and I remembered her well. She was not in danger of being replaced by Mrs. Coulter in my affections, but I could not deny the magnitude of my feelings for this woman, either.

Watching Mrs. Coulter exit the drawing room, I sat at the end of the table and refilled my teacup. The remainder of the party, largely made up of my father's acquaintances, laughed and spoke amongst themselves. A few of my father's friends sat on the sofas on the other side of the room discussing something they clearly found humorous. Mr. Radmahl hovered on the edge of their circle, perched comfortably on one of the tall wing-back chairs. He glanced at me, our eyes locking, and sent me a small smile, lifting his glass. Was it an offer of congratulations?

I looked over my shoulder, but no one stood behind me. Though the prickle that ran down my neck was evidence of my discomfort, there was no cause I could plainly see. Mr. Radmahl was a nice gentleman. His direct gaze made me feel vulnerable, but I shook the thought away. He was merely being polite.

Mr. Thornton approached, pulling out the chair beside me and gesturing with his right hand. "May I sit?"

"Of course, Mr. Thornton."

He glanced around the room and his gaze landed on my face, resting there. I thought back to the child-rearing sermon from earlier and my cheeks heated. Clearing his throat, he sent me a smile which revealed even teeth and caused butterflies to flap in my stomach. "Have you enjoyed your meal?"

"Yes, I have. Our cook has outdone herself."

She was not the most talented chef in the world, but she could produce a decent cake. And the array of pastries and meat pies today were particularly succulent.

The quiet stretched further and I looked about me for something to speak of. My father's home was not the grandest, but it was nice enough. It still felt odd that my things were packed to move to a home I had never before seen.

The women were gathered near the windows discussing something of vast importance if their tones and expressions were any clue. If I had to guess, I would assume it was gossip. If only Mrs. Coulter might have been able to remain, then I would have had my own friend to chat with and Mr. Thornton would not have been obliged to entertain me.

Mr. Thornton reached for the pastry on my plate, crumbling the flaky edge between his fingers absently. "The journey will take a good deal of time, so I think it best if we rise early tomorrow and get on the road as quickly as we are able."

Nodding, I said, "That is a practical idea. I feel I must warn you, before we begin our journey, that, on occasion, I have not felt entirely well when riding in a carriage."

"Do you feel unwell when riding a horse?"

"I wouldn't know, to be honest." I tried to think of the last time I'd gone for a ride but my mind drew a blank. "Though I ride, I have not done so for any great length of time."

Mr. Thornton smiled, leaning closer. "I have a good friend who cannot abide carriages. He must ride horseback the entire way if he travels, but it does keep him from becoming ill."

"Perhaps I could try it sometime. At present, however, I do not lay claim to a horse."

"Well, you are in luck. I own a good amount of horses and I have one I am sure would fit you well." His eyebrows screwed together as though he was concentrating. "Though I do not own a side saddle. We could perhaps borrow my sister's."

"That won't be necessary. A side saddle, I do own."

Mr. Thornton laughed. "What good is the saddle without the horse?"

"Good enough to teach me to ride on my father's steed, though not quite sufficient to give me enough practice to call myself a proficient."

Father approached the table, swinging his eyeglass around on its chain. "The footman are ready. Where might I direct them to load Lydia's trunks?"

Mr. Thornton said, "I shall have my carriage brought to the front. My townhouse is but two streets from here." He turned to me. "Perhaps we might walk?"

I opened my mouth to speak but he cut me off. "Unless you are not fond of walking?"

The very words he spoke indicated how little he knew me. "It is one of my greatest pleasures."

His answering grin made me grateful I enjoyed walking at all. Perhaps that was one thing we had in common.

"I do not *ever* wish to walk if I can help it," he said.

"It is good for the body and the soul," I argued without thinking. What had come over me? It was not in my nature to speak out.

Amusement glittered in his eyes as he said, "Though our acquaintance is short-lived, I believe you have so far proved my inferiority quite sufficiently."

My stomach sank slightly. I did not intend to make him feel inferior. I had simply thought we would share something. Perhaps we did and had yet to discover it.

With father standing over us, the stilted conversation shuddered to a complete halt. Father grinned, his side whiskers twitching with his smile. I would miss him, of course, but I had a strange feeling he would not miss me as much. Still, I knew he loved me. It was an odd relationship we had.

Mr. Thornton stood. "Allow me to assist you, Mr. James. If you will but direct me to your footmen?" He turned to me and reached for my hand. I gave it to him willingly. I held my breath, waiting for him to place another kiss on the top of my knuckles, but was sorely disappointed when he only squeezed my fingers tightly, and said, "Allow me a quarter of an hour to get things settled and we will be off."

I smiled up at him then watched him retreat. His gray coat fit snug about his waist and the light brown of his hair gleamed from an oil of some type. He was kind, with a genial disposition. I had never dreamed of an arranged marriage, but I was not too obtuse to recognize that the arrangement could have been far worse. I even harbored hope that Mr. Thornton and I might become friends.

CHAPTER 6
LYDIA

Mr. Thornton's townhouse was nicer than my own, but the furnishings and interior were sparse. One would almost believe he had fallen on hard times and married me for my money, but I was no heiress and my father was a penny pincher. My dowry was modest, at best. I ran my eyes over the thread-bare carpet and plain drapes of the parlor, and wondered if there could be any merit to my theory. Maybe Father had offered more? To entice Mr. Thornton into marrying me?

But, no. Father would never spend a large sum on something so *frivolous* as a marriage. He hadn't even allowed me to bring my personal footman to my new home.

Christine had been permitted to come, but Jacob had remained behind with my father. It had shocked me when father told me of the arrangement. Jacob had been my escort through London for quite some time, but on further reflection, it made sense. Mr. Thornton likely had his own footmen.

I sat in a chair near the fire contemplating the day and how very much my life had changed in three weeks. The door cracked open and Mr. Thornton glanced inside. He approached me slowly. "May I sit?"

I nodded, noting a strange sense of familiarity in the situation.

"I feel that we have done that before," he said. His eyes were solemn, and his gaze intent. He seemed sincere. "How are you?"

"Well enough."

"May I get you anything? Did you find the violet room to your liking?"

I nodded. I was surprised it did not lead to a master suite, but he must have chosen it intentionally if he knew which room was mine. "I must admit, I was surprised to find it has no dressing room."

Was it such an obvious way to inquire on why I was not put in a mistress suite or any chamber joining his?

His cheeks turned pink. "I had thought it might be wise to better acquaint ourselves before sharing a chamber."

Speechless, my gaze sought the fire. I watched the flames flicker, licking the brick barrier. What an uncomfortable conversation to have. "If you feel that is wise, then I will readily agree."

It was a thoughtful gesture, to be sure.

Mr. Thornton stood, wiping his hands down his thighs. Was he nervous?

"If you have all you need then I will be off to bed. Your maid is set to wake you early, I presume?"

"Yes, Mr. Thornton. She is prepared."

He turned to go but paused at the door. Looking back over his shoulder, he said, "May I escort you to your room?"

I stood. "That would be nice."

He offered me his elbow and I placed my hand inside the crook of it. Leading me up the stairs and down the dim hallway, he paused at my door.

"Good night, Mr. Thornton," I said, wondering if our encounters would grow less awkward with each passing day.

"Good night." He seemed to hesitate a moment before adding, "Would it be very forward if I requested to call you by your Christian name?"

I tried to swallow my surprise. But it was not so very odd, was it? We were married after all. "That would be fine. You may call me Lydia."

"If you would call me Edward, I would be much obliged."

"Very well. Good night, Edward."

He nodded, his lips raising in a small half-smile. He almost looked sorrowful, but I would not do myself the disservice of assuming to know his emotions. Surely, he was only feeling as insecure as I was about being married to a stranger.

"I shall see you in the morning, Lydia."

Lydia

By the second day of our journey, I had lost the contents of my stomach three times, and finally determined it was better I eat nothing at all.

"Are you ready to try the horse now?" Edward asked, his eyebrows pulled together. Concern laced the pitiful smile on his face. I had refused riding earlier because I had felt so ill; I was certain I would not keep on top of a horse.

At present, I was willing to try anything. "Yes. I think that would be wise."

Edward pounded the top of the carriage loudly with his fist and we rolled to a stop on the side of the road. He opened the door and hopped out, turning to hold my hand and gingerly lead me to the grassy earth.

"We are going to ride now," he said to the coachman.

I stood in the wide space, the fresh air immediately easing my discomfort a slight degree. My stomach still churned and rolled, but I tried to minimize the effects of the carriage ride in front of my new husband. He helped a servant untie our horses and led a light gray horse with dark gray spots toward me. She was breathtaking—both in the sense of her beauty and also her size. Edward must have thought highly of my accomplishments to believe me capable of riding such a beast.

"Are you certain she is not too big?" I asked, my voice sounding small and unsure.

He glanced from me to the horse. "No, I think you and she will suit."

Gathering my courage, I took a step toward her. Edward stood close behind me. "Are you ready?" he asked.

I nodded, and he came around to face me, his hands sliding around my waist. He lifted me in one effortless motion and I grabbed onto the saddle to keep myself aloft. Hooking my knee on the pommel, I rested my foot in the stirrup and arranged my gown over my legs. I'd worn my riding habit just in case, but it was a tad snug and caused me to sit up very straight.

Perhaps that had been contributing to my ill stomach.

Edward circled around me to his own black steed and climbed up with swift agility. The carriage took off soon after, the additional vehicle full of servants and trunks behind it, with Edward and I trailing in the back.

We passed a mile, at least, in silence, before Edward broke it. "How are you feeling?"

"Better than I did in the carriage." I'd released the strong grip on the reins I'd been holding minutes before, and my hands felt better for it. As for my stomach, I was slowly beginning to feel the ebb of relief.

We continued to trot along the pocked road, a steady rhythm of hooves clopping and birds singing in the distance. The rolling hills of the northern counties were a lovely backdrop to our ride and the expanse available for us to see was breathtaking. I hadn't had the opportunity to see this before now. Partly because I'd never been so far north in my life, but also because I'd hardly left London.

"Are you enjoying the ride?" Edward asked.

I nodded. I searched for something to ask him but my mind was distracted by the beauty of the autumn hills and the wide, blue skies. "We are fortunate to avoid bad weather," I said.

"Indeed. It is a miracle we've yet to encounter rain. Perhaps we ought not refine upon it too much or Mother Nature will change the circumstances just to spite us."

I laughed, the idea of the earth changing on a whim entertaining. What an odd thought.

"Have you enjoyed what you've seen outside of London thus far? I know you said you don't travel often."

"I have enjoyed it, actually. The view is marvelous, even from this road. I hope we are able to see something of the moors I've read about. My mother often spoke of her love for the moors she would visit as a child."

"We shall. I am certain of it. Perhaps tomorrow, if not later today."

He sent me a kind smile and warmth grew in my chest. The pelisse I'd worn over my riding habit was sufficient for the weather we were having, but it was not warm enough to cause such an overwhelming heat within me. I could only think it was due to the kindness Edward had shown me. He was a gentleman of the truest form, concerned for my well-being at every step.

"Shall we play a game?" he asked suddenly.

"Very well. What did you have in mind?"

His nose wrinkled in thought. "How about a questions

game? You may ask me a question that I must answer honestly and then we can repeat the process."

The nature of the game was unusual, but I could see the wisdom of trying to better know one another. "Who shall begin?"

"I will," he said, "since the game was my idea." He leaned forward and stroked the black mane of his horse, his face a picture of serious concentration. "Where is the farthest you've traveled from London?"

"That is easy. Bath. My mother and I spent a holiday in Bath one summer taking the waters."

"And did you like it there?"

"The waters were atrocious," I replied, laughing, "but the assemblies were great fun."

"A concise description, I would think."

We trotted along as I tried to think of a question, but nothing came to mind. What did I wish to know about this man? I could inquire why he chose me for a bride, but that was perhaps too large a question for so early in the game. Or maybe why he had asked me to dance after our very first introduction and then subsequently forgotten about me. Perhaps I ought to work up to that one as well. I should begin small, as he had.

I finally settled on, "How many siblings do you have?"

"Just the one sister, Sarah," he said, right away. "Our parents have been dead for many years and we've alternated between spending time with our aunt in Cheshire, our house in London, and various friends' estates."

"She is lucky to have a brother who looks after her so dearly."

He looked away from me, abashed. Did he not appreciate the praise?

"'Tis my turn." Clearing his throat, he asked, "Besides reading and walking, what do you like to do with your time?"

Nothing. I could think of nothing. "I suppose I like to

embroider," I said. "Though, not excessively." I'd finally decided to bring my trousseau to work on while we were in Northumberland. It was likely I would have quite a bit of time on my hands and I could finish embroidering the linens.

"Perhaps you can show me some of your work," he said. Now he had gone too far. No man was so kind as to actually *wish* to look at embroidery.

"Why are you being so solicitous?" I asked.

I'd caught him off guard with my question and his mouth fell open, his eyes widening. "What do you mean?"

"Do you *really* wish to see my embroidery?"

"Yes," he said concisely. "We are married now, Lydia. And I find I have the desire to understand who you are."

It was a reasonable explanation. I felt silly for my question and trained my gaze on the carriages ahead of us, watching the wheels turn on the ground, the carriages bouncing along.

"Are you feeling well now?" he asked.

Taking a moment to consider my nausea—or lack thereof—I realized how much better I felt. The relief had snuck up on me so slowly it did not occur to me before now how the rolling and churning within my stomach had ceased. "Does this count as your question?"

He glanced to me, surprised. "I suppose it does."

"Well, I am feeling well now, actually. The horse is significantly better than the carriage." I faced forward as I said, "Thank you, Edward. I would not have considered this option on my own."

Grinning, he mimed relief, wiping his hand across his forehead. "We must send our thanks to my friend, Mr. Garrett, for discovering this treatment. It has served us well."

"I will write him a note forthwith."

Edward chuckled. "Perhaps the gratitude can wait until I see him next."

A small town appeared on the horizon. "We should stop and

dine," Edward said. "Our next opportunity won't be for some time."

I agreed, finally sure I might be able to retain what I ate, though disappointment snaked through me. I had been enjoying the conversation and wasn't eager for it to stop. We continued in comfortable silence and I stole a look at Edward on his large, black horse. He was clearly comfortable, his arms relaxed as he directed the reins.

Perhaps this wedding trip wouldn't be too dull after all.

CHAPTER 7
LYDIA

The final leg of our journey was completed on a tree-covered lane, the branches so overgrown that I was forced to crouch low on the horse to avoid losing my bonnet.

"I must get these trees trimmed immediately," Edward said. "It is dangerous to ride."

"Your coachman likely agrees," I said, indicating the crouching coachman on the carriage ahead of us. The wagon containing trunks and servants had gone on ahead of us the day before and should have arrived at Thornville already. I pointed to the vicious-looking branches above us. "Is this where the estate's name comes from?"

"It should be. But no, Thornville is simply a derivative of our name."

That made more sense.

"Besides," he added, "though sharp, these are not considered thorns."

"They are quite the thorn in my side at present," I argued, leading my horse closer to Edward's as a particularly long branch scraped the side of my mare. She skittered a moment but continued on.

"How clever of you," Edward responded dryly.

We approached an iron gate and waited for a servant to open it, the creak of the hinges slicing through the quiet.

"I have not visited in a year, at least," Edward said. "Forgive me for not coming ahead to ensure the house's cleanliness and order."

"Do you employ servants?"

He nodded. "A smaller staff for when I'm not here, but there are sufficient people to care for it."

I tried to give him an encouraging smile. "Then I am sure all is well."

We approached the house and I was surprised to see that it was actually rather aged. Perfectly rectangular, with eight windows across on each of the two floors, broken only by the front door, the gray house appeared solemn against the backdrop of forest. Though many trees had lost their leaves, a good deal of gold and orange remained, clinging on until the last breath of autumn.

The forest was kept at bay by a guardian hedgerow of Blackthorn, the empty thorns and deep blue berries adding to the solemnity of the view.

Though I would not describe the scene before me as an oasis, as Edward once had, the house itself appeared earnest and faithful, as though it had weathered many storms and could yet withstand more. I was eager to see the interior though, and the outbuildings. There did not appear to be a flower garden of any sort; if I was planning to spend more time here, I would rectify that deficiency. But, alas, the poor children of London needed me if they were going to have a chance at a decent future.

And those children were far more important than beautifying an old country estate.

A stablehand stepped forward and took the reins of my

horse. Edward smoothly dismounted beside me, staring at the house with a look of sorrow and disappointment on his face. I felt a sense of his emotion and my stomach swirled in empathy, though I did not understand why. He noticed me watching him, and his face turned to stone as he jumped to help me down, offering me a bland smile. I put my hands on his tall, broad shoulders and gripped them as he lifted me from the mare.

"Not too bad, eh?" he said, looking down at me with clear, green eyes.

I took his proffered elbow, unsure if the butterflies in my stomach were a result from the contact of his hands on my waist once again, or the look he gave me after he helped me down.

Oh, dear. Was I very much in danger of developing feelings for my husband? I could not blame myself, I supposed, for no one had ever held my waist before in such a way. It was likely not *Edward* eliciting the feelings, but the heady rush of contact.

He led me to the front door and inside to the foyer. The walls were dark and lined in mahogany paneling, the deep red drapes hindering all sources of light. It was difficult to see, but from what I could tell in the dim sunlight sneaking through the gap between the drapes and the wall and from the open door behind us, the foyer was shabby and sparse.

If I thought Edward's townhouse was suffering from a lack of funds, his country house was struggling even more.

I schooled my emotions, willing myself not to look disappointed. I should not judge the entire house from one room.

The housekeeper was waiting inside, her dark gray hair pulled back into a severe knot. She had a serious, disapproving mouth and sharp, eagle eyes.

"This is Mrs. Patton, our housekeeper," Edward said.

Mrs. Patton curtsied. "Allow me to show you to your room, Mrs. Thornton. The trunks have already been taken up."

I glanced to Edward. He gave me an encouraging look and I proceeded toward the stairs. Mrs. Patton jingled as she walked, her keys bouncing around on the chatelaine attached to her waist. She brought me to a door near the top of the stairs, swinging it open and allowing me to step inside.

It was lighter than the foyer had been. Pulled away from the windows to admit sunlight, the drapes were a deep plum, matching the bed hangings which surrounded a large, raised bed. A carpet covered most of the floor, worn but sufficient, in sage green and ivory, with purple accents.

Christine stood near the wardrobe, unfolding gowns and hanging them inside.

A table beside the bed and a washstand near the window were the only other furnishings in the room.

"Is there a chair we might bring in?" I asked. I didn't know how else Christine was to do my hair.

Mrs. Patton nodded. "I can have one brought in. Is there anything else you stand in need of?"

The room was drafty but claimed a small fire, which would heat the room eventually. A writing table wouldn't go amiss, but I did not want to be needy. "That should be all."

Mrs. Patton nodded and made to leave before pausing at the door and speaking over her shoulder. "I will inform Mr. Thornton, of course, but as you are the mistress of Thornville, I thought it prudent to tell you that we have had no cook in residence for a few months. We make do, of course, but you might choose to employ one if you are going to reside here at length."

Shaking my head, I dispelled her thoughts. "We shall only be here a week, perhaps a little longer. This is not a permanent trip."

Mrs. Patton cast disbelieving eyes on me and clamped her mouth shut. What cause had she for not believing my words? I dismissed her and she closed the door behind her. I moved to the bed, shifting the hanging to the side and revealing a plump, feather mattress with sage green coverings. It appeared newer than the rest of the things within the house and I found that I liked the look of my bedchamber very much—despite the dour housekeeper.

Lydia

Dinner was a simple stew with bread and wine. Edward sat at the head of the long, oak table and I at the foot. We did not speak, for the distance lent itself to nothing but stilted, awkward conversation. Our meal was not at all what I was accustomed to, but the thick broth was flavorful and the bread moist.

I removed to the drawing room following dinner, where more red drapes and dark wood paneling decorated the space. Had the original designer failed to realize that rooms could be done up differently from one another? The dark colors were stifling in their overpowering nature and were quite masculine, as well.

Edward remained behind for his pipe and brandy, and I waited until the maid who had shown me to the drawing room left me alone before I crossed to the window to peek outside.

Rich, black darkness met my eyes. It was strange, for I knew the forest was just across the lawn there, but I could not see anything. No stars in the heavens or Blackthorn lining the earth made themselves known to me through the window. If I was to step outside, would I hear the wildlife lurking there? A shiver crept down my arms and I released the drape, stepping back into the safety and warmth of the room as it swung into place.

"Did you enjoy your dinner?" Edward asked, stepping into the room and crossing it with purpose. His long stride was confident and his eyes serious.

"I did, yes."

He approached me, pausing just out of reach and holding a glass of brandy. "Splendid."

I waited for him to speak further, but he said nothing. Instead, he stood quietly before me, sipping his drink.

I cleared my throat. "Shall we sit?"

A moment's pause caused me to regret my words, for the hesitation across Edward's face proved that he had not intended to remain in the drawing room with me. And he did not necessarily need to. I didn't want him to consider me a needy wife, for I was quite capable of spending an evening with my own company.

"Or perhaps you are busy?" I said quickly. "Which would also work rather well, for I was considering reading."

His eyebrows pulled together in concern. "If you are sure? I do not wish to leave you alone on your first evening at Thornville. Though it is not at the height of fashion, it is a comfortable home and I think it will serve us well."

"Yes, it shall," I agreed. He bowed to me before turning to go and the room fell quiet once more. I let myself fall onto the sofa and sighed. I did not have my library with me any longer and I hadn't thought to bring a book. I could fetch my embroidery, but my fingers were achy from clutching the reins for such a long ride and they deserved something of a break. Perhaps the town had a lending library? I would inquire in the morning. For tonight, I decided I might as well go to sleep.

This was going to be a long week.

CHAPTER 8
EDWARD

Swinging my hammer down, I pounded the nail into the wood with as much force as I could. Wiping the back of my hand along my forehead, I slicked the sweat away and wiped it on the leg of my pants.

Rising with the sun, I'd made my way to the barn across the lawn and directed a few of the men to begin trimming the overgrown trees along the lane to Thornville. It had been a few years since I was there, and while the house looked very much the same, there were a number of things that would benefit from improvement.

Like this broken fence post in the corral. My horses would escape at once if it was not corrected.

Bringing the hammer down one last time I secured the final nail in the post. Stepping back, I surveyed my work. It looked well enough. Gripping the rail, I tugged to check its stability and was pleasantly surprised. I hadn't done much labor before in my life and my arm was bound to be sore in the coming hours. For now, however, I was pleased.

And ravenous. I glanced back to the house. It was nearly time for breakfast to be ready. I started inside to wash up and inhaled, the rich, clean air which vastly differed from the thick London smog I'd been using to fill my lungs.

The journey to Thornville had been wrought with unease, both from my wife's countenance and my own worry.

I hadn't known the condition I would find Thornville in, and while many of my fears were realized and there were plenty of improvements which needed to be made upon the house, the place had not lost its feeling of home.

I was grateful Lydia agreed to ride with me for the latter half of the journey; she seemed better for it. I was determined to do my duty as her husband. In whatever ways I could, I would try to be considerate and mindful of her needs.

Coming down the stairs with damp hair and the dirt washed from my person, I came upon Lydia in a simple, lavender gown with her dark curls secured high on her head, a few loose ringlets brushing her temples.

"Good morning," I said, offering her my arm. She smiled coyly, but in a way that I was positive was not meant to be a subtle flirtation, as so many women in London's ballrooms were prone to do.

Sensible and rational were not sentiments most women would appreciate, but I had the distinct feeling Lydia would appreciate the compliments. She was not a silly woman, that much I'd discerned through our game of questions and subsequent conversations, and she had a knowing glint in her eye when she spoke to me that I appreciated.

We approached the dining room and the long, slab of a table loomed before us. Dinner the night before had been a quiet affair, our places so far from one another that conversation was unsuitable.

Approaching the chair beside my seat at the end of the table, I offered it to Lydia with a slight flourish. "Perhaps at breakfast we don't need to be quite so formal," I reasoned.

The footmen rushed to move the place setting from the end

of the table to before the seat Lydia occupied. I directed them to move our breakfast dishes to the space between our plates instead of the sideboard, and we filled out plates with muffins, coddled eggs, and cold slices of ham.

I understood there was no cook present, but whoever was covering for the lack was doing a decent job.

I glanced up at Lydia over the rim of my goblet and caught her eye, but her gaze skittered away quickly. We did not have a love match, but that did not mean we could not obtain a friendship. She was kind, smart, and as far as I could tell, artless. Vastly different from the simpering Society misses who had vied for my hand and flirted their way into the hearts of many gentlemen before me.

I was fortunate, I had come to determine, that James's daughter was the woman sitting beside me today. She had proved at dinner last evening that she would not require my presence by her side in the drawing room each evening, and we were free to go about our activities in whichever ways fit us best. I could see us creating a friendship that would last us throughout the years of our marriage.

Though I wanted to give her time to adjust to the idea of being married and better come to know one another, I knew that we would one day have children and raise them to be intelligent, kind humans *without* any addiction to gaming. I would overcome my own desire to gamble, in the meantime, and all would become right in my world.

Satisfied with the direction my life had taken, I reached for another muffin.

Lydia

I reached for a second muffin at the same time as Edward and brushed his fingers, jumping back immediately from the contact. Our hands were both lacking gloves and the feel of his skin burned the tips of my fingers. He lifted a muffin and offered it to me, clearly less bothered by the connection than I was.

"Thank you," I said, my voice squeaking as I accepted the muffin, careful not to touch him once more. I closed my eyes a moment, taking a breath to calm my racing heart. They were just *fingers*. Whatever had gotten into me?

A month before, this man had forgotten me on the dance floor. Only a week later he asked for my hand in marriage, and now we were in Northumberland at his ancestral estate sharing muffins. I would have laughed at the oddity of my own life if I had not lived through the whole ordeal and known very well of its reality.

"Shall we ride into town today?" he asked. "I can show you where the market is held and the church."

"If you wish," I said congenially. "I had wondered if there was a lending library nearby."

"There wasn't when last I visited but perhaps that has changed. We can inquire with Mrs. Patton before we leave."

"Did she speak to you about the situation with the cook?"

"Yes," he said, "but I found dinner and breakfast to both be pleasing. It might be worth discovering who has been cooking our meals."

I wanted to inquire right then why he had forgotten me at the ball. I should have asked when he played our questions game, but I had not had the courage then. Perhaps after a little longer acquaintance, I would be in a position to ask.

He rose, saying, "I will order the carriage—or, wait. Would you rather go on horseback?"

"If it is preferable to you over walking, then yes, horseback would be fine."

He grinned. "Horseback is always preferable to walking."

"Then I must change." I would need to order a new habit if the riding continued much more. The journey here had been enough to convince me that if I should like to ride and breathe at the same time, then I would need to do something about obtaining a larger gown.

"Meet me outside in half an hour?" he asked.

I agreed and watched Edward leave the room, his steps long and swift. I didn't know why I was so sorrowful of his distance. He had led me to believe that perhaps he could care for me when he was so kind and attentive. I was beginning to wonder if that was merely the way he was to everyone.

Changing my gown with the help of Christine, I went downstairs to meet Edward. I paused in the foyer before the front door, however, and glanced over my shoulder at the shrouded windows on the opposite side of the foyer. Crossing to the window directly across from me, I flung the drapes open with one smooth motion, sending dust particles into the air, swirling within the sudden light. I slid open the drapes on the window beside it, and the other on the opposite side of the room beside the door. Standing in the well-lit foyer, I felt the warm rays of the sun penetrate the windows and heat my skin. Inhaling a deep breath, I instantly regretted filling my lungs with dusty air and coughed repeatedly as dust particles coated my throat. I flung the front door open and escaped into the bitter chill outside.

Inhaling the cold air, I pulled my breathing under control and looked up to find Edward standing beside our horses, watching me with concern.

"Are you unwell?" he asked.

Shaking my head, I approached him, rubbing my hand down my horse's mane. Well, the mane of Edward's spare mare. "I merely got a lungful of dusty air," I explained. "It was my own doing."

He nodded before helping me onto the horse.

We rode toward the open gate and I remembered the snarly tree branches that scratched my side when we'd first arrived at the house.

As though reading my thoughts, Edward said, "I sent some men out this morning to trim back the branches. I suppose we'll find out if they did a decent job."

We trotted through the gate and although the branches came a tad too close at times, I did not have to crouch to avoid them, and neither did they reach me.

The town was a twenty-minute ride from the estate. Most of the journey passed in silence but as we neared the outer region, Edward said, "I have good news for you and I almost forgot to share it."

"Oh?"

"Yes. There is a recent addition to the school at the end of town. A couple has rented out a room and created a small lending library within."

"Splendid!" I said, clapping my hands together and quite forgetting I was on top of a horse. She jumped at my sudden movement and took off toward the town at a greater speed than I had ever ridden.

CHAPTER 9
LYDIA

I grasped the reins tightly in my hands and pulled with all of the strength I possessed, pressing my legs into the stirrups to secure my place as the horse finally slowed. Heart racing, I pulled the horse to a complete stop, my rapid breath forming clouds in the cool air.

Thundering hooves pounded the road behind me and I unhooked my leg, sliding to the ground with unladylike haste. I did not want to be aloft the beast if she was to spook again.

"Are you hurt?" Edward asked, stopping suddenly.

I held the reins in shaky fingers, watching Edward slide smoothly to the ground and approach me, leading his enormous horse behind him.

"No, I was able to stop her quickly." I cleared my throat. Even my voice shook.

"I saw that," he said, his eyebrows raised. He appeared suitably impressed and I refrained from puffing up my chest in conceit. I had merely reacted to a runaway horse. It was nothing but a survival technique.

"Perhaps walking would have been wise." He reached

forward and took the reins from my hands. "I will tie the horses and we shall walk from here."

I stepped back and waited for Edward in the shade of a large tree. My heart was returning to a normal tempo, but I clutched my hands together regardless. A few women stood down the road near the fence of what appeared to be a church, their faces directed at me and their heads bent in conversation.

I'd had an audience during my runaway horse escapade? Lovely.

Edward returned, offering his elbow. "Shall we? The school is just at the end of this street."

I fell into step beside him, listening as he pointed out the shops and shared a brief history of the town. "And that is the church," he said, pointing across the street. I had been correct in my assumption. He indicated the large, thick tree situated in the front of the church yard, towering over the building, its branches reaching over the street. "That yew tree is older than most of the town. It is rumored to be older than Berkeley Castle."

"It would be interesting to know all that tree has seen."

Edward shot me a look and I glanced away. I was letting my imagination run away with me again. But I did not disbelieve my words. There was so much of history that had taken place before such a tree.

"Mr. Thornton, is it true then?" a voice called from near the church fence. We paused and I followed Edward's lead as he crossed toward the people who had been watching me earlier. Upon closer examination, it was clear that the two women were identical twins. Their dark blonde hair was streaked with white and tied back in similar knots, and their gowns, though one was yellow and the other green, were of similar design. It was their wrinkles which set them apart, for the woman in the yellow gown had significantly more of them lining her eyes and mouth; I was sure she had smiled more than her sister.

"Good day," Edward said, bowing. "Lydia, allow me the pleasure of introducing you to Melton's finest, the Misses Robinson."

I dipped a curtsy. "Pleased to meet you."

"And this," he gestured toward me, "is my wife."

The women's mouths dropped in unison, adding to their similar appearance. Miss Robinson in the yellow gown was first to regain her senses as she dipped her head and said, "I am Miss Abigail, but my older sister, Miss Robinson, is forever being called by my name. When I am called by hers, it is not entirely a mistake."

"But no less confusing," Miss Robinson added. "Welcome, Mrs. Thornton. Oh!" Her mouth forming a perfect circle, she turned to her sister. "Shall we throw her a breakfast?"

"We *must* if she is going to be a new addition to our community."

Edward cleared his throat. "We have already celebrated in London with a wedding breakfast."

And we were not planning to remain at Thornville for long. Why did he not tell them that we were only in residence for our wedding trip?

"But this is for the people of Melton as much as it is for your wife, Mr. Thornton." Miss Robinson lowered her voice and gave Edward a severe eyeing look. "We would love the opportunity to celebrate and meet her."

"You have met her just now," he argued, "and the rest of town can do so on Sunday."

Why was he not simply explaining that there was no need? If they knew I wasn't going to be here for long, then perhaps they would let it go. "Actually," I said, cutting off Miss Abigail before she could speak. "We shall not remain in Melton long enough to meet everyone."

Three sets of eyes blinked at me. "Why do you say that?" Edward asked.

"Because this is only our wedding trip, of course," I said.

He stared at me. His mouth opened, but his gaze flicked to the women, likely noticing the way their bodies leaned forward and their passive faces concealed interest. He cleared his throat. "Good day, ladies," he said, offering me his elbow.

Turning me toward the other side of the road, we crossed it in silence.

"I shall begin planning the breakfast," Miss Robinson called, waving her fan at me. "It is a Melton tradition!"

"Couple of old gossip-laden biddies," Edward said under his breath. "You don't have to go to any town breakfast if you don't wish to."

I didn't wish to, but Edward's vehemence caused me to reconsider. "What is it about the women that distresses you so?"

He paused, forcing me to halt beside him in front of a blacksmith's forge. Heat reached me in waves, a welcome reprieve from the chilly autumn air.

"They don't distress me. But you did not appear to want another wedding breakfast, and I do not wish to force Melton society upon you. The whole concept is absurd."

"Strange, indeed," I agreed, "but sweet."

His mouth lifted in a half-smile. "I suppose it could be looked at that way." He began walking again and I felt the cold more once we left the warmth of the blacksmith's entryway. "Here we are."

We stopped before a tall, brick building at the end of the row of businesses. A garden ran alongside the building and around the back with a plaque beside the door that read, *Kirklin School*.

"Is it for boys or girls?" I inquired.

"Both, I believe. But the lending library is in the front parlor, according to Mrs. Patton."

We knocked on the door and a servant ushered us into a dim hall and through a doorway immediately on the right. The smell of leather and paper overcame me at once, causing a strange sense of homesickness for my favorite room in Father's house.

Rows of bookcases lined the walls, full to the brim of various sizes and colors. Long, open windows sat in the corner of the room along a curved wall, letting in sufficient light and surrounding a desk situated in their center. A woman sat behind the desk, her honey-colored hair pulled back in a loose knot. She glanced up as we entered, closing the book she was reading and rising in her chair.

"Welcome," she said, coming around her desk to approach us. She wore a nice dress, though not overly frilly, and a kind smile graced her face. "I am Lady Cameron. Have you come for a subscription?"

"Yes," Edward said immediately. "My wife would like to borrow a book."

Nodding, Lady Cameron shot me a knowing smile. "Wonderful. That is why we are here." Turning to me, she said, "If you would like to browse our titles, I can show your husband how to sign the form and pay the fees."

I nodded, moving along the wall to browse the books. There was a wide variety available. Everything from poetry compilations to gothic novels adorned the shelves, with a section dedicated to nonfiction along the farthest wall.

"This shelf is hardly touched," Lady Cameron said, coming to stand beside me. Edward stood behind the desk, watching out the window with his hands clasped lightly behind his back. "Your husband says you are recently inhabiting Thornville. Welcome to Melton."

"Thank you."

"We are neighbors," she continued. "If you find yourself in need of anything, I live just on the other side of the wood."

I smiled, pulling a small novel from the shelf titled *Sense and Sensibility*. "The wood completely surrounds Thornville, so I wouldn't know which way to venture, I'm afraid."

Her nose screwed up in thought. "I am not the best with direction, but I did happen upon your estate during one of my rambles. I believe you would travel north to reach my house."

I did not yet know which way from Thornville pointed north, but I likely wouldn't need to know, either. And regardless, the sentiment was kind.

"Have you read this one yet?" she asked, pointing to the book I held.

I shook my head.

"I recommend it. Perhaps I only picked it up at first because it is written by A Lady," she said, pointing to the inscription on the front cover, "but whoever this lady is, she is brilliant."

"Thank you. I shall take this one then."

Lady Cameron crossed to the desk and pulled a ledger from the top drawer, filling in a line with slow, deliberate pen strokes.

"Have you found a book?" Edward asked, approaching me. I nodded and bid Lady Cameron farewell as he led me outside. We walked along the street to the tree where our horses were tethered in comfortable silence. Edward took my book and slid it into his coat pocket before pausing before my horse.

"Would you prefer to walk?"

"No," I answered, surprising even myself. "I must return to the saddle now or I may not ever." He seemed to understand and helped me onto my horse.

"What did you mean earlier when you said this was only a wedding trip?" he asked as we pulled our horses onto the road and began trotting home. I squeezed my knees together in the sidesaddle, reassuring myself that I was safe and secure if the mare was to bolt again.

"It is what you told me," I said.

His eyebrows drew together in contemplation. Oh, dear. This was not good.

"This *is* only a wedding trip, is it not?" I asked.

He cleared his throat and I pulled on the reins, stopping my horse. He circled around to face me on his own, saying, "I suppose we did not understand one another originally. I can see how you would have thought that, but it is not what I meant. I intended to come here and reside. Permanently."

"Then why, sir, did you call it a wedding trip? Such a thing implies that we go on holiday and then *return home*."

"There is no cause to be angry, Lydia. We shall return to London eventually."

My voice rose alongside my panic. "I cannot return to London eventually. I am needed there *now*."

He shook his head. "You are *my* wife. Whatever could need you in London?"

I scoffed. "Marriage has little to do with it. I have committed to a friend and she is counting on me to—" I paused, unsure of Edward's feelings on the merits of Sunday schools. Would he forbid me from volunteering if he knew? He watched me expectantly, but my tongue froze.

"Well?" he probed.

"I have promised to help a friend. She is counting on me."

"Surely she has someone else to call on. Does she know that we married?"

I nodded. "She attended the breakfast."

He appeared satisfied. "Then she has likely already sought a replacement."

But she would not. She was counting on my return. I studied Edward's placid smile as he turned his horse. The set of his shoulders on his retreating form was careless. He did not realize how important my calling was. He did not know about the young children and their need for education.

But perhaps he didn't need to. I could find a way to return. Many marriages survived through distance. Why would ours be any different?

CHAPTER 10
LYDIA

One week later, and seven more dinners of stew with bread, and I was no closer to contriving a cause which would allow me to return to London. I sat in the drawing room with a basket of embroidery beside me and a fresh set of handkerchiefs awaiting my new initials. I considered writing to my father and requesting my old room for a short visit, but his face swam through my mind, serious and unwavering, when he told me I would not be welcome to live with him anymore.

I would have to think of something else.

"I have a request," Edward said, coming into the room and dropping onto the chair opposite me.

We hadn't spent much time together since our ride into Melton. He'd taken to spending every moment of sunlight out of doors learning the needs of the land and making repairs where they were necessary. He was dirty in a way I had never seen my own father become, and the sight had equally frightened and surprised me initially. I'd grown used to the layer of dust Edward now trailed behind him, and I found that it did not bother me.

And people said *I* was singular.

"Lydia?" he asked.

"Yes?"

Bewildered, he shook his head. "I am tired of stew."

"Indeed. It is tasty, but I have grown tired of it as well."

He raised his eyebrows. "Perhaps it is time to hire a new cook."

I had thought so the last few nights, but Edward had been situated so far from me at the dinner table, and I hadn't wanted to yell across the room. Our routine was to immediately separate following dinner each night, so I had not had the opportunity to speak to him.

"Would you take care of obtaining a new cook?"

"Me?" I asked, surprised.

"You are the mistress of Thornville."

I nodded my head. It was true. "I suppose I can take care of it." Though I had no idea where to begin to look.

He rose to his feet, bowing. Pausing before the door, he turned back and said, "Oh, I almost forgot. We received an invitation to dine out this evening at Downing Wood. It was from Lady Cameron, the woman from the lending library, you'll recall? I've ordered the carriage for six o'clock. You can abide a short ride, yes?"

"That should be fine." A little queasiness would not ruin my entire evening, surely. "On a positive note, we are most likely not going to be eating stew for dinner tonight."

Edward laughed, his voice ringing through the room. A smile spread over my lips, remaining long after he left.

I spent an hour embroidering an intertwining L and T on the first handkerchief, purposefully avoiding glancing at the writing desk in the far corner of the room. Yet, I knew I must write to Mrs. Coulter. I could put it off no longer.

Tucking my embroidery into my work basket, I set it on the floor near the hearth and wiped my hands down my gown.

Lowering myself in the spindle-back chair, I pulled a fresh sheet of paper from the writing desk and lined it up beside the ink, pen, and necessary writing implements. I dipped my pen in fresh ink, then wrote Mrs. Coulter's name at the top of the page. I froze, my hand hovering over the page.

What was I so afraid of?

Shaking my head to ease the tension building within me, I rolled my shoulders, re-dipped my pen in the ink, and began. If the letter was horrible, I could always toss it in the fire and begin again.

Mrs. Coulter—

I am grateful for the consideration you paid my husband and me in attending my wedding breakfast. It was lovely to see a face I knew well amidst the strangers. I have been in Thornville for one week now and while the house is old, it holds a certain charm and I find that it is beginning to grow on me.

Unfortunately, we are not returning to London as soon as I had hoped. It is my express desire to help Mr. Coulter in his Sunday school, and I will write to you the moment I know we are to return so that you can plan accordingly.

At present, I know the children are in capable hands and I appreciate that Mr. Coulter believed me worthy of being one of their teachers.

I read the letter, unsatisfied with my words. I did not want to send this in the post, but I knew I must. Drawing in a breath, I signed the bottom with a flourish and sanded the paper before folding and sealing it with wax.

Mrs. Coulter would understand. I only wished it hadn't come to this.

Edward

I'd sent for my phaeton days ago, but it had yet to arrive and I was beginning to worry. Lydia had grown so ill in the carriage that I wanted to do my best to avoid rides in an enclosed space as best I could. But after watching her horse run off with her in Melton, my heart had stopped beating and I wasn't eager to put her back on a horse again, at least not on the lane we would need to take through the woods.

I would never forgive myself if Lydia became hurt from falling off a horse.

"Can you ensure the lumber is made available to repair the steps in the barn?" I asked, looking my stablemaster in the eye as he brushed down my stallion, Rebel. "The state they are in is dangerous. One misstep will break through the rot and injure the person on the stairs and whatever animals lie below him."

"Of course, sir," Appleworth responded with a curt nod. He had not necessarily kept up with the necessary repairs, but the animals were in good health.

"And what of the cottage down in the woods?" I asked, doing my best to appear indifferent.

Appleworth paused, his hand resting on Rebel's neck. "The Morley place?"

I nodded, watching him for any sign of recognition.

He lifted one shoulder before resuming his brushing. "It was rough when they first arrived, but recently they've been left alone, as far as I can tell. Mrs. Morley gets help sometimes from a man in town, but they do well enough."

"Are they in great need of anything in particular?"

He watched me curiously but refrained from speaking his mind, only saying, "Who doesn't need *something*, Mr. Thornton?"

Indeed. I could only imagine the woman and her daughter would be in need of some extra finances, or perhaps food. But how was I to assist them without drawing attention to the connection? Surely it would bring notice if I suddenly singled them out and I didn't wish to form a connection between my name and their own.

The scandal was reason enough for me to desire distance, but now I had Lydia to think of, too. If she was to deduce the situation, she would surely wish to do something about it. And I had made a promise, which I vowed to keep.

I could not break that promise now.

CHAPTER 11
LYDIA

Edward surprised me at six o'clock by leading me to the phaeton instead of his covered carriage.

"When did this arrive at Thornville?" I asked.

Climbing up beside me, he said, "Just today. I didn't know if it would be here in time, so I said nothing, not wanting to give you false hope."

"It is perhaps chillier than a carriage ride. But I will feel better. I must thank you."

He smiled at me before snapping the reins and directing the horses through the iron archway. We were not too far out of the gate when Edward led us to the left, through a narrow road in between two, stately trees. The woods were sparse of leaves but thick with trunks, and the waning sun dipped behind them, shining through the trees to light our path.

Coming through the other side of the woods, we turned onto a larger road that led us to a house, slightly smaller than our own. Covered in climbing ivy, the light-gray, stone house was simple, but clean. Smoke billowed from the chimneys and swirled above the house, the sun shining from behind us and bouncing off the windows. Compared to Thornville, surrounded by barren trees and Blackthorn, this house was absolutely marvelous.

"It is beautiful," I said, under my breath.

"Just wait until March," Edward said, his words clipped. "You will find Thornville beautiful as well." He hopped down from the phaeton as a servant held the horses steady. Reaching a hand for me, I placed my own gloved one in his and let him help me down.

Had I detected bitterness in his tone? I had not compared the houses aloud, but Edward had deduced my meaning, regardless.

We approached the house in silence. His mood was bland, and his expression guarded. I felt the desire to reach forward and squeeze his hand in support, but refrained. The impulse was not ordinary for me and I was certain Edward would find it strange.

Melton was his childhood home, filled with the people he'd grown up around, was it not? What would he have to feel nervous or upset about?

An aging butler took our coats and led us toward a room at the end of the hall. Voices trailed toward us and a group of faces I recalled seeing at church a few days prior met me at once. Edward had been eager to return home following the sermon on Sunday, so I had been unable to obtain introductions to anyone that day.

"I am so glad you both could make it," Lady Cameron said, approaching us immediately. A tall man with dark hair and a kind smile followed closely behind her. "This is my husband, Lord Cameron." She turned to him. "This is Mr. and Mrs. Thornton. I met them in the lending library last week."

Lord Cameron stepped forward, bowing. "I've known Thornton an age," he said to his wife. Turning to Edward, he grinned. "I did not know you were the Thorntons Lady Cameron told me about. Though I should have made the connection on my own, I didn't realize you had gotten married."

"It was only recently," Edward explained. "I received a letter from Stallsbury just a month ago. It appears your brother has wed as well."

Lord Cameron nodded, a smile pulling at his mouth. "Eleanor has been a wonderful addition to the Nichols family. They are already expecting a new addition, in fact."

Edward clapped Lord Cameron on the back. "You are to become an uncle, then? Congratulations."

"We have been made an uncle and an aunt five times over already, so the title is not a new one," Lady Cameron explained. She reached forward, lightly grasping my wrist. "Shall we leave them to reminisce? I would love to introduce you to my friends."

I nodded, glancing over my shoulder to Edward as I was led toward the women standing near the fire. His shoulders had relaxed and the tightness in his eyes was gone. Perhaps he merely needed a friend.

"Cameron is very pleased with his brother's recent marriage," Lady Cameron said. "He was afraid the man was destined to bachelorhood."

"Do they reside nearby?" I asked.

"They are not terribly far. An hour's ride, I believe." She paused before we reached the women. "It is part of the reason we chose Melton above Collingdown, where they live with Cameron's parents in the ancestral castle. We hoped for a measure of independence ourselves."

I nodded. "You have not lived here long, then?"

"Only half a year. But it is a wonderful community and we have really grown to love Downing Wood. You missed the peak of the autumn leaves, Mrs. Thornton. It was positively breathtaking. Now tell me, what did you think of *Sense and Sensibility*?"

"It was marvelous. Has the author written anything else?"

"Yes," Lady Cameron said, grinning. "I will set one aside for you titled *Pride and Prejudice*. If you liked the first one, you will love this."

Two women turned to meet us when we finally approached. "Mrs. Thornton, allow me to introduce Mrs. Whitaker and Miss Gould."

They curtsied as their names were spoken and I did likewise. Standing in order of tallest to shortest, Mrs. Whitaker positively towered over Miss Gould, who stood nearly a foot beneath her. Both women wore welcoming smiles that led my concerns of not fitting in to wane considerably.

"How do you like Melton?" Miss Gould asked, her mouth forming a smile which rounded her pink cheeks. Tight curls framed her face, the remainder of her hair pulled back to form a delicate knot at the crown.

"It is colder than I expected," I replied, "but I am growing accustomed to it."

"Just wait," Mrs. Whitaker said, her eyes widening as she shook her head. "Winter hasn't even begun."

I recalled Edward inquiring about the warmth of my clothing and suggesting I purchase a thick, fur-lined cape. Oh, dear. Was I desperately going to regret ignoring that advice?

"Ah," Lady Cameron said. "Our last guest has arrived. Perhaps we might be called in to eat now."

I looked over my shoulder and stilled when I caught the man's eye, immediately recognizing his fashionable head of dark-red hair.

Mr. Radmahl.

"Shall I introduce you?" she asked.

"There is no need," I said, turning back to my hostess. "I am already acquainted with Mr. Radmahl, from London."

"He recently returned from a trip to Town," Miss Gould said dreamily. "And I hear he is yet unattached."

"Not that it matters," Mrs. Whitaker said, her tone shifting from her pleasant demeanor of before to a deeper, more serious tone. "He will never settle for a Melton woman."

Miss Gould did not move her gaze from Mr. Radmahl as she said, "But how can you be sure of such a thing?"

"Easily," Mrs. Whitaker snapped. "He did not marry Sarah. Why would he settle for anyone less?"

Edward's *sister*, Sarah? I opened my mouth to inquire when the butler announced dinner.

"We are informal," Lady Cameron explained. "You may sit wherever you choose."

A man approached, his gray hair liberally sprinkled with white, and asked to escort Miss Gould into dinner, which she regretfully accepted. Lord Cameron and Edward approached at the same time and held their arms out for Lady Cameron and I respectively, and I felt relieved that my own husband was leading me into dinner and not a stranger. Resting my hand upon his arm, I felt a peaceful comfort in his guidance and nearness, though I could not place precisely *why* I felt that way.

Sitting between Edward and the end of the table, Lady Cameron on his other side, I removed my gloves and laid them in my lap. Miss Gould sat opposite us, her sorrowful gaze watching Mr. Radmahl lead Mrs. Whitaker to the chair opposite me before sitting in the last remaining empty chair to my left.

"What a lovely surprise," Mr. Radmahl said as the first course was brought in and placed before us on the table. "I did not realize you knew Lord and Lady Cameron."

"We are recently acquainted," I explained. "Edward and I saw you in London only a fortnight past. It is strange seeing you here so soon."

"There was nothing to hold my interest in Town," he said nonchalantly.

"Did you have a pleasant trip?" Mrs. Whitaker asked, drawing his attention away.

I took the opportunity to lean toward Edward. "Is the gray-haired man across from you Mr. Whitaker, by chance?"

"He is," Edward said, nodding. "His wife is sitting just opposite you. They run the school where Lady Cameron holds her lending library."

My head snapped up, taking in the couple in a fresh light. Mr. Whitaker was older than his wife by a decade, at least, though I was not one to judge. If she ran the school, perhaps I could request a volunteer position within it. I could not expect Mr. Coulter to hold a place open for me in my absence, but surely he would not hesitate to take me on if I came back with some experience. Even, perhaps, a recommendation.

"You have a decided gleam in your eye and I very much doubt it is emotion over the succulent meal," Edward said, his tone low and even. "Even though I, myself, am finding it vastly more pleasurable than stew with bread. Please do enlighten me."

I faced him, watching the candlelight flicker against the green of his eyes. Perhaps I ought to wait and ask him about it *after* I had obtained the position. Surely he would not oppose the opportunity for me to volunteer and help the needy once he knew people were counting on me.

But then again, my father forbade all forms of volunteer work on the faulty reasoning that there were plenty of people to see to the work, so I didn't need to. His true reason, however, was that he did not appreciate the uncleanliness of the less fortunate and did not want me to bring the dirt home with me.

I did not share Father's aversion to dirt. But what would I do if Edward did?

"How is the estate, Thornton?"

Bless Mr. Radmahl and his perfect timing.

Edward hesitated, looking between Mr. Radmahl and me before picking up his goblet and sipping his wine.

He turned away to speak to the Lady Cameron on his other

side and my cheeks warmed at the blatant disregard he paid to Mr. Radmahl. I felt the need to apologize on behalf of my husband, but something held me back. Mr. Radmahl tilted his head, delivering a knowing smile.

"I think you will find the society of Melton to be very welcoming," he said, graciously ignoring the snubbing Edward dealt him. "It is a small community, but they are tight knit."

"I have found that to be the case thus far," I said. "Did you see my father before you left London?"

"The last I saw your father was at your wedding breakfast. But he seemed joyous, if I can say that."

"You may."

"And if I remember correctly, he had recently won a large and valuable game. I cannot imagine he would be anything but happy."

"I beg your pardon?" I asked, confused. What large, valuable game could Mr. Radmahl be referring to?

He glanced behind me and lowered his voice, bringing his face closer to my own. "I really should not say. But I suppose if you inquire of your husband, he would be more than capable of filling you in."

Mrs. Whitaker laughed loudly, stealing our attention. "And *then* Miss Robinson was so offended by Jonathan's poem, she actually stood and left the recital in that moment."

"Whatever did her sister do?" Miss Gould inquired, her eyes wide.

"Followed after her moments later, of course. Miss Abigail's face was redder than a strawberry." Mrs. Whitaker laughed again. "And neither one of them has graced our school again."

Light chuckles bounced around the patrons of the room and I desperately wished to know the aspects of the child's poem which forced the Misses Robinsons to flee.

"You are curious, are you not?" Edward said around a grin, his voice low and intimate.

I could not tamp down my smile, no matter how much I wished to remain poised and appear carefree. "Yes," I finally admitted, whispering as I leaned closer to my husband. "Whatever was the poem about?"

He drew the moment out longer than was necessary. "The boy delivered a poem he authored himself about hunting with his grandfather's dogs."

"Is that all?"

"And how they took the animals back to the house and prepared them to be eaten."

"Good gracious," I said, my whisper rising in volume. "I think I wouldn't enjoy such a poem either."

"Would you run from the school with cheeks blazing hotter than a fire?" he asked. His head tilted to the side as though he was genuinely curious.

I shook my head slightly. "I couldn't do that to the child."

A small, satisfied smile played at his lips as he sat back in his chair and I was grateful I'd given such a response. Evidently, Edward approved.

Dinner continued in an informal, yet comfortable manner. Mr. Radmahl hadn't returned to his cryptic conversation, but that was all the better for me. The gleam in his eye had made me slightly uncomfortable, though it very well could have been my imagination. Still, Mrs. Whitaker's interruption, with her poem anecdote, had been perfectly timed. I'd yet to obtain an introduction to Mr. Whitaker, but hoped to find a moment to question his wife about their school and the reading program they had in place. If there was a lending library in their front parlor, it was likely safe to assume that they valued reading.

Lady Cameron stood at the close of the meal and the rest of the women followed suit, removing to the drawing room.

We gathered on the sofas near the fire, Lady Cameron on my left and the other women across from us.

"Now you must tell us," Mrs. Whitaker said, leaning forward. "How did you capture such an unattainable bachelor?"

Did I tell these women that I hadn't the faintest idea how I had obtained Edward for my husband? I'd had no part in capturing any bachelor. How would Edward feel if I told the present company that he'd arranged our marriage without even asking me? Nay, without even showing me any interest?

I could not tell them about our first and only introduction when the man forgot me on the dance floor.

"I am afraid there is no grand story to tell," I said apologetically. "I was merely fortunate, I suppose, perhaps in the right place at the right time."

"I do not believe that for a moment," Lady Cameron said. "Mr. Thornton must have become smitten by your beautiful eyes."

That was a nice sentiment, but clearly false. They could believe what they wished, however. I had done my part by telling the truth.

"Have you met many people from Melton yet?" Miss Gould asked.

I sent her a grateful smile and shook my head. "I'm afraid not. Aside from the Misses Robinson, I've only been introduced to the present company."

"Well, avoid them at *all* costs," Mrs. Whitaker said. "They are gossips in the severest form."

Edward had said something similar as we'd walked away from them, hadn't he? Something to the effect of *gossiping old biddies*.

The men entered the room then and tables were set up for cards. Edward stood behind the table and watched us play. His mild refusals to join the card games were met with calm acceptance by our hosts and Lord Cameron sat out with him during one round, chatting easily as they watched the rest of the party enjoy the game. I was able to partner Lady Cameron once and

Mrs. Whitaker another time before the night drew to a close, but never had the opportunity to discuss the school with the Whitakers in relative privacy.

At the end of the evening, I glanced back at Downing Wood. Fire lit the rooms from the inside and caused the windows to glow as Edward helped me into the phaeton. I could see the outline of the remaining guests as we pulled away from the house.

"I want you to stay away from Radmahl," Edward said, his tone sharp.

My head snapped toward Edward. His face was hardly visible, the lanterns lighting our way too far ahead of us to cast any sufficient light our direction. "Why?"

"He is not a good man. Trust me on this."

I felt torn, my conscience pulling me in opposite directions. While I had no reason not to trust my husband, I'd been given no cause to doubt Mr. Radmahl, either, aside from my own sense of unease at our dinner conversation. But that hardly merited completely avoiding the man. "Why?" I asked again.

"Trust me," he said, turning to look into my eyes. "Do you promise?"

"I will do my best," I said. "But we reside in the same town. Am I to cut the man when he's given me no cause?"

"Is my word not cause enough? I am your husband, not he."

"But how am I to feel comfortable committing such a drastic measure when I do not know the cause? I've had a very amiable relationship with the man and have yet to learn of any of his misdeeds. Furthermore, he is a friend of my father's."

Edward scoffed and I clamped my mouth shut.

We finished the remainder of our drive in silence and parted ways in the foyer. Edward stomped upstairs, shutting his door with more force than I'd ever heard from him before. It was clearly a sensitive topic for him, but I could not, in good conscience, agree to cut a man who'd done me no wrong.

CHAPTER 12
LYDIA

Birdsong filled the air as I left Thornville and walked the perimeter of the Blackthorn hedge, skirting the rough exterior and stepping into the woods. Mrs. Patton would not reveal who had been making our stew, but she did point me in the direction of a cottage just off our property who might know of someone capable of stepping in as our cook, at least for the interim, if nothing else.

And perhaps Edward would quickly forgive me if I was to replace the stew with something different.

I followed Mrs. Patton's directions, turning right on the worn footpath outside of our gates. I'd asked Mrs. Patton to fill a basket with an offering for the family I was going to visit, but without a cook in residence, there was little to give. A loaf of bread and jar of strawberry jam would have to suffice, though pastries or a pie would probably have taken us further in their esteem.

Perhaps the lack of baked goods would prove to this woman that Thornville was in dire need of assistance.

Pausing, I lifted the linen over my basket to peek at the bread inside. Was I giving away the loaf which was to accompany our stew later that evening? I supposed I would have to wait and find out.

It was not too much farther down the path that a small cottage appeared just around a bend. Its thick, thatched roof was snugly holding the building together as a thin stream of smoke drifted up from the chimney. I let myself through the short gate and drew in a fortifying breath before raising my fist and knocking on the solid, wood door.

Silence met me. I waited a moment longer before knocking again. Slow, steady footsteps could be heard inside the cottage and I raised my fist to knock a third time when the door slowly creaked open.

A short, stout woman with long gray hair and an old, dingy apron opened the door. She glanced at me for a long moment before she began to close the door once more.

"Wait! Mrs. Morley?"

She paused. I'd caught her attention. I stepped forward, holding up the basket. "I've brought you some bread from Thornville."

She waited a moment longer and I pushed my luck. "I brought you jam, as well."

"Blackberry?" she asked, her voice as craggy as she appeared.

"Strawberry."

I held my breath as she looked between me and the basket as though she were weighing the worth of accepting my offering. I lifted it closer in case the smell of the bread would entice her further.

"Ack. Come in."

Leaving the door open, Mrs. Morley turned away, walking through the hallway and into the next room with slow steps, her back hunched over.

I hesitated only a moment before following her and closing the door behind me.

"What do you need?" she asked. "Thornville has been empty for years. Or so I've heard."

"Well, we have come to live here for the time being and are in need of a cook. I was told I might find one here."

"Haven't cooked in years," she said gruffly. "And I'm not interested anyway."

I tried to keep my shoulders from deflating. "Oh. Well, alright. Thank you for letting me into your home. Enjoy the jam."

I stood to go, leaving the basket on the table just opposite us.

"My daughter might be interested," Mrs. Morley said.

I paused, turning back toward her. "May I see her?"

"She's out delivering her mending. If it won't interfere with her mending, she can come help up in the kitchen."

"It would only be temporary," I said.

The woman held my gaze.

"I don't mind if she brings her mending to work on in the kitchen as long as she can produce meals. At least, until I find a more permanent solution." I felt like I was playing a game with the older woman. But the heady rush of bartering infused me. I continued, "Of course, if she wants to do the job *permanently*, she will devote her time to my kitchen while she is at my house."

I stood in the doorway, awaiting a response. When I was convinced none was forthcoming, I turned to go.

"She'll be there tomorrow."

Yes. "And I suppose I will receive her answer when she comes tomorrow, whether she brings her mending or not." I nodded to the basket on the table. "Good day, Mrs. Morley. Please enjoy the bread and jam."

I closed the door behind me, invigorated. My shoulders set back, I almost did not see the small, brown lump on the ground before nearly tripping over it.

I jumped out of the way, clutching a nearby tree as my breath came rapidly.

A rock had *not* been in the center of the path on my way to Mrs. Morley's cottage. I was positive.

The rock shifted, and I stilled. A small head lifted from the ground and clear, brown eyes gazed up at me through a thoroughly brown face. Whoever this small child was, he was positively covered in mud.

"Did I hurt you?" I asked, stepping forward.

He watched me quietly before shaking his head. He pulled himself up to his full height; I guessed he was around five or six years old.

Pointing back to the Morley's cottage, I asked, "Is this your home?"

His small eyes were solemn as he nodded.

"Shall I take you inside? I happen to know that there is a loaf of bread with a jar of strawberry jam waiting on your table."

His eyebrows perked up and hope slithered through me, though his face did not lose its wary expression. Why was he outside alone? And why was he so dirty?

I reached forward for his hand, but he stepped back. I had gone too far.

"Can I walk you to the house?" I asked.

He shook his head, then took off at a run. I listened for the door and heard it slam shut a few seconds later. I could hear the rumble of Mrs. Morley speaking to the boy, but was too far away to make out her words.

A boy that age should be playing with other children.

I took myself home and directly down to the kitchen. Swinging the door open from the outside, I came upon Mrs. Patton standing beside the fireplace, dropping chopped potatoes into the stew pot over the fire. Her cheeks went pink, and I swallowed my grin.

Was she embarrassed that she'd been pulling double duty

and cooking as well as running the household staff? Or simply ashamed that she had served us nothing but stew for over a week?

"I have just come from Mrs. Morley's cottage. I believe we will have a new cook in the morning, but whether she is temporary or permanent is yet to be determined."

"Very good, ma'am."

"And Mrs. Patton? What is the name of the young boy who lives with Mrs. Morley?"

"Young Samuel? He is Mrs. Morley's grandson."

"A son of our new cook?"

She shook her head, her eyes shifting between the pot and me.

I waited. That was not an answer though it was clear she knew something more.

"His mother is dead," Mrs. Patton said. "No one knows who the father is."

So the mother was unmarried, the boy illegitimate. That would explain Mrs. Patton's hesitation. "And why is he not at school in Melton?"

"They won't take him," she said at once. "They won't take any of the dirty kids. Don't want to spoil their school."

With dirt, or because the children were poor? Fire spread through my bosom and I felt anger at the Whitakers for their blatant disregard for all of the less fortunate children of Melton. Why were the poor children less deserving of an education? Particularly when it would be of such use?

If these young children could learn how to read, then they would be able to escape their bland worlds and lose themselves in stories. Coupled with a basic understanding of arithmetic, these skills would open up opportunities for them to better their circumstances and qualify for work they would otherwise not be able to do as they aged.

Shaking my head, I said, "Well perhaps I ought to do something about that, then."

Mrs. Patton watched me stalk off. The last thing I saw before shutting the kitchen door was her surprised face.

Perhaps I had vented my anger on an undeserving soul, but Mrs. Whitaker and her husband weren't nearby.

It might not be a common belief, but I had been taught and enlightened by Mr. and Mrs. Coulter, and I could never go back to my ignorance of before.

I passed Christine on the stairs and stopped her. "I would like to go into Melton, Christine. Do you know where my husband is?"

"In the barn."

I thanked her, turning around and marching down the stairs and outside. After the warmth of the kitchen, the cold air hit me like a wall of bitter ice and I wrapped my spencer tighter over my shoulders. Thankfully, the barn wasn't far and I went directly for it, hoping the interior was warmer than the chilled air outside.

The stench of hay and horses reached me the moment I stepped inside. A line of stalls on the far wall were occupied by horses. I followed voices to a set of stairs which led to an upper loft. I halted halfway up the stairs. Edward stood on the far end of the loft, leaning against a large, open doorway while another man shoveled hay into cut out holes on the far end. I could see below the loft floor to where the hay was falling into the horse's stalls.

"Lydia?" Edward asked, surprised.

I glanced up to find Edward crossing the loft toward me. He did not appear upset over our conversation the night before. I cleared my throat. "I would like to go into Melton and exchange my book. Do you have a need to go into town or should I do so with my maid and return before dinner?"

He paused. His face was covered in dirt, and his shirtsleeves were so dingy they could no longer be called white.

How could I have even considered Edward having an aversion to dirt? The man was positively covered in it.

"I do not have a need to go, but would you like my escort?"

"I had planned to walk," I said. "I can bring my maid." I didn't mention that I could likely walk to Melton and return before Edward was able to fully remove the dirt from his person.

He nodded, his face taking on a relieved expression. "Wonderful. I shall see you at dinner."

Hopefully following a bath. He looked as brown as little Samuel had earlier that morning.

I went back inside and retrieved my maid before setting off for Melton. I was going to walk the frustration out of my limbs whether Christine could keep up or not.

CHAPTER 13
EDWARD

The loft stairs had been repaired just in time for Lydia to ascend them without hurting herself. I'd panicked momentarily when I found her halfway up the steps, but then remembered there was no danger remaining and had let out an anxious breath.

I watched her cross the lawn toward the house and then returned to the barn to check on Rebel. He was clean and happy, munching away at his oats and neighing gratefully when I picked up the brush and began stroking his side.

"Mr. Thornton," a footman called from the doorway.

I turned to find a tall young man holding a sheet of wrinkled paper, his eyebrows knit together. Returning the brush to its hook on the wall, I motioned for the footman to approach.

"What is it?" I asked.

"This was found tacked to the front door of the house, sir." He reached forward to pass me the sheet of paper and I took it, though it felt strange to retrieve it from his hand and not from a platter.

You are unwanted. Leave Melton if you know what is good for you.

"Where did this come from?" I asked.

"The front door, sir," he repeated.

A child's prank, perhaps? It was a drastic request and could not possibly hold any merit.

I crumpled the note in my fist. Perhaps if this servant saw what little heed I paid the threat, he would spread about the servants quarters that it was nothing to trouble the household over. "Send Jeremy to prepare a bath for me. I should be inside in a quarter of an hour."

"Yes sir," the footman said, turning back for the house.

With the footman gone, I smoothed out the paper and examined the writing. It was done in a hand much older than that of a child, but I couldn't help but consider it anything but prank, nonetheless.

I did not have any enemies. And as far as I knew, neither did Lydia. Though perhaps it would be in my best interest to learn a little more about my wife.

CHAPTER 14
LYDIA

I hurried to the lending library in Melton with *Sense and Sensibility* in my hands and the questions which had arisen from meeting Samuel that morning on the tip of my tongue. When I pushed inside the small front room of the school, I came face to face with Lady Cameron and Mrs. Whitaker drinking tea on the chairs in the center of the room and my ire deflated.

These kind, welcoming women had done nothing but show me consideration and offer me friendship. I planned to speak to the Whitakers about their school, but I would do so with respect.

"Would you like to join us?" Lady Cameron asked. "We've only just sat down, so the tea is very hot."

"That would be lovely, thank you."

I sat on a ladder-back chair beside Lady Cameron and set the book I'd brought in my lap before accepting a cup of tea.

"We were just mentioning the lack of assemblies in Melton this year," Mrs. Whitaker said. "The only balls we had in the past were thrown by the Fuller's, but they have since gone to the colonies." She stopped, setting her tea on her lap. "Can you credit it? Who would want to do that?"

Lady Cameron smiled, bringing her tea to her lips. "We do not have the space or I would offer to throw a ball myself."

"Perhaps a small one?" Mrs. Whitaker asked. She looked about herself with dramatic flair. "Mr. Whitaker and I *really* do not have the space, I am afraid."

"Mrs. Thornton," Lady Cameron said, "I recently heard that the Robinson sisters are planning a wedding breakfast for you."

"It is quite bizarre," I said. "I cannot understand them."

"Tradition," Mrs. Whitaker stated, matter-of-factly. "The town has helped with wedding breakfasts for one another for years, and the Thorntons are one of the oldest families this town can claim. The sisters probably feel it is their duty in some way."

"But perhaps a dinner party in our honor would be more appropriate," I said.

The women glanced at one another. "That would be far more appropriate," Lady Cameron said, eyeing Mrs. Whitaker deliberately. "Maybe someone ought to drop the idea in their ears."

Mrs. Whitaker placed her teacup on the small table beside her, sighing. "Very well. I will see what I can do. For now, though, I should get back to the students."

"Are there many of them?" I asked.

"Students? We have twelve."

My heart began to beat rapidly. I did not want to create discord, but I could not keep my questions away. "And do they all live here in Melton?"

She nodded, rising to her feet. "There are two little boys who stay with us most of the year and board in the house, but the rest of the students go home at the end of the day."

I swallowed. "And what of the other children?"

Mrs. Whitaker's pale eyebrows drew together. "Which other children?"

"I met a little boy outside of the Morley cottage today who was not in school."

The women watched me quietly and I wondered briefly if I should have kept my question to myself. But no, I would never regret speaking up for someone who did not have the capacity to do so for himself.

"We run a school, Mrs. Thornton, not a charity. Unfortunately, children like Samuel Morley cannot afford to come to school."

So she knew of whom I spoke. "Which is why Sunday schools are being put in place. To educate those who cannot afford school. Does Melton not have a Sunday school?"

"I'm afraid not," Lady Cameron said.

Mrs. Whitaker cast me a curious glance and bid us farewell. I listened as her footsteps trailed up the stairs outside of the parlor.

"Shall I exchange that book for you now, Mrs. Thornton?"

I handed Lady Cameron the book and waited for her to retrieve *Pride and Prejudice*, and then mark the exchange in her ledger. She walked me to the door. "You know," she said, "you might try speaking to Mr. Cartwright over at the church. Perhaps a Sunday school could be implemented."

My heart warmed. "Thank you for the suggestion. I believe I shall."

I retrieved Christine from the front steps and walked back down the road, crossing the street toward the church and the overbearing Yew tree before it. "I just need to speak to the vicar and then we can return home."

Christine nodded, waiting beside me as I knocked on the door. A woman answered the door, wearing a purple apron and holding a potato.

"Is the vicar in?"

"Yes, ma'am. Who might I say is calling?"

"Mrs. Thornton."

She closed the door and walked away, before returning to lead me into the rector's study.

"Good afternoon, Mrs. Thornton," Mr. Cartwright said, pulling his aged body to a stand as I entered the room. He gestured to the leather chair opposite his desk and I lowered myself into it.

"What can I do for you?" he asked.

My back straight and shoulders level, I said, "I wanted to inquire about a Sunday school for children." His face immediately stiffened, but I continued. "I have been told there is no school to teach the young, poor children of Melton to read. How are they meant to read their bibles if they do not know how?"

"They can learn by coming to church."

"But that does not allow for daily study," I argued. "Perhaps if I were to offer my services—"

"No, Mrs. Thornton," he said, shaking his head. "We will not be implementing a Sunday school. Those children can receive the good word by attending church. They have no time to read daily, as they will spend their entire lives working from sunup to sundown, and it is a wasted effort to teach them something which can do them no good."

"Is it not good to have the ability to escape into the story of *Romeo and Juliet*, or *Robinson Crusoe*? Perhaps their evenings will be better spent learning from the book of *John* and you will find a rise in attendance."

"It can only lead to unrest and dissatisfaction. They will soon believe they can change their future outcomes and that is a dangerous road to travel."

His words had a final, stubborn ring to them and I realized at once how fruitless further arguing would be.

Twice now I had approached a person I thought would surely agree with me about the merits of educating young minds, and twice I had been rebuked and denied. The rejection would have hurt more if I was not so very angry.

Clenching my hands tightly in the folds of my gown, I got to my feet. "Good afternoon, Mr. Cartwright."

"I shall see you on Sunday," he said.

I paused at the door. "I suppose you shall."

No one waited near the door, so I let myself out. Walking straight past Christine, I turned for home while she scrambled to catch up.

Mrs. Whitaker had stated that the poor had no money, and because of that, school was not an option. Mr. Cartwright blatantly admitted that the poor had no need for education because they spent their lives working.

If it was such a terrible, pointless idea, then why was Mr. Coulter finding such wide success with his Sunday schools in London? They were growing so rapidly that he was opening a new school every few months, at least.

I paused in the middle of the road and Christine bumped into my shoulder.

"Sorry, ma'am," she said.

I turned to her and looked in her wide, blue eyes. "Christine, can you read?"

She shook her head. "No."

Drawing a breath, I did not give myself time to question my sanity. "Would you like to learn?"

Her uncertainty was not comforting. I said, "We can take no more than thirty minutes a day. It will take quite some time, but I believe it will be worth it."

She glanced from me down to the book I held in my hand. I raised it and placed the leatherbound copy of *Pride and Prejudice* in her hands.

Opening it, she fanned the pages before looking up at me. "I would like that very much."

I grinned, taking the book back and turning toward Thornville. "It is settled then. We will begin today."

CHAPTER 15
LYDIA

Teaching another person to read was not quite as easy as I had anticipated. I had been reading, myself, for years, and I could do so quite well, so I assumed passing my knowledge onto another, particularly someone who was at least sixteen years old, would be simple.

It might have been simple in theory, but it was vastly difficult in execution.

Christine and I had returned from town and went directly to the drawing room. I'd pulled a few sheets of paper from the writing desk there as well as a charcoal pencil and had set Christine up at the table beside me. We'd sat across from one another a few minutes while I determined where to begin, and eventually settled upon vowels.

I explained letters and their purpose, then wrote out the vowels and demonstrated their sounds. But Christine, instead of immediately soaking in the information, grew flustered and overwhelmed. We quit our lesson so she could prepare my gown for dinner and I determined to try another course of action the following day.

Whatever I did, I needed to slow down. That much was abundantly clear.

I went upstairs to change for dinner and returned to the drawing room to find Edward standing over the card table, analyzing the papers I'd left there with the vowels written out.

"What is this?" he asked.

Rejection and a lack of understanding had met me twice that day, and further defeat fell upon my shoulders with the difficulty of Christine's first lesson. I opened my mouth to disregard his question when an image came to my mind of Lady Cameron, suggesting I approach the vicar.

She couldn't have known Mr. Cartwright would turn me down. But surely she was supportive of my endeavors or she simply would have bid me goodbye.

Edward's clear green eyes watched my indecision until I finally blurted, "I have begun teaching Christine to read."

"Christine?"

"My maid."

The drawn-out silence and surprise on his face were equally distressing.

"Whatever for?" he finally asked, confusion written on his features.

I bit my tongue before I could shout, *So she can read!* It was an impertinent remark and, unfortunately, Edward seemed genuinely confused.

"You might not enjoy reading," I said, "but many people do. Why should Christine not have the opportunity to decide for herself as well?"

He seemed to ponder my explanation before setting the paper containing my written vowels on the table. He said nothing else and I found myself yearning for his opinions, be them good or not.

"Do you object?" I asked.

He shook his head, meeting my gaze, and I felt immediate relief.

"I suppose not, as long as it doesn't interfere with her responsibilities."

Christine's responsibilities were to me, so I could see no reason it would interfere. If I chose to forgo an elaborate hairstyle to give Christine time for a lesson, then why it should matter to anyone else?

"Thank you," I said.

He nodded, leading me into the dining room for dinner. Stew was brought forth in bowls, but no bread. Edward looked about him for the sliced bread we usually had beside our stew and glanced up at me, confusion etched on his face.

"I traded our loaf of bread for a cook," I called across the vast length of the table.

I seemed to only add to his confusion, so I lifted my spoon and ate, instead.

When my soup was finished, I rose, as I normally did, to leave for the silence of the drawing room, the roaring fire, and my book. But this time, I hesitated. I felt unfinished. Our conversation had not led anywhere useful as Edward's mind was still very much unknown to me. But when I turned to inquire further on his thoughts regarding my teaching, he glanced up and caught my eye and I paused.

His smile was perfunctory. If it was bothering me that our conversation never seemed to find a comfortable completion, it obviously did not bother him. He returned his gaze to the drink in his glass and I turned back for the door.

Edward was disinclined to worry about my teaching the poor, so I should let it be. He was a busy man, constantly finding something within the estate grounds to fix or improve. Even in the evenings, I had seen him leave the house following dinner and make his way toward the barn.

Sitting on the sofa in the drawing room, I pulled out *Pride and Prejudice* and began to read.

I had not read more than five pages when the door opened to the drawing room and Edward walked inside. He sat on the chair opposite me, leaning back and casually crossing one ankle over the other knee.

"What, no projects to work on this evening?"

He sighed. "I have determined to fix the broken step on the servants' stairs, but I cannot do so until the morning."

"Why?"

"Because I do not currently have ample light. I attempted to bring in additional candles, but they were insufficient."

"Perhaps the servants will appreciate that as well, for they might have a hard time sleeping through a banging hammer."

Edward's lips pulled up into a smile. "I hadn't thought of that."

We sat in silence for a minute longer. He did not leave, and he did not speak, so I opened my book to read once again.

"Is this how you always pass the evenings?" he asked, watching me with interest.

Closing the book, I set it on my lap. "Either reading or needlework. But yes, I pass most evenings in here."

When it was apparent that Edward was not leaving, I set my book on the table beside the end of the sofa. "Would you like to play a game of cards?"

His face immediately froze up. "No, I'd rather not."

"Very well. Would you like to read?"

"You will read aloud?" he asked, his eyebrows pulled together.

I would *rather* not, but if it would help him to pass his evening then I was willing to sacrifice. "Unless you have a better idea."

"Well," he said, bringing his hand up to rub his chin, "we have a billiards table in the parlor. Would that be an appropriate way to pass the hour?"

Far less enjoyable than reading, to me. But I did not want to be rude. He'd never before reached out to me in such a way and I found myself wishing to not disappoint him. "Very well."

I rose and followed Edward from the room, down the hall, and into a small parlor at the back of the house. It was dim and Edward rang to request another lamp as I pulled the mace from the wall and ran my fingers along the smooth wood of my stick.

"Shall we play to six points?" he asked, pulling a mace down and situating the red ball on the table.

I nodded. He indicated that I could begin and I lined up the stick, tapping the flat edge of my mace along the ball, toward the red one. I missed it by quite a lot.

"Shall we raise the stakes?" Edward asked.

"I'm not sure if that is enticing for me," I said, chuckling. "I doubt I'll be able to get *any* points, let alone win."

"Then we shall make them low stakes." He leaned a hip against the table and held his mace with two hands, resting one end of it on the floor. "Perhaps more questions?"

"Very well."

Edward smiled, turning toward the table. He surprised me, turning the mace around so the tail of the stick was positioned toward the ball, instead of the flat side. "I have found," he said, hitting the ball, "that this way gives me a little more control over the direction my cue ball goes."

"Odd," I said. "Perhaps I ought to try it."

I watched his ball hit the red one, shooting it across the table and just near a pocket.

Trading places with Edward, I positioned the tail of my mace to hit my cue ball toward his and hit. I drew in a sharp breath when the crack of ivory hit ivory and I moved his ball out of the way. It rolled slowly and I watched as it hesitated momentarily outside of the pocket before falling inside.

"Very good," Edward said, suitably impressed. "Two points for potting my cue, and a question of your choice."

"Have you always been such a hands-on landowner?"

He seemed caught off guard, and then screwed up his face in thought. "No, I haven't been a very good landowner at all."

He had not answered my question, but I had the impression he equated them to being the same thing. "Then what caused you to change?" I asked as he lowered his mace to take his turn.

He looked up at me with a playful smile on his lips. "You'll have to earn another question first, Lydia."

His ball hit the red one into a pocket and he grinned at me. "My turn. Why are you teaching your maid to read?"

"Because I want to practice."

"Practice teaching or reading?"

"Teaching."

"Why?"

I walked past Edward, choosing the best place from which to shoot my ball. "You'll have to earn another question first, Edward."

He chuckled, a warm, low sound that I felt in my stomach. I leaned forward and focused on the red ball in the distance before holding my breath and letting my cue fly.

"Yes!" I said, jumping up as the red ball hit the pocket. "Hazard and two more points for me." I spun to face him.

"You would like to know why I've changed?" he asked, moving to pull the red ball out of the pocket and placing it on the table.

"Yes, I would."

He seemed to weigh his words for a moment. "I almost lost this house," he said quietly. He glanced up at the plastered ceiling and then back at me. "I vowed when we returned here to do what I could to restore it. I have been negligent in my duties to the house, and I am ashamed. It has been in my family for three hundred years. If I want to pass something suitable onto my own children then I must keep it in good order."

My heart warmed at the mention of children. We were not

prepared to take a step yet toward bringing children into the world, but the idea of raising sweet little ones was pleasant. Doing so in the shadows of a miserable forest and a row of thorns was not as idyllic, however.

"That is a noble cause. Are you planning to remove the Blackthorn? It cannot be a safe hedge for children."

"Never," he said with finality. I waited for more, but he said nothing.

Now that my turn and resulting prize were completed, Edward moved to take his shot. He made it, nearly hitting my cue before shooting the red ball into a pocket, then smiled at me. "Almost had it," he said. "Now, please elaborate. Whatever do you need to teach for? Our own children will have a governess and our boys will be sent to Eton, as I was."

I paused. The plan he laid out was acceptable to me, but I was caught off guard that Edward had even thought so far ahead. If he cared so much about our future children's education, would he approve of my endeavors with the Sunday school?

My father would have forbidden it. But Edward was not my father. Furthermore, he did not have my father's aversions.

"I would like to implement a Sunday school for the children of Melton." He opened his mouth to reply but I cut him off, pressing forward with my reasoning before he could stop me. "The Whitakers' school in town will not take the poor children because they cannot pay. I already spoke to Mr. Cartwright, but he believes Sunday schools are a pointless endeavor."

"The vicar is a wise man," Edward said carefully. "Perhaps his reasoning—"

"His reasoning is flawed," I said at once. "He believes it is useless to teach the poor to read because they will spend the majority of their lives working. But is that not a *better* reason to teach them? That they might spend their precious, spare moments in the beauty of books?"

Edward looked at me as though I'd grown an extra head. It was not comforting.

"Will you forbid my Sunday school? If I can contrive to start one, I mean." I thought of little Samuel Morley. I *would* begin a school, one way or another.

"No, I will not forbid it."

He did not say that he agreed with Mr. Cartwright, but I could see it in his eyes. I supposed I ought to be grateful for a surprisingly indulgent husband, however flawed he deemed *me*.

"Your turn," I said.

It was quiet as Edward hit one white cue ball into the other, then potted the red ball.

"Hazard!" he shouted, smiling.

I could not help but laugh at the joy he displayed. "What a shame that you won't get any points for that," I said.

"What do you mean?"

"You hit my cue first."

"Yes," he nodded, "and then the red one."

"No," I said, approaching the table and pointing to the cue ball further away. "*That* is your ball. You hit mine *first*."

He glanced back and forth. "But mine was the ball with the black mark."

"Exactly," I said.

He looked to me and then back at the table. "I truly believe I hit my own ball."

"And there is only one way to find out." I reached forward to lift the white ball closer to the pocket and show Edward the black mark, when his hand came forward and lightly gripped my wrist.

"Wait," he said. "Let us wager."

"Another question?" I asked, meeting his gaze.

"No, this time we shall wager the game. If you are correct then I will forfeit and you are the winner. If I am right, however, then I win."

I smiled. This was too easy. "I've never actually won before. My father was a ruthless player and did not give me any advantages."

"You will find that I do not give you advantages either," he said softly. His words had an edge to them, and my breath caught in my throat.

"Are we agreed?" he asked.

I nodded, my skin burning from the warmth of his touch. "Agreed."

He released me and I lifted the ball, the black mark clearly evident on the bottom, proving it was his.

I could not contain my smile as I showed the mark to Edward. His rueful grin was handsome as he took my mace and hung it on the wall alongside his own.

"Well done, Lydia. You deserved this win."

"Because I had more points at the completion of the game?" I asked facetiously.

His lips quirked into a half-smile. "And a watchful eye. You were cunning in your distraction."

I laughed. "Edward, you cannot blame me for your fault mixing up the balls."

"I can," he argued, leading me from the room. "But I have the distinct impression it was not done deliberately."

Edward continued past the stairs, toward the drawing room. I paused. I was tired and ready to sleep.

"You are not coming to read?" he asked, once he noticed I was not following him.

"I am tired. I think I ought to go to sleep."

"Very well. Perhaps you can read tomorrow evening," he conceded.

Yawning, I nodded. "Goodnight, Edward."

"Goodnight, Lydia."

CHAPTER 16
LYDIA

"Miss Morley is awaiting you in the kitchen, Mrs. Thornton."

"Thank you, Mrs. Patton." I sat on the ladder-back chair Christine had brought into my room when we first arrived, my spine straight as she put up the last of my dark, wavy hair. The weather outside was overcast and gray. If it had not rained yet, it was probably going to soon.

The housekeeper left my chamber and I waited for Christine to finish my toilette. "I am glad the woman decided to come cook for us," I said. "I don't think I can take much more stew."

"Indeed," Christine said with feeling.

I contained my smile, leaving Christine to tidy the room while I went downstairs to meet the new cook. The doorway to the servants' staircase was propped open with a chair. A loud banging echoed through the hallway and jarred my ears. I poked my head through the doorway and found Edward halfway down with a new plank.

He had mentioned needing to fix the servants' staircase last night, hadn't he? But why was *Edward* doing it, and not hiring a man to take care of it instead? Not that it bothered me, but it was so very odd.

He must have sensed me watching him, for he glanced up and quit hammering at once. "Do you need to get past me?" he asked.

"I was trying to make it to the kitchen, but I can go outside and access the door around the back."

"No, come this way. It is far less complicated." Pushing himself up to a standing position, he moved his tools to the side of the step and wiped his hands down his trousers.

I descended, halting a step above the one he was repairing. "Is it safe?"

"It is mostly secured." Reaching forward, he grasped my hand. "But allow me to help you, just in case."

His warm fingers wrapped around my own. I leaned on him as I stepped gingerly past the fresh plank and down to the step below it. Letting go at once, I clutched my skirt tightly to give my hand something to do.

"You do know that you can direct the servants to fix their own steps, yes?" I asked.

He was one step below me, which caused us to stand at eye level. My breath caught when he locked eyes with me; I realized in that moment how narrow and enclosed the staircase was and how very close we stood. I wanted to back up a step, but the step behind me was the plank not yet fully secured and I didn't wish to trip.

"But if I have one of the servants fix it, then what will I do with my time?"

Was it a trick question? I didn't know what he was implying. "You would watch them?" I guessed.

He chuckled. "I suppose that would be one option. I simply meant that I enjoy filling my time."

"Yes," I agreed emphatically. "Of that I have no doubt."

He watched me a moment and I felt vulnerable under his

gaze. Clearing my throat, I indicated past him. "The new cook has arrived. I am going down to meet her."

"Ah, I see." He stepped out of the way, backing against the wall to give me room to pass. "Shall you request stew so we can judge the merits of her skill?"

"I shall request anything *but* stew," I said, brushing past him. Prickles ran down my arm from the connection and I skipped down the rest of the stairs quickly, the sound of Edward's laughter trailing behind me.

In the kitchen, a young woman stood at the counter with flour on her apron, kneading a blob of dough.

"Miss Morley?" I asked, stepping further into the kitchen. "I am Mrs. Thornton."

She stopped at once and glanced up, looking me in the eye. She was beautiful, with pale blonde hair and striking blue eyes. Her features were dainty, and she was so slight I was impressed by the force she put into kneading the dough.

"Good day, Mrs. Thornton. Thank you for giving me a chance. I promise I won't disappoint you."

"Have you brought mending with you?" I asked, glancing about me for a basket.

A small smile touched her lips. "Mama told me what you said. She doesn't want me to give up the mending, but I told her this job would bring in much more if I could keep it. I left the mending basket home."

"Then we are very glad to have you."

"I am so grateful for this opportunity," Miss Morley said.

"Do you have everything you need?"

She broke the dough into two parts and mounded them both into loaves. "Yes. Mrs. Patton showed me where to find everything."

"Very good." I turned for the servants' stairs again and paused. My nerves could not take another close encounter with

Edward at present. My heart was still fluttering from before, and I did not want to add to it.

I turned around to use the outside door and paused. "Miss Morley?" I asked.

She glanced up from the bowl she was mixing.

"How is Samuel doing?"

Her pale eyebrows lifted. "My nephew? He's a little troublemaker, but he's got a good heart. Why?"

"I met him yesterday." I took a moment to consider my words. If I told her about the school, I would have no choice but to continue with it. But Edward had allowed it, so why would there be any reason not to move forward with the plan? My own doubts aside, the children were worth it. "I am planning to begin a Sunday school. It will take some time to organize, but I would like to invite Samuel to attend."

Her silence was cause for concern. Her arm continued to stir while her eyes darted about her.

I waited patiently for an answer.

"We can't afford school," she finally said.

I softened my voice. "Sunday school does not cost anything. We will meet following church…somewhere. I have yet to secure a place. And the children will learn only a very basic education. Reading, writing, and sums."

Her gaze altered from worried to hopeful. "I will talk to my mama."

"Thank you, Miss—"

"Oh please, just call me Nora. I'm not used to all the misses."

"Very well, Nora. Please let me know what your mother says."

I listened quietly, but movement and a thump of something hitting a step behind me reached my ears and I moved toward the door leading outside. My stomach rumbled as I pushed open the door and I nearly turned back for the kitchen when a movement on the perimeter of the woods caught my eye.

I let the door close, stepping across the lawn toward the place I saw the motion. Was it a large shadow or a trick from the sun? No, it could not be, for it moved swiftly.

Halfway between the house and the wood I felt a drop of rain on the tip of my nose. Pausing, I searched the woods once more, but the person—or animal—was gone.

I would have assumed it was nothing, except for the prickle of fear that ran down my neck and the unease which skittered through my body.

Or that could have been my lack of breakfast. But…I thought not.

I stepped closer to the woods, skirting the barn as I looked for the cause of the shadows. If it was a person coming to visit, they would not have tried to hide. The rain began in earnest and I ducked into the barn, taking the dim steps up to the loft. Crossing the hey-strewn floor, I unlatched the wide door and pushed it open, sweeping my gaze over the woods from the better vantage point.

Nothing. No rustling of trees or pounding retreating footsteps could be heard. I stared through the sheet of rain at the blurry, barren forest and waited. Perhaps it would have been wiser to run for the house instead of the barn, but something tugged at my gut. I had to be certain the threat was gone.

Leaving the door open, I stepped back, seating myself on an overturned hay bale secured with twine. Resting my elbows on my knees, I sat mesmerized by the pouring rain. Whoever had been in the woods—for surely it was a person—was likely lost. If they had business with a member of Thornville, they would have approached the house.

They probably realized their mistake and left. The feeling of discomfort within me was, more likely than not, a product of my own fears and not rooted in any true danger.

The rain was not letting up. With a sigh, I determined there were two options before me: wait out the storm for quite some time or make a run for the house. I chose the latter. Closing the large barn door, I picked my way across the loft and paused at the top of the stairs. Glancing back over my shoulder, I surveyed the space. With the hay bales set up in such a way, it looked almost as if someone had intended to create benches.

I gasped. The space was perfect for a school.

It was warm, easily accessible, and would make the young children like Samuel comfortable.

I skipped down the stairs and bolted across the lawn, but my speed was no match for the pouring rain. I entered the front door of Thornville absolutely dripping.

The aged butler, Dickson, paused, giving me a once-over. "Will you have Christine sent to my room?" I requested.

"Certainly."

I passed the staircase and slipped into the dining room, pilfering a muffin from the bowl left over from breakfast, before turning and running up the stairs.

Taking a bite of the dry muffin, I swallowed the lump of sandy bread. It was a vast relief to have a cook in the house whose responsibilities were not tied up in running the household. Perhaps we'd even have a hot breakfast tomorrow.

"Lydia?"

I stopped in the hallway and glanced over my shoulder. "Yes?"

Edward walked toward me, his eyebrows raised. "Caught in the rain, I assume?"

"Actually, I was drenched by the new cook."

His eyebrows rose further and I broke into a smile. "Yes, Edward. It was the rain."

"Good. I did not want to have to fire the cook before we had a stew-less meal."

"I should think not."

He smiled, bowing. But I stopped him as he turned to go. "Is there any reason I cannot use the loft to teach my Sunday school?"

"Aside from the fact that it is dirty and smells of horses?"

I chuckled. "Edward, the children who I am hoping to teach will feel more at home in the barn than they would in a clean classroom in Melton. And if I do not object to the stench, I see no reason not to utilize the space."

He regarded me curiously. Could he hear the rapid beating of my heart? I'd run in the house and again up the stairs, and Edward's proximity was not allowing my breathing to calm in the slightest.

"Very logical of you, to be sure," he said.

My damp gown caused a shiver to run through my body. "I ought to change into a dry gown."

His eyes ran from my hair to my feet. "You must be freezing," he said at once. "Forgive me. I shouldn't have delayed you." Bowing, Edward shot me a smile before departing immediately.

I watched him go, his light brown hair flopping as he hurried down the stairs.

Sighing, I returned to my room where Christine was waiting with a fresh, warm gown and a large fire in the hearth. She must have been forewarned about my wet state of dress.

Changed and sitting before the fire as Christine brushed out my hair, I allowed myself to contemplate my station in life and the very real possibility that living at Thornville was perhaps not the worst thing in the world.

CHAPTER 17
LYDIA

That evening following dinner, I tried to mask my surprise as Edward trailed behind me to the drawing room when I left the dinner table.

"I think leg of mutton and boiled potatoes are a vast improvement over stew," he observed, settling into the chair opposite my seat on the sofa. "What do you think?"

Nodding, I picked up my book from the table beside the sofa and set it on my lap. "It was wonderful to eat something different, of that I can heartily agree."

"The new cook will work out fine, I think."

"Yes, Miss Morley is a blessing, indeed."

He stilled and I caught the confusion in his eyes. "Morley?"

"Yes. I met her mother yesterday."

He sat up straighter. "You went to their cottage?"

"Yes," I said slowly.

Concern was evident on his features. "I don't think that is wise. There is a significant amount of gossip attached to that family. I don't want our name getting caught up with the Morley's."

My heart plummeted. "I must send Nora away?"

He seemed to ponder my words, his gaze seeking the fire. Was he considering more dinners of stew, as I was?

"No," he said at length. "We needn't go to such extreme measures. But perhaps we ought to keep an eye on her. Her sister caused a great deal of trouble a few years back."

"Samuel's mother?"

His head snapped in my direction, but I sensed he was guarding his expression carefully. "How do you know of Samuel?"

"I met him in the woods when I went to speak with Mrs. Morley. I've asked Nora to invite him to my Sunday school."

Indecision warred across Edward's face. "I wish you would have consulted me first."

"But he is a young boy. Not above five years, surely. What trouble could come of inviting him to the school?"

"More trouble than I care to take on," Edward mumbled, running a hand over his face.

"Have I erred greatly?"

His face became soft, tilting to the side in a slight manner. "No, Lydia. You've done nothing wrong. You could not have known."

Somehow, those words did not make me feel better. I inhaled a deep breath of air laced with fire smoke and looked down at the book in my lap, suddenly anxious for an escape from Thornville.

Sighing, Edward leaned back further in his chair, making himself comfortable. "We do not need to discuss it further. I am ready whenever you are."

"Ready for what?"

"For you to read to me," he answered, his eyes drifting closed as his hands clasped comfortably over his stomach.

I sat there, stunned. He peeked up at me. "I agreed to listen to you read tonight if you played billiards with me yesterday."

I had not gathered that agreement from our conversation. I

was not fully opposed to it, of course, but it took a moment for my mind to catch up to Edward's expectation of our evening. Opening *Pride and Prejudice*, I skipped back to the first page. If I was going to read to Edward, I may as well start from the beginning.

"'It is a truth universally acknowledged that a single man in possession of a good fortune must be in want of a wife.'" I paused, glancing up to catch Edward's eye. My cheeks grew warm and I darted my gaze back down to the page and continued. I did not look up again until I had completed the first chapter.

"You are finished?" he asked.

"Would you like me to be?"

He watched me a moment before saying. "You have a soothing voice. You may continue, if you wish."

The compliment warmed me and I returned to the book, beginning chapter two.

I read for the better part of an hour, until soft snoring reached my ears and I glanced up to find Edward peacefully asleep. Closing the book, I set it on the table and watched Edward with unabashed interest. He looked kind, even in his sleep. I ought to wake him, but I was never afforded such open opportunity to look at his face, and I found that I liked what I saw very much.

He was less a stranger to me now than the day we'd married, but he was still very unknown to me. Spending time together would only bridge the gap and it was fortunate that Edward had desired to spend time with me two evenings in a row, but I doubted it would last. A man with such strong aversions to sitting still could never comfortably sit and allow his wife to read him a novel every evening.

He stirred, his eyes fluttering open. When he saw me watching him, he sat up tall, blinking rapidly. "I was not asleep," he said.

"Of course not," I agreed. I was tempted to inquire the last thing I read, but I did not want him to misinterpret my playfulness for irritation, so I swallowed the urge. "But I am tired and will go to bed now."

He nodded, yawning. "Goodnight, Lydia."

"Goodnight, Edward."

Lydia

The next few days fell into a predictable pattern. I spent my days preparing lessons for Sunday school while Edward was off managing the estate or fixing some new thing he'd discovered as broken. When I had sufficient lessons prepared, I mustered my courage and sent a message home with Nora, inviting her young nephew to the barn loft the approaching Sunday at two o'clock, and to inform anyone else who might be interested.

She had told me she knew of a few families nearby she could pass along the information to, but overall, she did not seem overly hopeful.

Still, I did not let her hesitation deter me.

What did surprise me was Edward's continued attention following dinner in the evenings. He invited me to play a second game of billiards, which I'd lost quite horribly, followed by another night picking up where we'd left off reading in *Pride and Prejudice*. It took a few more nights for me to realize that Edward was trading each night with me, alternating our activities between what he enjoyed and what I enjoyed.

It was a sweet sentiment, and whether or not it was purposefully done, I found I enjoyed the variation quite a lot.

On Saturday I awoke with high nerves and shaky fingers. I

breakfasted alone on sliced ham and toasted bread then took myself to the drawing room to go over my lesson plan one last time. Christine had patiently sat for small lessons every day since our first attempt, and I discovered through my over-eagerness that the best way to begin was with very basic instruction. I told her to forget my lesson on vowels and we started over with the alphabet, learning the letters and tracing them.

I was going to try a similar approach with Sunday school.

"Lydia?" Edward asked, poking his head through the drawing room door. "Will you come with me?"

I stood at once, setting my papers on the writing table. "Of course."

"You will need a cloak. It is getting colder outside."

My cheeks warmed. Dare I admit that I had ignored his advice? "I do not own a cloak. I will fetch my spencer."

He regarded me dubiously. "I don't think that will be sufficient."

I was learning that on my own. The weather was growing cold, and fast.

He looked down at his own clothing and then said, "Allow me a minute to change and I will drive you into Melton. We should order a cloak as soon as possible."

Chagrined, I nodded in acquiescence.

I retrieved my spencer and an additional shawl, as well as my bonnet and gloves and returned downstairs to await near the door. Edward followed me down a few minutes later and I stepped into the bitter cold. Why hadn't I simply listened to the man when we were back in London?

"Come this way," he said, pulling my hand. We rounded the house before he finally let go; I stretched my fingers to remove the tingling sensation left behind by his touch.

He led me to the barn and halted at the foot of the stairs, sweeping his arm up to indicate that I should precede him. I walked up the steps toward the loft, glancing over my shoulder in confusion, only to find Edward grinning in a way that immediately warmed my stomach.

Stepping into the loft, I gasped, halting on the top step. A soft hand rested on my lower back, guiding me further into the room. The straw had all been swept away, the bare wooden planks clean and tidy. Benches had been placed in two rows along the wall opposite the horses' feeding holes. A single chair sat before the benches, between them and the neatly stacked hay. I had wondered how I was going to keep the children from falling into the horse stalls below, and the problem had righted itself.

No, *Edward* had righted the problem.

"I do not know what to say," I said, awed. No one had ever done such a thing for me before and I was utterly speechless.

"You needn't say anything at all."

I faced him. "Thank you, Edward."

He looked away, smiling as he glanced around the loft. "It was nothing. I merely made benches and swept away dirt. You have the hard part."

"Which is?"

"You have to teach."

CHAPTER 18
EDWARD

Melton was quiet today. The skies were overcast and the streets bare. I directed the phaeton to the livery and left it there, guiding Lydia to a small modiste down the road from the lending library.

A short, gray-haired woman with a loose apron over her gown welcomed us. I did my best to explain what we needed and she nodded knowingly, displaying various choices in thick, rich fabrics.

A deep burgundy caught my eye. I was sure it would look lovely beside Lydia's dark hair and fair complexion. "That color is quite fine," I said, as though I knew anything about the state of women's fashion. My cheeks warmed slightly, and I was grateful when the modiste nodded in accord.

"It will complement the lady's complexion," the modiste stated.

Lydia agreed. "I have to admit, I was drawn to it as well."

That was all she needed to say to spin the short woman into action. I perused the fabrics as Lydia's measurements were taken. The short woman smiled at me greedily as payment was exchanged, and a promise delivered to have the cloak finished quickly. "You come back if you find yourselves in need of anything further," she said.

Lydia nodded to the woman before turning her attention on me and asking in a quiet voice, "I was hoping to step into the lending library if we can spare a minute."

Had she tired of our nightly ritual? I could not say the same for myself, a sentiment which caught me off guard. "We have not finished *Pride and Prejudice*."

"I am not planning to get a new book," she explained. "I simply wish to speak to Lady Cameron."

We stepped outside and nearly bumped into a man walking past the store.

"Forgive me," I said at once, my arm wrapping around Lydia's waist to ensure she would not fall.

Radmahl turned, flashing a smile of crooked teeth. "You are forgiven," he said, and my gut immediately tightened alongside my hand at Lydia's waist. I curbed the desire to pull her closer to me so I might protect her. Instead, I reluctantly let her go.

I wished I hadn't, however, when she dipped a curtsy and said, "Good day, Mr. Radmahl."

He lifted his hat, bowing to both Lydia and me. "I have heard a rumor, Mrs. Thornton, and I can hardly credit it. Will you do me the honor of dispelling it right away?"

My whole body went stiff. He would not inquire about the Morley daughter working in our kitchen, surely.

"What is it about?" Lydia asked.

"A Sunday school, in fact."

"You need not say anything further," she replied. "I can confirm the rumor is true. If you know of any children in need of such services, please send them my way."

Radmahl's smile grew, stretching wide. "What a superb notion, Mrs. Thornton."

"Thank you, sir."

Had Lydia noticed my silence since we'd stopped to speak to

Radmahl? It took everything within me not to drag her away from the snake of a man.

"We shall see you in church tomorrow, I hope," Lydia finally said. "Good day, Mr. Radmahl."

He dipped his hat, delivering a bow with dramatic flair before turning and sauntering away.

We stood on the side of the road a minute while we watched Radmahl's retreat, and then I spoke quietly. "I do not want you to further your connection with that man, Lydia."

"We have very little connection as it is. He is a friend to my father."

Then it shouldn't be a problem. "And he is only using you now to get to me."

She stepped back, eyeing me with disbelief. "Whatever would he do that for?"

"He knows I do not care for him," I said.

Her mouth hung open a moment. Was it truly so difficult to imagine that Radmahl might have nefarious intentions?

"Edward, you cannot ask me to be so rude when I've been given no cause. If there is just cause, I would ask that you share the whole of it."

I watched her a moment. I did not want to inform her of his misdeeds. It would only give her reason for concern and would put a blight upon my own sister. Sarah was gone from Melton and did not plan to return and I did not wish to bring to light old scandals which had only just begun to be forgotten.

"I cannot say," I finally said.

Lydia lifted a shoulder. "Then I cannot say I will ignore the man. I am sorry, but I must do what I feel is right."

I scoffed. Could she not simply trust my judgement? "And you do not feel it is right to follow your husband's guidance?"

"I do not believe this is guidance, Edward. You have made a baseless request."

My body heated in irritation. "But it is *not* baseless."

She said nothing. Raising her eyebrows, Lydia waited for me to continue.

But I could say nothing, unless I wished to tell her the whole of it. And I did not. Grunting, I set off toward the lending library.

She followed close behind me, catching up by the time we knocked on the front door of the Whitakers' school.

We were led into the library and Lady Cameron stood, approaching us at once. "Good day, Mr. and Mrs. Thornton."

Lydia

"I have a request for you," I said, eyeing Edward surreptitiously. Irritation was still evident on his features. "I wanted to know if you had a minute to discuss it."

"I do," Lady Cameron answered, surprised. She gestured to the chairs in the center of the room. Joining her there, I lowered myself onto a soft, cushioned chair.

Edward cleared his throat. "I will leave you to your business and return in a quarter of an hour."

I hardly had time to respond before he dipped a short bow and let himself out.

"A man need only hear of the possibility of a lengthy conversation and he will make himself scarce," she said, grinning. "Now, what did you need to speak to me about?"

"I am starting a Sunday school."

"So I've heard," she said. "It is all the talk about Melton, actually."

"How?" I asked, shaking my head. "I've yet to even begin. Tomorrow will be our first lesson."

"You have students already?" she asked, surprised.

"I believe I have one." Nora had reported that her nephew would be in the barn, but I could not count on anyone else yet. I was not even certain I could count on him. "But that is not what I wished to speak of. I wanted to borrow a few simple texts, if you have them. And to ask you to spread the word to any families who you think may benefit from a Sunday school. We are going to meet in the loft of Thornville's barn at two o'clock."

"Will you serve tea?"

I hadn't thought of that. "Do you think I need to?"

"I think it will entice some children to attend if you do."

"Then by all means, inform them that I will serve tea."

Lady Cameron grinned. "I am eager to see the results of your idea, Mrs. Thornton."

"You are welcome to come and see them for yourself," I said before thinking. Immediately, I regretted the impulse, for I would never wish for her to come only because she felt she must.

But the way her eyes lit up upon my invitation relieved me at once. "If you are certain, I would love to come. I might assist with the children."

"Do you have any experience?" I asked. "Perhaps in this school?"

She shook her head. "I have many nephews, but no experience in a school."

"Neither do I," I admitted. "Perhaps we shall figure it out together."

Her smile was contagious, and I soon matched it.

I stood to leave. "I shall see you tomorrow."

Lydia

. . .

The number of curious glances and whispers I heard in the surrounding pews at church caused my shoulders to tense. I felt a desire to scoot closer to Edward on the bench, but he had been tense, himself, since our meeting the previous day with Mr. Radmahl.

I followed him into the churchyard following the sermon, delivering a feigned smile to Mr. Cartwright as I passed him at the door. The vicar gave Edward a commiserating smile, but ignored me. I felt certain he'd heard about my Sunday school.

We paused under the enormous yew tree as Edward spoke with another man. Lady Cameron approached me on the arm of her husband and I smiled at her eagerly, removing myself from Edward's side to speak with her.

"Are you nervous?" she inquired.

"Immensely. But I am equally excited."

She grinned. "I will see you soon."

They left the yard and I waited a minute longer for Edward to complete his conversation, catching Mr. Radmahl's eye on the other side of the churchyard. He dipped his head to me and I smiled briefly, focusing my attention on Edward and his friend, instead.

"Mr. Coates is holding a night of cards tomorrow evening if you have any desire to join, Thornton. You are more than welcome."

Edward's gaze darted from the man he was speaking with to me, hesitation written on his features. I didn't mind if he left me alone in the evening, if that was the cause for his hesitation. I opened my mouth to say as much when he spoke. "I must pass for now. I am afraid I have other obligations, at present."

"Shame," the man said, shaking his head.

Edward led me from the churchyard and helped me into the phaeton, his expression stony. I waited until we were out of town before speaking. "It would not bother me if you went out in the evenings. My father used to go off and play cards quite frequently. I am used to being left at home."

The look Edward shot me silenced me at once. "I appreciate the sentiment, but it is not for you that I denied him."

I closed my mouth. Clearly, this was a conversation which Edward did not wish to continue, though I had no idea why.

When the phaeton pulled into Thornville, I stepped down with Edward's help and went straight for the barn. I had only made it halfway across the lawn when Edward's shout stopped me in my tracks. I turned back to find him coming toward me, a paper clutched in his hand and a confused look on his face.

"Has anyone made any threats toward you?" he asked. His breath was quick and ragged, his eyes stormy.

"No," I said, at once.

He read my face before glancing back at the house. "Perhaps it is only a joke, though if so, it is a poor one." He turned away.

"Edward," I called. "What is it?"

He glanced from the paper to the barn, finally settling on my face. "I do not want to worry you when it is likely a youthful prank, but I suppose it would be foolish to keep it a secret." He handed me the paper, saying, "I found this tacked to the front door."

I read it and my body went cold. It merely said, *Leave Thornville, or else.* "Or else what?" I asked.

"That is precisely why I feel it must be a prank. There is nothing to indicate we are unwelcome here." He ran a hand over his face. "The more I think on it, the more ridiculous I think this is. I have known most of the people of Melton my whole life. I am certain it is simply a poorly executed prank. It cannot be dangerous, surely." He offered me an encouraging smile. "Perhaps if we ignore the prankster, they will go a step further and we shall find our horses painted blue."

"Who would paint a horse?" I asked, shocked.

Edward's smile was telling.

"*You?*" I asked. "Whatever for?"

"Like I said, Lydia. It was a youthful prank. Poorly thought out, but superbly executed. The headmaster never saw it coming."

Shaking my head, I could not help my smile. Mischievous, that was Edward. I could see it in the twinkle in his eyes.

"Christine should be preparing tea for the children," I said, "but will you ask Dickson to send her out?"

"Yes," Edward said. Pausing, he lifted my hand and squeezed my fingers. "You shall do well today. I know it."

The encouragement was unexpected and sweet. I chose not to say anything, fearing I might ruin the moment, and only mumbled a mere "thank you" before leaving for the barn.

The children were set to arrive soon, and I was not nearly ready.

CHAPTER 19
LYDIA

I sat on the bench beside Lady Cameron while she nibbled at a biscuit and I drank another cup of tea.

"How much longer do you wish to wait?" she asked gently.

I glanced to the sun through the open loft door. It was a little higher just moments before, wasn't it? "Is no one coming?" I asked, my shoulders deflating.

She lifted one shoulder. "I cannot say. Though we've waited well over an hour so I think it might be safe to assume that no one will make it today."

I turned on the bench, facing her. "Mr. Coulter fills his classrooms the first day he opens a new school. I have specifically invited at least one boy and even offered tea! How can I have failed so miserably?"

"You must remember that London is a very different place than Melton. I think your idea has merit. You only need to be patient. They will come. Maybe not today, but they will come."

A small sound on the staircase caught my attention and I hopped to my feet. "Samuel!" I all but squealed. He backed up a step—no doubt due to my overexuberance.

"Please," I said, softer, "come up." I recalled how easily I'd persuaded him to go home when I mentioned the bread and jam. "We have tea and biscuits."

His little brown eyes widened momentarily before he stepped forward, hesitantly.

"Has Nora come with you?"

He nodded, glancing behind him. She must have delivered him and returned to the kitchen.

I turned to ask Lady Cameron to prepare a plate for Samuel but the look on her face gave me pause. Her eyebrows were drawn together, a glassy look in her eyes. Clearing her throat, she shook her head and tossed him a shaky smile. "Samuel, is it?"

He nodded.

"Would you like to come sit beside me? I have biscuits here for you. And you must tell me how you take your tea."

He obeyed and before long, Lady Cameron's smooth voice had lulled him into comfort. Or, perhaps that was due to his aunt's fine biscuits.

"Nora told me I'm going to learn to read," he said quietly. "But I don't know why."

"Because education is good for you, Samuel," I said, sitting on the bench beside him. "Would you like to finish your tea, and then we can begin?"

He appeared hesitant and nervous. Glancing about him, his eyes brightened when they fell upon the stacks of hay. "Are those to feed the horses?"

"Yes," Lady Cameron said softly. "And if you are very good during your lesson with Mrs. Thornton, perhaps she'll allow you to help feed a horse before you go."

He looked up at her in awe. "My gramma *never* lets me near any horse."

Lady Cameron shot me a small grin over Samuel's head. "You must earn the privilege first. Am I understood?"

He nodded his little head and shoved another half of a biscuit into his mouth. Perhaps I ought to consider adding a decorum and proper manners segment to my teaching plans.

"Samuel," I said, moving to sit in front of him, "do you know what letters are?"

Lydia

The lesson had begun slowly, but this time, so had my expectations. And Samuel successfully exceeded them. We discussed how letters formed words and how each letter had its own series of sounds. I read to him from a book to entice him to want to learn for himself, and then Lady Cameron helped him feed some hay to each of the horses below.

The grin which spread over his small face was worth every second of worry and frustration when no one had arrived for school earlier.

I leaned down, resting palms on my knees as I said, "Samuel, shall we take you to Nora, or does your gramma expect you at home?"

"I need to go home."

Straightening, I said, "Very well. I can walk with you."

Lady Cameron stepped forward, reaching her hand for Samuel's. "I don't mind walking him home."

Edward's warning to stay away from the Morley cottage swam through my head. "Perhaps we can go together."

Straightening the book and stack of papers I'd used to show Samuel the alphabet, I tucked them into a small box at the end of the bench and crossed the loft to close the door.

Lady Cameron walked ahead with Samuel and I lagged

behind, watching them move hand in hand down the rough path through the woods. Winter was fast approaching, the days shifting into night earlier and earlier. The sun had already begun to fall behind the cover of trees, creating shadows between the branches that caused a shiver to run down my spine.

The small cottage came into view and I reached forward to stop Lady Cameron from approaching the house with Samuel. I could hear a man's voice within and it surprised me, though I knew not why.

"Is that your grandfather inside?" I asked.

Samuel shook his head. "Probably Mr. Hammond. He brings us a pheasant sometimes for our dinner."

"How very kind of him," Lady Cameron said. "Samuel, will you return to Mrs. Thornton's barn next Sunday? We would very much like to teach you again."

He looked up at her with soft, hopeful eyes. "Will you have tea again?"

She nodded.

Samuel turned to me. "Can you have jam next time? The strawberry kind?"

"Yes Samuel, I think we can make that work."

He grinned, his boyish face much sweeter than the solemn look he typically wore. The poor child should be smiling more and frowning less.

And I was going to make it a priority to give him reason to smile more.

He turned to leave but I said, "Samuel, wait."

He glanced over his shoulder.

"Do you have any friends you would like to bring with you next week?"

He shook his head. "None of my friends want to go to school."

My heart squeezed and I offered him a smile as he turned back for his home.

Lady Cameron strung her arm through mine as we walked back to Thornville.

"Thank you for helping me today."

She laughed quietly. "I am afraid you helped me more than the other way around. But if it is not too bothersome, I would like to return next week."

"Of course," I said.

The woods darkened quickly about us and I clung to Lady Cameron's arm. "Perhaps next week, Samuel will be on time and we needn't walk him home in the dark."

She nodded. "Did you get an odd feeling in front of that cottage?" Lady Cameron asked softly.

I had, but I didn't know if I would sound disturbed were I to admit as much aloud. "Yes."

She shuddered. "I've never seen Samuel before. He is a sweet boy, but quiet."

"His aunt is our new cook," I explained.

"He reminds me of my nephews. He's a touch older than they are, but sweet, just the same."

Stepping under Thornville's iron gate, I led Lady Cameron to the front door. We stepped into the house where hearty male laughter could be heard from within the parlor down the hall.

Dickson approached, bowing.

"Lord Cameron Nichols has arrived. Mr. Thornton is entertaining him in the parlor."

"Thank you, Dickson."

I led the way and Lady Cameron followed. We came upon the men playing billiards, stepping into the room as the red ball rolled across the table and fell into a pocket.

Lord Cameron moaned as Edward cheered.

"Close game," Edward said, slapping Lord Cameron on the back.

Lady Cameron approached her husband and he smiled down at her sweetly. Theirs was *clearly* a love match.

"Was your Sunday school a success?" Edward asked, hanging his mace on the wall.

Lady Cameron smiled encouragingly at me.

"Yes," I said decisively. "I think I can say it was."

"Good," Edward agreed. He turned to our guests. "Shall we plan on next Sunday?"

Lord Cameron grinned. "I think that's a marvelous idea."

We walked them to the front door, bidding them farewell until Dickson closed the door behind them.

I turned to the stairs to change for dinner, but exhaustion ran through my body and I paused before mounting the steps.

Edward turned toward me, his face a picture of confusion.

"Would it be very wrong for me to not change for dinner?"

His pause lengthened. "No," he said finally, taking a step toward me. "Let us go into dinner now."

My heart surged as Edward picked up my hand and placed it on his arm, leading me into the drawing room to await dinner. We sat in comfortable silence and I considered the progress Edward and I had made toward friendship since our wedding day.

"Edward?" I asked, on impulse.

He looked up, a placid smile on his lips.

"Do you recall the ball when we met?"

He hesitated slightly before nodding. Was his hesitation because he was also reminded of the moment he had forgotten about me on the dance floor? Perhaps he was embarrassed over the action now. I would not force him to recall a blight upon his own character, however badly I wished to hear him acknowledge it, to understand why.

I glanced to the roaring fire in the hearth. Edward's voice pulled me back toward him.

"Was there a reason you wish to recall it?"

I shook my head. "I merely marvel at how much has occurred since then."

"Yes," he said, smiling. "Who could have known?"
Who could have known, indeed.

CHAPTER 20
EDWARD

That evening, following dinner, I allowed Lydia to return to the drawing room on her own as I considered the danger we were in as occupants of Thornville. Surely it was nothing to worry about, but that did not mean I should dismiss the notes completely.

It occurred to me that the notes could refer to any person in Thornville, not just my wife and me. They were not addressed. Perhaps one of the servants had formed an enemy nearby and was thus being tormented. It was silly, of course, but I needed to question Dickson, at the very least, and wanted to receive his input before concerning Lydia unnecessarily.

"Dickson," I said as he poured me a glass of brandy. "Have you any cause to believe that someone in this house would be receiving threats?"

"Threats, sir?"

"Yes, Dickson. Threats. Like the notes which have been found tacked to the front door." I refrained from reminding my butler that it was his duty to keep an eye on the front door and he had obviously been derelict if the person was able to post multiple notes and remain undetected. He was likely working that out for himself at present.

"I will question the staff, sir, but there are no concerning connections at present, that I know of."

"Report back as soon as you know anything."

"Very good, sir."

He bowed away and left me to the silence of the long, awkward table and my glass of amber liquid. I swirled it around my glass before taking a sip. Motioning for my footman to approach, I said, "We are going to change the way we dine."

He waited for me to say more, and I spoke before I could think twice about it. "Tomorrow night place Mrs. Thornton beside me. This blasted table is too long."

"Yes, sir," he said, waiting a moment before I waved him away. I could only hope Lydia would not find it distasteful, but I found myself desiring to bring her closer to me. Watching her across the expanse of empty, shiny wood had been difficult this evening in a way it hadn't been before. She was a fascinating conversationalist now that she had warmed up to me and we'd created something of a relationship. I desired to be around her now in a way I had never desired to be around a woman before.

She was unlike any woman I had known in my entire life.

I grinned as I thought of my wife's many virtues. As it turned out, marriage wasn't so horrible after all.

CHAPTER 21
LYDIA

Rain pelted the earth for four straight days, causing a large pool of water to form before the front windows of Thornville and causing an unrivaled crankiness to develop within Edward. He paced the windows in the drawing room, looking through the drapes and then swinging them closed again.

Groaning, he crossed the room and sat hard on the sofa, causing a loud creak to rent the air.

Edward paused, looking to where I sat at the writing desk. We watched each other in silence, waiting to see if the sofa would crash to the floor. Nothing occurred, and Edward leaned back, covering his eyes with his forearm.

"I cannot remain indoors any longer," he said. Again. He had said as much five minutes before. And then another twenty minutes before that. The man was positively restless, and his anxiety was causing me a measure of my own.

"Shall I request the card table be brought in?" I asked.

He moaned again, the sound muffled from underneath his arm. "You do not realize how deeply I am tempted to say yes right now."

I had not expected that. I set my pen down, turning on my chair to better see him. "Whatever do you mean?"

He removed his arm from his forehead, sitting up on the sofa and shooting serious eyes at me. "I made myself a promise that I would never again touch playing cards."

I could not help the surprise that fell over my features, drooping my mouth open. "Not even whist? Or speculation?"

He shook his head. "I cannot. If I allow myself any room for exceptions, however slight, then I could very well succumb to the larger captivation of gambling."

Oh. He was a gambler. That did not surprise me, for he had played on occasion with my father. But I had not realized the extent of his burden.

"But you've played with my father," I said. "Was this a recent decision?"

He watched me carefully, opening his mouth to speak before glancing away, and closing his mouth once more. I allowed him time to gather his thoughts and nearly turned back to the letter I was drafting to Mrs. Coulter when he finally said, "It is recent, yes. Just before we wed, in fact. I realized my weaknesses and I determined that if I was to retain Thornville and cultivate something to pass on to the next generation of Thorntons, then I would need to curb my expenses."

Given the extent of the wear in both his London townhouse and Thornville, it was clear that Edward did not have funds. My dowry could not have been much, I assumed, but as father had always been rather tight-fisted with his money, he had never told me precisely what it was.

It must have been enough to make Edward feel as though he was receiving a second chance, however, if I was understanding him now.

I turned back to my letter to fully contemplate the information. I had never been under any sort of illusion that Edward loved me, but I did not understand at all why he had offered for me, and I hadn't tried to before.

I picked up my pen, sharpened it and dipped it into the ink to continue my letter, but my mind would not focus on the paper.

I'd had no choice, at the time, but to proceed with the marriage. But I'd had no real reason not to, either.

But now, I wondered what sort of union I had agreed to.

"Lydia," Edward said, and I paused. "Perhaps when you have completed your correspondence you could read to me?"

"I should be delighted," I responded at once. We were over halfway finished with *Pride and Prejudice* and I was eager to continue the story. That *he* was requesting I read to him was oddly attractive.

I stood, crossing to the sofa and taking my seat on the other side.

"You can finish your letter first," he said.

"I have come to a place where I cannot think what else to write. The letter will be more meaningful if I give myself time to contemplate what might be of interest to Mrs. Coulter."

He regarded me closely. "You are a thoughtful person, aren't you, Lydia?"

My cheeks warmed and I reached for the book, opening it and setting it on my lap. I found our place easily with the bookmark I'd left there—a delicate lace rectangle my mother had used before me. Draping the lace over my knee, I cleared my throat and began to read.

I was not used to sitting on the sofa beside Edward as I read, for he typically chose the chair directly across from me. The proximity was nothing to worry me, but the way he inched closer and leaned his head back on the sofa to read over my shoulder caused my heart rate to increase substantially.

I read an entire chapter while Edward's breathing sounded near my ear, before I set the book lower on my lap and turned toward him. I had not anticipated his face being *that* close, despite his steady breathing, and his green eyes pierced me at once, causing me to draw a sharp intake of breath.

"Is something the matter?" he asked, his eyebrows pulled together.

Afraid to speak, I merely shook my head.

"Then why have you stopped reading?"

"I don't know," I said, because my brain was cloudier than the storm outside our windows and I could not form a coherent thought.

He smiled at me and my heart squeezed. With the knowing grin and the creases beside his smiling eyes, my heart could not help but race. I had an attractive husband.

His eyes darted to my lips and I suddenly panicked. Was he going to kiss me? I was aware of my responsibilities as Edward's wife, but I had *never* kissed anyone before. Ever.

When his eyes glanced to my mouth a second time, I looked back at the book in my lap, opening it to the place where we had paused. I was not purposely sabotaging Edward, but I didn't know what else to do.

"Mr. Thornton," Dickson said from the doorway, causing me to bolt upright. "You've got a visitor."

"No card?" Edward asked.

The older butler shook his head. "Lord and Lady Cameron."

"By all means, send them in."

Edward sat up on the sofa, straightening his posture, but he did not move further away from me as I had anticipated he might. The couple came into the room and took their seats opposite us, and I dipped my head in acknowledgment, smiling at Lady Cameron.

"You braved the weather," I said.

"I hope you had a good cause," Edward added.

Lord Cameron glanced to his wife. "Shall I tell the truth?"

Lady Cameron shot her husband an indulgent look.

"I grew tired of sitting inside all day," Lord Cameron admitted, "and Lady Cameron took pity on me. Any chance you would like to play a game of billiards?"

Edward grinned. "Absolutely."

The men left and Lady Cameron pointed to the book on my lap. "How are you enjoying it?"

"It's lovely. Though I wonder at Darcy's aloofness."

She tilted her head. "Continue reading. I am sorry to have infiltrated your afternoon, and with no invitation."

"You are always welcome," I said. I looked behind me at the window streaming with rain. "Has the weather let up at all?"

Lady Cameron shook her head. "And I have not been able to think of anything besides that sweet little Samuel Morley for days. He has no doubt been cooped up at home with all of this rain."

"I am sure it is not the first time he has lived through a rainstorm," I said gently.

"Of course," she said absently.

"Are you familiar with the Morleys?"

"No," Lady Cameron said, tucking her feet under her and settling into the chair. "I've never seen them before meeting Samuel on Sunday. They do not come to church."

I was about to tell Lady Cameron of Edward's warning to stay clear of the Morley family, but I did not want to spread gossip. And when I wasn't completely aware of his reasoning, I couldn't very well pass along the plea.

"Do you know much about Samuel's parents?" Lady Cameron asked.

"Only that Nora, our cook, is his mother's sister. And I am assuming he only lives with his grandmother and aunt, for I have heard no mention of anyone else."

"And his parents?" she repeated.

I lowered my voice. "I know nothing beyond the fact that Samuel is illegitimate. And my own assumption, based off something Mrs. Morley said when I first met her, is that Samuel's mother must have been involved with a man of superior birth."

Nodding her head slowly, Lady Cameron trained her gaze on the fire.

"Will Samuel's situation force you to stop assisting me in the Sunday school?"

She glanced up quickly. "Of course not. He is a sweet boy and he cannot help where he comes from."

An uncommon belief, but I would not complain. "I am grateful, for I appreciate your support."

"I love being around children. I have none of my own, so I must enjoy them when I can."

Lost for words, I simply said, "Of course." Now her eagerness to help with the school and her attentiveness to the boy made quite a bit of sense. I was grateful I had not inquired after her own children, for I had assumed she had some at home. Though I'd yet to meet any at church, of course.

Now I knew why.

"Have you taught long?" she asked.

"I have never taught before—aside from attempting to teach my maid to read these last few weeks. But I was associated with a man called Mr. Coulter in London who has taken it upon himself to begin Sunday schools all about Town. He is an inspiration to me."

"If only we could find a way to spread the word about it. I am certain we could get more children in the loft this Sunday."

"I'm not sure there's much more we can do," I said. "Perhaps over time the school will grow through word of mouth. I am sure there are more children who would be interested."

CHAPTER 22
EDWARD

Lord Cameron sank my ball, along with the red one and glanced up from his mace, grinning. "Two more points and I take the game."

"It is good we did not set a wager at the start," I said. "I'd be sunk."

He chuckled, taking the balls from the pockets and placing them on the table before moving aside so I could take my turn. The tail of my mace hit the white ball and spun it sideways on a faulty hit.

Grunting, I backed away. "It is not my day."

"Indeed," Lord Cameron agreed. He took his place and bent forward, preparing to take the shot which would end this round. "I have found our visits to Thornville quite enjoyable," he said, grinning, as he took the winning shot.

I could not help but chuckle. He had beat me twelve to zero. It was *certainly* not my day. "Well done."

"You seem distracted," Lord Cameron said, hanging his mace on the wall. "Surely that has aided in my win."

"It's kind of you to find a cause, but you won fairly."

He grinned. "My skill is superior, naturally. But I *do* think you seem distracted. Is it something I can assist you with?"

I turned around to sit on the edge of the table, crossing my arms over my chest. "Someone is threatening my household by leaving notes on my front door."

Lord Cameron's face immediately transformed from comfortable to serious. He silently waited for me to continue.

"Initially, I assumed it was a joke. But the more I think on it, the less I can shake the unease. What if the notes are intended for Lydia? What would I do if harm was to befall her?"

"What are the notes saying?" Lord Cameron asked, his dark eyebrows drawn together in concentration.

"They are vague. The last one told us to 'leave Thornville, or else.'" I shook my head. "Or else *what?*"

Lord Cameron paced across the floor. The concentration on his face implied his thoughtfulness, though I didn't know how he could resolve a problem when he had no more information than I did.

"I think there's nothing more you can do besides keeping a vigilant watch. Have you stationed servants to keep watch?"

"No," I said sheepishly. "I hadn't thought of that."

"Perhaps it will amount to nothing, but it could be wise to keep a rotating man in an undisclosed space to watch the front of the house. You said the notes were tacked to the front door?"

I nodded.

"Then that should be sufficient for the time being. And you must know you can call on me for help should the situation worsen."

I did know that, now. I hadn't expected to find such a trustworthy friend in my neighbor, but I was grateful for his camaraderie. "Shall you keep Lady Cameron from assisting in the school?" I asked. Lydia would be sad, of course, if it came to that. "I would not fault you for it," I added.

He seemed to consider the question before shaking his head. "I trust you," he said. "And I could not forbid my wife from helping in the school. She's quite fallen in love with a little boy by the name of Samuel."

I froze, watching Lord Cameron closely for his response. "Have you met this young boy?" I inquired.

Shaking his head, he casually leaned back against the wall. "Not yet. But I would like to meet the boy who has so smitten my wife."

Nodding, I searched for something to say to shift the conversation. The secret remained safe, at least for now, but it wouldn't be for long. Lord Cameron would *know* who Samuel belonged to the moment he laid eyes on the boy.

"Shall we play again?" I asked.

The distraction worked the way I hoped it would. Turning to retrieve his mace from the wall, Lord Cameron said, "Gladly."

The remainder of the afternoon passed in pleasant conversation and amiable teasing. Lord Cameron was entertaining. More so than I'd expected. I had always been closer friends with Cameron's brothers, Lord Stallsbury—Lord Tarquin, when I had known him well—and the oldest brother who had died tragically from an ill-suited duel. Of course, I'd known Lord Cameron for quite some time, but not well, and now that I was spending more time with him, I wondered why we hadn't done so sooner.

Probably because he was a better man than I, and spent his time writing books instead of wasting his money at cards. I could take a page from his book, metaphorically speaking, and spend my time in more worthy pursuits.

In fact, I supposed I was already doing so.

With a self-satisfied smile, I bent down and prepared my mace to strike.

"It appears your luck has caught up with you," Lord Cameron said, pulling the red ball from the pocket which I had sunk moments before.

Chuckling, I moved aside for Lord Cameron to take his turn. "Well, I suppose it is better late than not at all."

CHAPTER 23
LYDIA

The air shifted when Edward and I stepped into the church the following Sunday. What had been welcoming smiles and encouraging nods the week before were now solemn faces of curiosity and distrust. Mr. Cartwright himself gave me a long, serious look before turning to speak to a woman in the front pew.

Were the inhabitants of Melton angry because I had started a Sunday school? Surely they could not care so much about the village poor as to have such feelings of disdain or apprehension.

It was a *school* for heaven's sake.

Edward led me to our bench and sat beside me. Rain pelted the roof above us, and I let the consistent pattering soothe me until Mr. Cartwright stepped up to the podium to speak.

Too eager to return home and prepare the loft for Samuel, I could not properly focus on the sermon. The time stretched for what felt like hours until I was able to finally stand and follow Edward from the building. We were stopped, however, halfway down the aisle by a thick man and what I assumed to be his short wife beside him.

"Thornton!" the large man bellowed. "Good to have you

back, son. I'd nearly given up on seeing you again. It's been years, hasn't it?" His voice boomed throughout the church and every ear nearby could clearly hear what was being said.

"I've been visiting an aunt," Edward explained. "But yes, it has been a few years since I've been here."

"Planning to stick around this time?" the larger man questioned.

Edward shot a glance at me. "I am doing my best," he finally said.

I had the impression that he was not referring to me or the house, but that he was struggling, himself, to remain. Hurt sliced through me, though I didn't know why I allowed it to. Edward did not say that he found me or Melton dull, of course, though his behavior the day Lord and Lady Cameron had come to visit might have indicated otherwise. I would like to ask him precisely what he meant by that comment, but it would have to wait until we were alone.

Maybe in the carriage ride home.

Edward introduced me to the couple, a Mr. and Mrs. Stockman.

"You've started a school then, eh?" Mr. Stockman asked me, his eyebrow raised in judgment.

"Indeed." I tried to smile to temper the unease which skittered throughout my body. Mrs. Stockman glanced away, unable, or perhaps just unwilling, to meet my gaze.

Mr. Stockman clicked his tongue, his voice turning from jolly to serious quite suddenly. "There's a lot of good people who take affront to your idea, Mrs. Thornton. It would be wise to consider how your actions are affecting the community."

Stunned, my mouth dropped open. I felt Edward's hand come around my elbow and turn me away. "Thank you for your concern," he said, and then swiftly led me outside to the line of waiting carriages and directly toward our own. We passed Miss Gould on our route and I smiled at her, but she quickly glanced away. Troubled, I climbed inside and leaned back against the squabs.

My mind was a jumble of nerves from the direct warning. I almost couldn't abide the idea of a carriage ride, so sure I was that my stomach would sour. Should every part of me be made to feel uncomfortable? At least it was only a short ride. Twenty minutes, perhaps.

My shoulders shook with the motion of the carriage as we took off, slowly rumbling forward through the muggy weather.

"You seem worried," Edward said.

I tore my gaze from the small window on my left. "I am trying to watch the trees outside. It has sometimes helped to ease my discomfort."

"I apologize that we were unable to ride today. Although with this rain, I don't think it would have been wise."

"What do you think he meant?" I asked, unable to shake the serious, rounded eyes which had borne into me. Mr. Stockman was not only warning me about the town's inclinations, he clearly felt affronted by my school as well.

Edward shook his head, watching me closely. "Mr. Stockman? He's a stubborn man. I would not take heed to his warnings."

"Yet how can I not? I don't wish to create a divide between us and the people of Melton."

Reaching across the bench, Edward's hand hesitated slightly over mine before his fingers came around my own. He squeezed them lightly, watching our gloved hands intently as he said, "Do not fear. There is nothing you can do which will create any significant divide. The people here do not like change, but change is upon them. They will grow accustomed to the idea in time."

My heart beat rapidly against my chest. The feel of his large, warm fingers was foreign, and yet comforting. "I cannot quit, regardless of Mr. Stockman's dislike. Samuel Morley is not going to be my only student forever, I hope, but he is worth teaching, too."

Edward's hand suddenly let go of mine and he leaned back slightly. Clearing his throat, he looked to the window. "Yes, of course. It is a very charitable thing you are trying to accomplish."

The connection between Edward and me was like a soft thread strung between us, one which suddenly snapped at the mention of Samuel Morley. Whatever it was, Edward was not pleased with the mention, and I shrank back against the squabs, defeated.

I wanted to argue that if my choices and actions were so very charitable, then why was the vicar and congregation so against it?

Our carriage pulled into Thornville's drive and stopped before the door. Edward helped me out and up the front steps. I pulled on his arm before he could enter, for there was a paper tacked to the door, soaked and plastered flat against it.

Edward peeled it off before Dickson opened the door for us and ushered us inside. We paused in the well-lit foyer while Edward tried to make sense of the note. His eyebrows drew together, and his mouth formed a slight frown.

"I cannot make out what it says."

"Did you retain the note tacked to the door from last week?" I asked.

He looked up sharply. "Yes. Dickson!" he called. "Send for Jeremy. I need him to retrieve a note from my bureau from the top left drawer."

"Right away, sir."

Dickson marched away and Edward looked back to the note in his hands, his mind obviously working to solve the dripping, running letters.

We moved into the drawing room, sitting on the sofa as a maid came in to tend the fire. Edward got to his feet as the maid left the room, pacing between the writing desk and the far wall. He could not seem to settle, his face a picture of confusion.

"Have you ever had trouble like this before?" I asked.

He paused, shaking his head. "Never."

Edward's valet stepped through the doorway and presented a creased note on a silver platter. Edward took it, dismissing his man and unfolding the note. He sat beside me on the sofa and placed the dry paper on the table before us, spreading out the wet paper beside it. The wet one had lost any recognizable words due to the streaming rain, the ink dripping and bleeding down the page.

"It is from the same hand," Edward said, "but that is the only thing of which I am certain."

"How can you tell?" I asked.

"Look at the lines here," he said, pointing to similar loops on each paper. "He wrote the same thing twice, though he added something to this second note. I wish I could decipher it, for I have no idea who would want us to leave Thornville." He paused, turning toward me. "Have you heard anything from the people in town that might give us some answers?"

"No," I said. I could not think of a single person who would wish us ill. "I was not very well received this morning, though."

"When?" he asked, surprised.

"During the church service. Did you not feel the stares?"

He scoffed, shaking his head. "I did not. And I have a hard time giving these notes any validity when there is nothing besides a few stares to indicate that someone has taken us in dislike. I did not tell you of the first note I received, but I had thought it an ill-suited, childish joke at the time."

I touched the lettering on the dry note, running my finger down the stiff paper. "Perhaps it is. Though it was clearly not written by a child. What did the first note say?"

"That we are unwanted and should leave Melton if we know what is good for us."

I felt my eyebrows raise. "It mentioned us by name?"

Edward looked up, chewing his lip. "No. It said *You* are unwanted. Leave Melton if you know what is good for you."

"And it was tacked to the front door?"

"Yes," he said. "Same as the others."

I reached forward and tapped the notes. "In that case, I can only assume the author of these notes either assumed the receiver would understand it was meant for them, or he assumed the master of the house would take it to be his."

"Which is why I do think it was intended for me. They began not long after we arrived."

"Not long after our new cook arrived, either," I argued. "They are so pointed, but so vague."

He gazed at the notes before turning toward me, resting his chin upon his clenched fist. His green eyes watched me closely. "We oughtn't worry. I am sure it is nothing."

Unease settled on my shoulders, causing my fingers to grow restless on my lap. Perhaps it was a childish prank, but the threat remained present in my mind with unceasing clarity.

Or else.

"Or else what, exactly?" I asked quietly.

He opened his mouth to speak when the door opened and Dickson stepped inside. "Lady Cameron," he announced, stepping aside.

She rushed toward me, a large, black umbrella clutched in her hands. "I am walking to the Morley cottage to fetch little Samuel if you would like to accompany me."

A moment's hesitation flew through me as my gaze flickered to Edward and then back to my friend. The rain was horrendous, and while I was looking forward to seeing Samuel, of course, I was also perfectly content continuing the conversation with Edward.

The determination on Lady Cameron's brow was unwavering. She would go whether I accompanied her or not, but I could not allow her to walk through the woods alone. Particularly after these threats. "Yes. I shall accompany you."

"Are you sure that is wise?" Edward asked.

I tried to read his expression, but his face was a stiff work of stone.

"It is far more ideal than forcing Samuel to walk alone through the rain," I said, hoping he would read my thoughts—that I wanted neither Samuel nor Lady Cameron to walk alone. "Or worse, him missing our lesson all together."

"It is one lesson," Edward replied. "Surely it doesn't matter if he misses just one."

I wanted to ask if he was more concerned with my approaching Morley cottage again, or if it was due to these ambiguous notes, but Lady Cameron's presence stopped me from asking.

"A little rain won't bother us," Lady Cameron said, lifting her umbrella.

Edward closed his mouth, his jaw working while he glanced between my friend and me. The silence stretched a moment longer before his face broke into a joyless smile and he turned to me. "I shall have some blankets sent to the loft. After walking through that downpour, you will need them." He stood, bowing to lady Cameron and me, before exiting the room.

I turned toward the door. "Shall we?"

CHAPTER 24
LYDIA

The rain was worse than earlier, pouring down the edges of the umbrella Lady Cameron and I shared and soaking me from the waist down. We stood outside Morley cottage, knocking at the door with force, for the second time.

I glanced over my shoulder at the rain streaming through the trees. A shiver ran down my arms. "I don't think anyone is going to answer the door."

Heavy footsteps stomped through the house, loud enough to be heard over the rain. It certainly could not be a woman's steps. Lady Cameron and I shared an apprehensive glance.

The door swung open and a tall, thick man with a graying beard which reached halfway down the front of his shirt towered before us. His scowl was frightening, and he did not speak. He simply glowered at us.

Lady Cameron cleared her throat. "We are here for Samuel."

He stared a moment longer. "He left hours ago." His voice was as weathered as his skin.

"Where did he go?" she asked.

I swallowed. The mountainous man simply stared, undoubtedly aware of how intimidating he was. His shoulder eventually came up in a half shrug before he slammed the door, suddenly, forcing both Lady Cameron and I to jump.

"Well," I said, leaning closer to Lady Cameron in case the mountainous man could hear through the door and the rain. "He was frightening. Shall we return?"

Determination fell over her features, hardening them into stone. She looked fierce, but in a way I hadn't before seen from the sweet woman. She did not respond to me, but instead turned for Thornville and walked. I scurried to keep up with her. I gave up my attempts to remain dry and by the time we reached the barn behind my house, I was absolutely soaked.

Lady Cameron let herself inside and hurried up the steps to the loft. "There you are!" she said, dropping the wet umbrella onto the dirty floor and swiftly crossing the bare plank floor. Lowering her hands onto her knees, she leaned down to speak to Samuel Morley, who sat on the floor before the large open door. The rain fell, blurring the countryside and streaking gray, blue and green together in a mixed, oil painting, framed by the loft walls and open barn door.

"Are you cold, Samuel?" Lady Cameron asked.

He looked up at her, a comfortable smile settling on his face. "Yes."

"I will return home and request tea," I said. "Otherwise, we shall have to wait another three-quarters of an hour."

Lady Cameron hardly offered me acknowledgment, offering only a perfunctory nod before turning her attention back to Samuel. She settled herself on the floor beside the young boy and I winced. The servants did a wonderful job cleaning the floor and preparing the space for my school, but this was still the storage space for the horses' hay, and a decent amount of dirt settled on the floor mixed with straw. Lady Cameron's wet gown was sure to be filthy when she arose.

My gaze caught on a stack of blankets and I lifted two of

them, crossing the floor and draping them, one at a time, over Lady Cameron's and Samuel's shoulders. I received thankful smiles before I left the two to their soft, murmuring conversation.

Lady Cameron was clearly a woman who cared deeply for others, particularly children. It did not take a superior mind to deduce her special concern for Samuel, and though I could not understand the cause or connection between the two, it was evident that Samuel appreciated Lady Cameron, as well.

Carriage wheels sounded behind me as I crossed the grounds to return to the house and Lord Cameron nearly flew from the carriage, running across the ground to where I stood, stunned, in the drive.

"Is my wife here?" he asked. "I was told she left for Thornville with an *umbrella* and nothing more." He looked up as if the sky held the answers.

"She is in the loft with my pupil," I said. "Let us continue this conversation indoors."

His shoulders relaxed. I mounted the steps with Lord Cameron close behind me and led us inside, warmth suddenly washing over my chilled body. "I have come inside to request tea, but then I can take her a message if you'd like."

Edward appeared in the hallway. "You are very wet," he said.

Lord Cameron looked between us, chuckling. "That is an accurate assessment, my good man."

"Are you finished with your school for the day?"

"I haven't begun yet."

"Then you ought to change into something dry before returning. You aren't much good to your students if you catch cold." His voice was calm, but his eyes were wary.

"I must speak to Mrs. Patton first," I said. "And I promise I shall change my gown before returning outside."

Edward nodded his approval. "Lord Cameron, can I tempt you to remain for a game of billiards?"

"I intended to try and persuade Elsie to return home with me," he said apologetically. "I can only assume she is equally in danger of catching a chill."

"I left her wrapped in a blanket." I hesitated, but the men did not push me. The picture of Lady Cameron and Samuel sitting on the loft floor in comfortable conversation, framed beautifully by the open loft door and the streaming rain came to my mind. Finally, I said, "I fear you will find difficulty in convincing Lady Cameron to leave. She's with Samuel now."

Lord Cameron gave me a knowing glance. Sighing, he turned to Edward. "I will take the game, Thornton."

Lydia

The lesson was short and focused on teaching Samuel a few more letters. Lady Cameron was distracted for the duration and I paused once to inquire if she would be more comfortable before a fire inside the house, but she immediately dismissed the suggestion. In her defense, she was neither pale nor shivering, securely wrapped in two quilts.

Samuel ate with abandon, loading cold ham and slices of bread slathered in jam on his plate. He gulped down multiple cups of tea until Lady Cameron refused to pour him another, laughing with pleasure over his wry little smile. He must have known he was drinking too much.

"I do not want you to have a stomachache," she said. "How about you try one of these biscuits, instead?"

He took a small, rounded biscuit from Lady Cameron's outstretched palm, and bit into it. "That's good," he said, taking another from the tray.

"Samuel?" I asked. He glanced up to me and I said, "I want to teach more students to read. Do you know any other children who might be interested in Sunday school?"

His little button nose scrunched up in thought. Glancing about the room, he settled on the tea tray. "My friends don't want to go to *school*, but I bet Lizzie and Jacob would like the tea."

I caught Lady Cameron's gaze over his head as Samuel reached for another biscuit. One would believe the boy had not been fed in a week if his appetite today was any indication.

Oh, goodness. Could he be underfed?

"Would you like to invite Lizzie and Jacob to join you next week when you come?" Lady Cameron asked.

Samuel shrugged, chomping his biscuit. "I can do that."

"Splendid."

We sat on the benches, waiting for Samuel to eat his fill. On a whim, I loaded a napkin with the remaining bread, ham and biscuits and tied the ends together to create a small pouch. "Would you like to take this home?"

Samuel nodded eagerly, accepting the bundle before shrugging the blanket from his shoulders.

"Can I walk you home, Samuel?" Lady Cameron inquired.

He shook his head. "No. I want to run."

He got up, thanking us, before taking off down the stairs and across the front drive.

Lady Cameron crossed to the open doorway and peeked around the corner, her eyebrows drawn together, eyes searching.

A few minutes passed before she gave up searching the woods for pattering footsteps and returned, sinking onto the bench beside me.

"I don't know what it is about that boy," she said, shaking her head. Suddenly she stilled, glancing at me. "Actually, I know precisely what it is about that boy, but if I say it aloud you will laugh at me."

"I will *not* laugh at you," I promised.

She seemed to gauge my sincerity before sighing. "It will sound silly, I am sure, but there is just something about Samuel which draws me in. Something about his eyes, I think, and the shape of his face." She shook her head. "I cannot put my finger on it, but he reminds me of my husband. I can almost imagine Cameron looking similar to Samuel as a little boy. I can imagine…"

I said nothing as Lady Cameron sighed, wiping at a suspiciously shiny eye. "I desperately want children, Mrs. Thornton, and Samuel is precisely how I imagine my little boy looking. My heart aches when I see him, but it also soars. Although, he did say something distressing earlier and I don't quite know what to think."

"What was it?"

"He told me that he spent the entirety of the morning in this barn, and when I asked him why, he explained that he did not like to be home when his gramma had Mr. Hammond over to visit."

"Did he give a reason for his dislike?"

She shook her head. "Only that Mr. Hammond is too loud."

"That could mean a multitude of things," I said.

"Exactly."

We gathered the blankets and tea tray and returned to the house through a slight drizzle of rain. The weather had let up in the last few minutes, slowing to a heavy mist.

Dickson opened the front door for us and took the blankets from Lady Cameron's arms. She immediately wrapped her arms around herself and I wanted to embrace her, but I did not know if it would be well received. Hesitation lengthened the moment longer and Dickson cleared his throat, slashing my resolve and ruining the moment.

"Shall I show you to Mr. Thornton and Lord Cameron?"

"Perhaps you can request their presence," I said instead. "Lady Cameron must return home quickly."

"Very good," he said.

She gave me a questioning glance as my butler walked away.

"You are soaked through," I reminded her.

She glanced down at her gown as if she hadn't known she was so wet. "That is correct," she agreed, smiling. "I was so preoccupied with Samuel, I hadn't considered what a fright I'd become."

"You are not a fright," I argued. "But I do worry for your health."

"I will not steal Samuel and make him my own," she said at once.

Surprise filtered through me. "I was not even considering that possibility. Though, perhaps I will now," I joked. "I was referring to your physical health."

She laughed. "Yes, that too. I cannot return next week if I am laid up in bed."

Edward and Lord Cameron came into the foyer, and the latter crossed to his wife immediately. "That was foolish," he said through a smile, shrugging from his coat and placing it around her shoulders. "I have a feeling that nothing would have kept you from checking on that boy, but I would have been more than happy to *drive* you here."

Lady Cameron smiled, chagrined. "I was not thinking—"

"Of anything more than Samuel Morley," Lord Cameron finished for her, as he gazed lovingly at his wife. "It is in your nature, my dear, and I have long known that you will put the needs of others before your own."

"It is an admirable trait," I said, causing them to look at me.

"Indeed," Edward agreed, coming to stand beside me. He watched Lord and Lady Cameron with interest, and I felt the heat from his body on my arm, as he stood so close behind.

Clearing my throat, I clutched my hands together. "Thank

you for your assistance today, Lady Cameron. With any luck, our numbers will triple next week."

"We can only hope," she agreed. "And please, would you call me Elsie?"

Surprised by the sudden request, I faltered. Quickly regaining my head, I nodded. "I would be honored if you would call me Lydia."

Smiling, Elsie took her husband's arm and followed him toward the door. Turning back, she said, "I nearly forgot. Will we see you at the Gunmans' ball?"

I had not heard anything of this ball before. Looking to Edward, I realized that he had not told me of it intentionally, for he glanced away with guilt. "Yes," he said at length. "We shall be there."

The air was thick and quiet when our guests left. Dickson closed the door behind them and the click of his heels could be heard as he left the foyer, following a dismissal from Edward.

"Would you prefer not to attend the ball?" I asked.

He shook his head. "No, the ball will be fine. I was concerned about..." He sighed, his words trailing into silence. "You are familiar with my determination to avoid playing cards. I only feared that the men at the ball would push me to play. How will I circumvent them?"

His face both vulnerable and hard at the same time, as though he was placing a wall between his fears and me. I wanted to be there for him, but I was afraid. It was not in *my* nature to be forward or to speak out. Defending a small child was one thing, but to reach out to my husband in such a way? The risk of rejection felt too great.

It frightened me.

The wall hardened on Edward's face the longer I stayed silent and I cursed myself for my hesitation. How utterly selfish of me. What did it matter if Edward rejected my help? It might hurt, but it would not break me, surely.

I stepped forward, surprised by my own actions, and placed a hand on Edward's forearm, gripping him tightly. I looked into his confused, green eyes and said, "I will be there. Should the temptation become too great, you can come to me."

His mouth quirked into a half-smile. "And you will defend me to the gentlemen?"

"No," I said, matching his smile with one of my own. "I will dance with you instead."

His head tilted slightly. "I hadn't considered that possibility. If they will not let me be, I can explain that I don't wish to leave you alone."

I nodded. "That is reasonable."

"Hopefully the men agree with that reasoning. If nothing else, I can always ask you to dance."

Just don't forget about me, this time.

CHAPTER 25
LYDIA

The Gunmans' ball was blessed, the rain ceasing well before the appointed hour we were to set off. The roads, however, had yet to fully dry and wet, muddy earth caused our carriage wheels to slide periodically on the way to the ball, both frightening me and causing my stomach to lurch.

A particularly wide turn was taken too quickly, and the carriage slid dangerously far. I slapped my hand against the side of the carriage to stabilize myself and felt Edward's large hand grip my arm at once. "Are you feeling unwell?"

"This sliding does not help," I explained, gulping a deep breath and squeezing my eyes closed, though that seemed to make the feeling worse.

"What can I do?" he asked.

I turned to look at him, my arm still pressing against the carriage. "I am afraid there is nothing I can do. This is my lot in life."

His smile was commiserating. "Do you feel unwell when you dance, as well?"

"No," I said, confused. "The floor does not move whilst I

dance."

"But you do. Quite a lot."

Had he watched me dance before, or was he referring to the act of dancing in general? "Most people do," I said.

"Exactly."

I turned away, leaning against the seat and focusing on my breathing. Edward's hand slid down my arm, resting finally on my forearm as my hand gripped the edge of the seat. His thumb began tracing small, soft circles around my wrist bone, distracting me immensely. Shivers raced up my arm and he paused, his thumb going still.

"Are you cold?" he asked.

"No," I said, my voice coming out hoarsely. "I am quite warm."

He did not resume his tracing, but his hand continued to hold my forearm, and I missed the motion very much.

Our carriage pulled into the Gunman's drive shortly after and Edward released my arm in order to help me down. I felt his lack of touch immediately, but gulped in deep breaths, filling my lungs with the clean, fresh air and waiting for it to cleanse me and remove the nausea from my stomach.

"Shall we?" he asked, offering me his arm.

I took it, and followed him through a large, columned entryway into a warm, stuffy house. People filled the ballroom, spilling into the surrounding rooms and even the foyer. I leaned closer to Edward, gripping his arm tightly. "I didn't know there were so many people in Melton."

"There aren't," he whispered into my ear. "The Gunmans' balls usually fill with people from all over the county. Lord Cameron has been attending them for years, in fact, and his family's home is not nearby."

We stepped before a man with stark white hair, worn long and tied in a queue behind his neck, in an older fashion, beside a woman with rich, dark hair and clear, intelligent eyes.

"My wife, Mrs. Thornton," Edward said. "Mr. and Mrs. Gunman."

I curtsied to my hosts. Mr. Gunman bowed, looking beyond me to the next in line in a clear dismissal. His wife merely gazed at me. "I've heard you are causing quite a splash," she said.

"Oh?"

"Yes," she said. The men started their own conversation, and she continued, "It has come to my attention that you have been attempting to begin a Sunday school."

I opened my mouth to confirm, but she cut me off. "It is a noble cause, my dear, but so very misguided. We have a lovely school in town. Surely if Mr. Cartwright deemed our parish in need of a Sunday school, he would begin one himself."

"Well, actually, I did approach the vicar—"

"Furthermore," she said, cutting me off yet again, "I cannot think that a school run in a *barn* creates a very healthy environment for anyone. I should think you would cease this endeavor before word is too widely spread and you've brought shame to Thornville. I cannot imagine Mr. Thornton would appreciate his new wife ruining his family's long-standing status within Melton."

Had the woman just *threatened* me? Stunned, I merely stared at her, mouth agape, until Edward slid his hand around my arm and led me away. Had he heard her?

"Circumvented," he said into my ear, his warm breath running shivers down my neck. He had not heard us then; evidently, he'd been too busy battling Mr. Gunman's plea to play cards.

I did not know if I was grateful or bothered that the threat had gone unheard. I would have to examine it closer at a later time. Filing the experience away, I let Edward lead me into the ballroom and install me along the wall in an empty space.

His gaze flitted about the room and I watched him search, wondering if he would take the opportunity to ask me to dance.

But what if he had forgotten? Or worse, what if he asked and then abandoned me as he had before?

It was not a situation I needed to worry over, for he hadn't yet asked.

"I've spotted Lord Cameron," he said.

"Perhaps he will be a safe ally."

Edward looked down at me and nodded. "Precisely." He took my arm and led me to the opposite side of the ballroom. Elsie stood beside her husband, clutching his arm as she glanced about the room. When her gaze landed upon me, her face lit up and my heart warmed.

I believed I had found a true friend in my new home, something I hadn't had in quite some time.

"Would you like to take a turn about the room?" she asked.

I clutched her arm and nodded.

"Wonderful. My sister-in-law will be here tonight. I don't know her well, but I would like to make an introduction if it would suit you."

"I would like that."

We circled the room but came up short. Making our way to the adjoining rooms, we meandered throughout the open floor of the house, chatting about various things while keeping an eye out for Elsie's sister-in-law, though I did not know whom I was looking for beyond a description of a beautiful woman with pale blonde hair.

"Is that her?" I asked quietly, gesturing toward a woman seated on a sofa beside a man with deep red hair.

"No," Elsie said. "And this is the final room. Perhaps they haven't arrived yet."

The man turned his head and I caught the familiar eyes of Mr. Radmahl at once, my steps faltering from his direct gaze. His lips formed a perfect smile and I returned the gesture before Elsie pulled me from the room.

"Who was that woman?" I asked. Perhaps Mr. Radmahl had an understanding with her.

"I don't know," Elsie replied. "But then again, I am new to the area. We've only been here a few months."

"Are you pleased with your choice in coming here?"

"Yes," she said. "I love my home." A sorrow in her eyes spoke of loss. I could see it written plainly on her face; her idyllic life was missing one thing. *Children.*

My life was missing the same thing, but I still had hope that I would one day become a mother. Edward had the same desire for children that I did. We only waited for the purpose of bettering our relationship. But it seemed Elsie and Lord Cameron were not waiting intentionally, and so my friend mourned the absence of children acutely.

"Do you think Samuel will be successful in persuading his friends to join our Sunday school?" I asked, hoping to steer the conversation toward happier pursuits. We made our way back to the ballroom and found Edward speaking with Lord Cameron and a few other men on the far side of the room.

"I hope so," Elsie said. "It would be good for Samuel to have peers learning alongside him, I should think, so he does not have to do it alone."

"I grew up alone," I said. "I learned from my governess alone and I played mostly alone. And I can say from experience that it would have been far more enjoyable had I another child to sit with."

"I, too, don't have any brothers or sisters. But I was fortunate to be sent to a finishing school and developed relationships with other girls who are still, to this day, like sisters to me. One of them is Cameron's sister, in fact."

"The one I am looking for this evening?" I asked.

"No, that is his brother's new wife." She looked about her. "If they do show up, that is."

I observed Edward interacting with the men near him. He

was relaxed, leaning against the wall with his arms casually crossed over his chest. He flashed Lord Cameron a smile, showcasing straight, white teeth. I felt the amusement which danced in his eyes from clear across the ballroom.

My heart swelled for the man. It was true, we did not have very much in common, but he had a tendency to think of small, simple things which made me more comfortable. Just a few days before, he had thought to have blankets sent to the loft because he knew the rain would drench Elsie and me. Before that, he had suffered through evenings listening to me read from my novels in order to spend opposite evenings playing billiards.

I hated to admit it, even to myself, but I was not eager for the bad weather to subside completely. Our evenings spent together would certainly cease once Edward was able to return to working outside.

"Your face is a picture of concentration, Lydia, and I am ever so curious why."

My cheeks grew pink and I tore my gaze from Edward. "It is nothing."

Elsie's smile grew as she glanced to where my line of sight had rested. "Oh, I see. You are gazing in silent adoration at your husband. I remember those early days of my own marriage. I frequently did very much the same thing." Her nose scrunched up in thought as she found Lord Cameron in the group. Chuckling, she leaned in. "Actually, I still do."

"What is it that you still do?" a feminine voice asked from behind. I glanced over my shoulder and found a beautiful woman standing close behind us, a satisfied smile on her lips. Kind eyes crinkled alongside her smile.

Elsie turned, grinning at once. "Eleanor! I am so glad to see you. Is Tarquin with you?"

The woman nodded, gesturing to where a tall man who closely resembled Lord Cameron crossed the ballroom with confident, sure steps. His chin was slightly more pointed, his jawline a bit more defined, but otherwise he might be mistaken for Lord Cameron.

Gripping my wrist softly, Elsie pulled me closer. "Please, let me introduce my friend, Mrs. Thornton."

I dipped a curtsy. "And Lydia, this is Lady Stallsbury. She recently married Cameron's brother, Tarquin, and they live at the family castle."

"Did you once tell me it is an hour's drive from Melton?" I asked.

Elsie nodded. "Indeed."

"We are planning to stay for a holiday," Lady Stallsbury explained, her hand lowering to rest on her belly. If I remembered correctly, Elsie had once told me that her sister-in-law was in the family way. She must not be very far along, but the way she held herself was telling. "I am not eager to make the return trip this evening."

"And we are so pleased to have you," Elsie said, grinning. Instruments began tuning and Elsie turned her head at once. "I am promised to my husband for this dance."

"I am sure Tarquin will bring him this way. I am promised, as well," Lady Stallsbury said.

I envied them and their promised dances. They were so assured that their husbands would appear before the music began in earnest.

And I was simply a placeholder should the need arise for Edward to escape eager card players.

Reminding myself that ours was not a love match, I swallowed the bitter taste which crept up my throat and smiled, likely *too* widely, at the women.

Elsie turned toward her sister-in-law. "Have you read the book I wrote to you about?"

"*Sense and Sensibility?*" she asked, smiling. Her eyes were alight and she appeared to be so full of joy, she positively glowed like the warm light of a candle. "Yes, and I enjoyed it immensely."

Elsie grinned. "Perfect. Once Lydia finishes the second book by that same author, I shall lend it to you."

"We are nearly done," I said. "I believe I will be able to return it by tomorrow evening."

"Do not hurry on my account," Lady Stallsbury said quickly. "If I must extend my holiday so that I can finish Elsie's book, then I will not complain."

"Tarquin might, however," Elsie said facetiously.

Lady Stallsbury chuckled. "He will not complain if he knows it is my wish. He is very giving." The light in her eyes was so sweet, it made my stomach turn.

I was not familiar with many people who made love matches for themselves, and now I was positive I did not want to know any more. It was all fine to read about in novels—Elinor Dashwood and Edward Ferrars, for one—but in real life, it was nearly sickening. Particularly when I was unable to find a love match of my own.

Unwittingly, my gaze caught Edward's over Elsie's shoulder. He was approaching us alongside Lord Cameron and Lord Stallsbury, and my heart began beating rapidly in my chest. Was he going to ask me to dance?

"Mrs. Thornton," a deep voice said just to my right. My head snapped toward the sound and I found clever eyes gazing at me. Mr. Radmahl looked tidy in his navy coat and tan waistcoat, his cravat tied to perfection with a large, shiny jewel pinned to its center.

His timing indicated that he was seeking a dance, but I wished so deeply for Edward to be standing there in his stead. I willed him to keep quiet until my husband could arrive and say the words first, but he must not have read my mind.

He held out a hand with a flourish. "Would you do me the honor of partnering me in this set?"

CHAPTER 26
LYDIA

Disappointment crushed my shoulders as I drew in a steadying breath and placed my hand softly within Mr. Radmahl's own. "I would be much obliged," I said quietly.

I turned, catching Edward's face as he stood just a few yards away and watched the interaction. I knew how deeply he disliked Mr. Radmahl, but I had been very clear when we last discussed it that I could not cut the man in public when I had no cause.

And Edward would not give me just cause.

Tightening his grip on my hand, Mr. Radmahl placed it on his arm and led me to the center of the dance floor to line up for the first set. Edward turned away from us as we approached, leaving the room completely.

Sick to my stomach, I faced Mr. Radmahl with determination. I would complete the required dances for the set and then I would find Edward and apologize. Perhaps he would ask me, then. All could not be lost, surely.

It was only a dance.

But then why did I feel so ill?

Minutes stretched on as I moved to the music, my gaze searching for my husband while the man he despised helped me through the motions. Mr. Radmahl watched me with leering, serious eyes in a way that made my skin crawl as though bugs ran down the length of my spine. I was ready for the music to end, but because of that, it seemed to last even longer.

"How does your Sunday school get on?" he asked.

"It is well," I said. "I have two pupils and they are beginning to learn. It is a slow process, for I am learning how to teach them, as well."

His brows drew together. "I had heard you only had one boy coming to your school."

How had he heard that? Perhaps he'd overheard Elsie speaking about our efforts to someone else. For I had certainly not spoken about it with anyone besides Edward, and I'd wager they hadn't had a conversation about my Sunday school. I was sure they hadn't had a conversation about *anything*.

"I have been teaching one of our servants as well."

"Ah, I see."

Edward appeared in the crowd along the wall near the entrance and I saw the moment Mr. Radmahl noticed him as well, for his eyes went dark. He narrowed his focus on me, glancing over my shoulder and then delivering a pleasant smile. All too familiar, in my estimation.

The music drew to a close and I pulled my hand from his grip before he could do anything drastic, like lean down and kiss it. I could see now, however much I did not want to admit it, that he enjoyed baiting Edward. Furthermore, I had surprised him by my sudden movements.

"Thank you, Mr. Radmahl," I said, clutching my skirt in both hands to keep them occupied. I turned toward the entrance where I'd seen Edward just moments before, but he was gone. Stepping through the doorway and into the foyer, I raked my gaze over the groups of people, some familiar but most of them strangers, but came up short.

He was not there.

The door sat propped open at the end of the hallway and I made my way toward it and the front porch, lowly lit by torches, and stepped into the cool night air.

If nothing else, it was a balm on my overwhelming emotions. I felt as though I'd been thrown into ocean waves and tumbled about, with no clear footing or direction. Elsie was a kind friend but seeing her with her husband, the two of them so very much in love, filled me with confusion and jealousy.

I hadn't even known before meeting Edward that I wished to fall in love. It was all such a shocking revelation, that I didn't know what to do with the information.

And the wretched novels recommended to me by Elsie were not helping, for regardless of the trials the characters faced, they each found their own happiness in the end. The books were dangerous, for they gave me something I very much doubted was good.

They gave me hope.

Sighing, I leaned against the column just off the side of the porch, shrouded in shadows and hidden from view. Dropping my head into my hands, I allowed myself one small, brief moment to pity myself before I drew myself up tall and rubbed the exhaustion from my eyes.

When I removed my hands from my face I nearly screamed, for I came face to face with a set of disgruntled, clear eyes.

Limiting myself to merely a gasp, I clapped my hand over my mouth to stifle the scream, and then gazed at Edward with all of the amazement I possessed. "Whatever are you doing, sneaking up on me in such a way?"

"I am not sneaking up on you," he argued, his eyebrows drawn and hands fidgeting near his sides. "I came out here first. You followed me."

"Yes, because I wanted to reassure myself that you were well. But I did not see you and chose to take a moment's respite in this space. I stood here first, and therefore, *you* snuck up on *me*."

"We shall not see eye to eye on this issue," he muttered.

"Because you are being ridiculous."

"What has gotten into you?" he questioned, bewildered. His eyes had grown wide and he looked up and down my body as though he needed to reassure himself that I was, indeed, still Lydia.

Shaking my head, I turned away. Yes, I was certainly more outspoken this evening, I supposed. But was that such a horrible thing?

Until now, I had been too nervous in his company to speak my mind much.

I wasn't as nervous anymore.

"I understand that you do not like Mr. Radmahl," I began. Edward immediately took a step back, as though speaking the man's name alone pushed him away from me. "But you have to realize that without proper reasoning, it is very difficult for me to treat him rudely. I must know for *myself* that he is deserving of such callous behavior."

He scoffed. "Yet one would think that as *my* wife, you would simply trust that my reasoning is sound."

"How can I when I hardly know you?"

He snapped his head toward me, a look of hurt washing over his face. Had I erred so greatly? It was the truth though. I did not know him well.

"Perhaps we ought to remedy that," he said softly. "I suppose you are correct, in a way, though I shall respectfully disagree with you."

"How, sir? How can you claim you know me when you asked moments ago why I am acting so differently?"

He regarded me closely before taking a step closer. The shadows cast from the torches along the entryway flickered and danced over his features. He was on edge, certainly, and I was sure a large part of that was the temptation to run away from me and lose a good deal of money in a game of cards. But I was to blame, as well, for my dance. Or, more specifically, my dance *partner*.

He spoke softly, with a calmness about him that caused me to listen intently. "I have had the pleasure of learning about you every other evening for the past few weeks, and I feel that I have gathered a good deal of information about your character."

The billiards games. He was referring to our ongoing game of asking one another questions while we played. It was true, and I was learning a great deal about him as well. There were a wide variety of topics we covered, from our growing up years to the more recent experiences we'd had at the various *ton* parties in London. He shared how he felt growing up in the wilderness of Northumberland and I confessed my lack of finesse in social situations, and how I hardly knew what to say when first meeting another person.

Even our evenings spent reading on the opposite nights were often punctuated by conversations about the characters or how we felt about their choices, which subsequently turned into discussions about ourselves.

It was unfair of me to have said that I hardly knew Edward. Likewise, he could safely claim he knew me fairly well.

Sighing, I took a small step toward him. "Forgive me."

"You are sorry you danced with him?" he asked.

"I am sorry we are in discord because of it."

He looked into my eyes again and leaned forward slightly, as though he swayed on his feet. Lowering his voice, he said, "But will you do it again?"

I wanted to give him the answer he desired, but I knew in my heart I could not agree to it without a proper explanation. Perhaps it bothered me more that Edward did not deem me worthy of his trust, than whether or not Radmahl was trustworthy himself.

But, nonetheless, I had to do what I felt was right.

Clearing my throat, I said, "I promise I will do my best to avoid him."

Strains of music drifted from the open front door and down toward us. Laughter and conversation floated behind it, filtering through the windows and doors, filling the outside space with muffled merriment.

I sensed that he understood my meaning. I would not outright ignore the man, but I would try to avoid him.

He stepped closer. "I did not stay in the ballroom long, but from what I could see, you did not enjoy the dance."

It felt rude, but I shook my head slowly. "How could I enjoy it? Particularly when I knew how it distressed you."

I seemed to catch Edward off guard with my statement and he tipped his head slightly, his gaze searching my face. His eyes flicked down to my lips and, for the second time, I began to panic that my husband was about to kiss me.

This time, the rapid beating of my heart was not because I didn't want it to happen. I held my breath and waited for the moment to occur. He seemed to sense my willingness and looked at my lips again. I found myself returning the action, wondering if his own were as soft as they appeared.

His hands came up to rest on my waist, and I could feel the shallowing of my breath in the rapid rise and fall of my chest. I took an infinitesimal step forward as his hands tightened around me, and I brought my hands up to rest on his arms, feeling the tightness of his muscles likely brought about by his dedication to bettering his estate.

I felt cool and warm flush through me at the same time as Edward lowered his head slowly.

Just before he reached me, a loud sound crashed behind us,

causing both Edward and I to jump and our heads to collide at the temples.

I stepped away and felt the distance acutely as soon as it occurred, a soft breeze billowing between us and highlighting our separation. Edward's eyes were dark and his jaw set as he stared at me, his chest rising and falling rapidly in beat with my own.

I'd never seen him look so serious before, and—I hoped—so full of disappointment.

Laughter echoed through the columned hallway, bouncing about and drawing my attention to the clattering behind us.

Rubbing my forehead where we collided, I glanced over my shoulder and found two men without control of their faculties, laughing and falling over one another.

"Foxed," Edward said in disgust. I bit back a smile, for one would assume by his disdain that Edward had never partaken in the activity of drinking, himself. And surely that could not be the case. Particularly when he ended each night with a glass of brandy.

"Shall we return?" I asked, watching as the younger of the men's faces turned white, and he rushed off the porch toward a set of hedges to cast up his accounts.

Edward grunted, sliding his hand down my arm and securing my hand before placing it on his outstretched elbow. He gave my fingers a reassuring squeeze then led me inside.

CHAPTER 27
EDWARD

I had been so close to kissing her. I would have, if those blasted lunatics hadn't crashed through the door and startled us. She was lovely, of course, with her blue silk gown and her ringlets styled with small, white flowers amidst the mass of curls.

But there was more than that. I had fallen in love with my wife, and it wasn't until she'd followed me outside that it occurred to me how deeply I was hoping she would do the same. Radmahl was a snake. And I understood—to the tiniest degree—how she would find difficulty giving him the cut direct when she did not know his history with my family.

I only wished she would trust me. Leading her to a group of acquaintances, I introduced her, proudly, as my wife. I longed to ask her to dance, but I was afraid of what would happen if I was to get her in my arms. I may never let her go again.

We spent the evening chatting with various people; all the while my nerves were heightened, my body extra aware of where Lydia was in relation to me. I followed her with my eyes when she moved away to speak to Lord Stallsbury and Mrs.

Wheeler—or, she was Lady Stallsbury now. They smiled at one another in that sickening way of lovesick fools, and I found myself grateful that while I loved Lydia, I was not sick. And neither was I a fool.

The evening came to a close in the early morning hours, before the sun had yet to make its ascent. I climbed into the carriage after Lydia and curbed my desire to reach for her hand. Would she welcome the advance? I did not want to press myself upon her.

I did my best to balance caring for her needs that evening, with giving her space to dance with other men, regardless of how deeply I disliked watching her prance about the floor at another man's direction.

I felt a river of emotion run between us as we shared a seat in the carriage. Did Lydia feel it as well? My hand itched to cross the space, but I refrained. Swallowing the impulse, I leaned my head back against the wall of the carriage and squeezed my eyes closed.

If we were not in a confined space, perhaps I could attempt to kiss her once more. If I allowed her a moment to catch her breath after the carriage ceased rocking her about and her stomach turmoil leveled, then surely I would not be pressing myself upon her. I wanted to show her what she meant to me, to explain that I was developing feelings which I hadn't planned on.

All I wanted was one, small kiss.

Lydia

The carriage ride home was quiet and full of energy. Much to my disappointment, Edward had not asked me to dance when we returned to the ballroom, but instead led me toward a group of acquaintances to introduce me.

The evening was a true measure of my patience. I was frustrated that Edward had gone from nearly kissing me to ignoring me so suddenly.

No, that was unfair. He was quite solicitous. But he had not asked me to dance.

After being forgotten on the dance floor at our very first introduction, and then avoided this evening, it begged the question: did Edward *intentionally* not wish to dance with me?

The wheels rolled to a slow stop and I swung the door open, letting myself out immediately to breathe fresh air on solid ground and wait for the unease within me to subside.

I began toward the house. The lamps lit within the foyer made the windows glow an eerie orange and the silhouette of people standing beside them could be seen.

Dickson opened the door and I stepped inside. I did not hear Edward's steps behind me, and neither did I look to see where he was. The weather had taken a sour turn with the storm and the frigid air seeped through my thin, silk gown and chilled my skin during the walk from the carriage to the house.

A high-pitched, authoritative tone rang through the foyer, assaulting me at once. "It is not unreasonable to request sustenance after such a long journey." The voice was moving upward and away, as though whoever was speaking was climbing the stairs. "I will see to my maid's unpacking and then I expect a tray in my room."

"Yes, Miss Sarah."

A frustrated groan ripped through the air. "Good."

Sarah? That could only be Edward's sister, surely.

His shoes clicked up the steps and into the house and he paused beside me. "Is something the matter?"

"I am not sure," I said honestly.

He turned to Dickson as the aging butler closed the door softly behind us. I could feel the moment it shut completely and the wind was prohibited from entering the house any longer. It was a blessed relief.

"Is it really so difficult to produce a meal this late?" Sarah continued as she stomped down a hallway upstairs, though her voice rang clearly throughout the house. "One would think I had requested a *pony* in my dressing room."

"Ah," Edward said, nodding concisely. "Sarah is home?"

"Yes."

He drew in a breath, letting it out slowly. Searching my face, he rubbed his jawline. "I had hoped we could continue our conversation from earlier, but I believe I will be tied up in welcoming my sister home. Perhaps it is better saved for another day."

Given that I didn't know which conversation he referred to, I could not help but agree. Watching him walk away, however, the pieces of the puzzle clicked together and my breath caught in my throat. Was he referencing our almost-kiss?

I shuddered. It was not an unpleasant prospect.

I followed behind Edward, but turned down the hall toward my own bedchamber, yawning. It was late into the evening—or morning, perhaps—and I was sure I would fall asleep the moment my head fell upon my pillow.

My hand paused on the door handle to my room as I heard the siblings' reunion.

"Edward, you are home!" Sarah said, her voice transforming from bitter complaints to pure joy. "I have so much to share with you. Tell me, where is your wife?"

"Half asleep, I am sure."

"Oh, do not say so. Bring her to me at once. I have been dying to meet her."

My back straightened at the abrasive, arrogant tone. I

dropped my fingers from the door handle, tempted to move down the hall and hear how Edward would respond. Luckily, both of the Thorntons had voices which carried and I did not need to sneak closer in order to hear them.

"I will not, Sarah. You can meet her in the morning."

"And shall I like her?"

I stilled. I should not be listening to this. But Sarah's door was clearly wide open, and Edward must have known there was a chance I would be nearby. He had left me standing in the foyer, after all, just minutes before.

"Of course," he answered, at length.

Did Sarah doubt him as much as I did in that moment? His tone was not convincing.

"Hmmm," she said. "I suppose I will have to decide for myself. You hardly sound convincing."

Indeed, she *did* doubt him as well. But why?

"Enough about Lydia," Edward said. "I would like to hear about Bath. I didn't realize Aunt had decided to go there until you wrote me Tuesday last."

"Her health, you know. Her neighbor, that bird-like woman with the titian hair, convinced her the waters could heal her."

They both chuckled and I opened my door at once, letting myself into my bedchamber and closing their conversation away. The atmosphere within the house was about to change. I could feel it already. I had never met Sarah before, but I could see immediately that she was a forceful person with a strong character.

I could only hope that Edward was incorrect in his assumption and that Sarah and I would get along together well enough.

Lydia

. . .

Forgoing an early morning to sleep through half of the day, I awoke after noon with a crick in my shoulder and a haze about my mind. Slowly pulling myself to a sitting position, I stretched my arms above my head, wincing as I turned my right arm the wrong way. I had slept on it in an uncomfortable position, and I was going to feel it the rest of the day, I was sure.

Pulling myself from bed, I felt the lethargy that came with sleeping late. It was not something I did often, but I had allowed myself to indulge this once. The dancing late into the evening and incessant wondering about what exactly it meant that Edward had nearly kissed me had worn me out, mentally and physically.

Christine helped me to dress and put up my hair, softly humming as she pinned up the last of my dark tresses.

"Has the rain ceased?" I asked, cutting her music short.

"To my knowledge," Christine answered. "I've yet to go outside, but the day looks bright and clear."

A moment's silence passed before she continued, "Miss Thornton has recently called for tea in the drawing room."

Drat. I had forgotten about her unexpected arrival last evening. "Very good."

Drawing myself up, I clasped my hands before me and took one last glance in the looking glass. My gown, a pale green muslin, was soft and worn. Not the height of fashion, but certainly not outdated. I had a penny-pinching father, but he did not fail to produce the funds I had needed to keep my wardrobe full.

With Christine's excellent skill and a gown I felt comfortable in, I was ready to face the loud, opinionated woman and hopefully discover how long she planned to remain at Thornville.

Descending the stairs, I was notified at once of an extra presence in the drawing room. Voices alternated through multiple women's tones, all of which sounded familiar, though I couldn't say precisely who they were. I hovered outside the door, straining to pinpoint who I was going to see. When bootheels clicked on the foyer floor behind me, I spun around, welcoming the distraction.

Edward stepped around the corner, a fierce glare covering his features which took my breath away. He appeared ready to spit fire like the dragons of my childhood fairytales and I took an inadvertent step back, bumping softly into the drawing room door.

Upon noticing me he paused at once, a bland expression overriding his irritation. He clutched a paper in his hand, but he quickly hid it behind his back, watching me closely.

"Good day, Lydia. I trust you've slept well?"

I had slept for half of the day, so clearly that was an attempt at circumventing whatever was angering him.

"Edward, what is it?" I asked.

His jaw worked and his gaze flicked away from me. The muscles in his arm bunched and smoothed repeatedly as though he was clenching and releasing the paper clutched in his fist.

"I was hoping to avoid speaking of this, for I didn't wish to frighten you."

I felt as though a cool breeze washed down my spine, though there were no open windows nearby and the house was decidedly warm.

I waited for him to continue, but his indecisiveness was alarming. "I do not frighten easily," I replied.

Sighing, he said, "Very well. Come."

Turning on his heel, he moved past me swiftly and I scurried to catch up. I followed him into his study, a room I had not seen before. It was simple, masculine, and smelled strongly of leather and spice.

"Please be seated," he said, pointing to a tall, leather chair near the hearth. He sat beside me and gazed into my eyes with a deliberate concentration. "We've received another note."

My hand stretched forth and he only hesitated momentarily before placing the crumpled paper within it.

Smoothing the creases on my lap, I read aloud, "The path to the cottage is riddled in danger. Keep away from the boy if you wish to remain unscathed." I glanced up at him. "Are they referencing Morley cottage? Samuel?"

Nodding, he said, "I can only assume so. There are no other cottages as close. And then the mention of the boy…"

"My Sunday school," I said at once. "Each of the notes has arrived on a Sunday" —I lifted the note— "or in reference to my only pupil."

He shot me a sheepish smile. "That is not true. We've received other notes, but I hid them away."

I tried to tamp down my annoyance. "Why?"

"So as not to frighten you."

"Is it not better for me to be prepared for the threat?" I asked.

His green eyes rested on me for a length of time. I could only assume he was contemplating my words. Eventually, he said, "I don't know. What I do know now, at least, is that whoever is sending these notes wishes us ill. Whether in regard to your school or otherwise, it is plain that we are being toyed with."

"May I see the other notes?"

His hesitation grated on my nerves. What harm could they do at this point? I meant what I had said. It would be *far* better for me to understand the depth of the threat so that I might protect myself and remain cautious.

He crossed to the desk and pulled a stack of crumpled paper from the top drawer. "These came after the note drenched in rain." Standing before me like a sentinel, he handed the notes to me and then remained, folding his arms over his chest, his eyebrows drawn together.

LOVE IN THE WAGER

I read them, my heart rate rising steadily.
Heed my warnings and leave.
A loft is an easy place to find harm.
That must refer to me.
But who was going to harm me?

CHAPTER 28
LYDIA

"But *who* would wish me ill? I have hardly lived in Thornville for more than a month."

Edward lifted a shoulder, dropping into the chair beside me once more. "The threat has grown more specific. I think it would be wise to cease operating your Sunday school."

My mouth dropped open. Was he in earnest? "It is but a stone's throw from the house. Whatever could possibly befall me there? I cannot pay heed to these ridiculous threats when I've done nothing to warrant them." Mrs. Gunman immediately came to mind.

"What is it?" he asked, clearly reading my change of thought.

"Likely nothing. Mrs. Gunman was very opinionated last evening in regard to my school and the blight I am creating on Melton and Thornville by persevering. She explained that I was going to ruin our family name if I did not close down the Sunday school forthwith."

His mouth hung open, his eyebrows pulled together. "When did she say this?"

"When you were speaking to her husband, directly following our introduction."

"I missed it," he said.

I nodded. "You were otherwise occupied. But that is neither here nor there. The fact remains that I had never even met this woman and she felt quite strongly about my efforts with the Sunday school. She even knew it took place in the barn."

He scrubbed a hand down his face, an annoyed, guttural sound escaping his throat. "This blasted town and their interfering."

"But what I don't understand is the intensity of their disapproval. If they do not support the school, that is their prerogative. But sending me threatening notes? This is absurd and I do not wish to pay it any heed—regardless of what the person sending these notes expects."

Edward speared me with a look, his voice low as he spoke. "It would be foolish to pay it *no* heed. They have become more pointed and oddly specific. 'A loft is an easy place to find harm?' I am sorry, but you shall not be alone in the barn anymore, and neither will you walk through the woods to Morley cottage. I wish I had put my foot down at the start of this."

"I have not been alone at all. Elsie has been with me in both the loft and walking to Morley cottage."

"Which has likely kept you safe."

I stood, gripping my hands to my hips while I paced to the far wall and back. "This is absurd! I shall not believe for one moment that someone is so bothered by my teaching efforts that they are threatening my life. It does not add up."

"It is the only explanation," he said. "Unless you have brought with you an enemy that I am unaware of, we must assume this is the cause."

"Mr. Radmahl," I said at once, dropping my hands from my waist. "It must be him."

Edward paused, watching me warily. "He is not my favorite person, but even I can admit that placing him as our villain is a little farfetched."

I dropped into the chair. "I saw it last night at the ball for the first time; I readily admit that he has a special desire to use *me* to anger *you*. I do not know your history, but I realize that I am the pawn. He mentioned something to me at our very first dinner party with Lord and Lady Cameron that I dismissed then, but I wonder now if it is worth considering."

Edward's face was stone as he asked, "What did he say?"

"He mentioned my father winning a large and valuable game recently that would undoubtedly give him cause for joy. He told me to inquire with you if I wished to know more."

Silence reigned thick in the room. Women's muffled voices could still be heard down the hall within the drawing room and I swallowed, the look of distress on Edward's face troubling me.

"There was a large sum of money at play at one of our recent games," Edward admitted. "I assume Radmahl was referring to that."

Something was missing, but I would not push Edward now. We had much more pressing matters to concern ourselves with than the stakes of a night of cards.

But then, it was my possibly naive assumption that Edward had won a large sum of money from my father which allowed him to restore Thornville and subsequently cut off gambling. But *Father* had won the game which Radmahl referred to, so that did not add up.

I closed my eyes. Breathing deeply, I inhaled the scent of leather and smoke, restoring what little balance I could. "Have you questioned the servants about the notes?" I asked.

Edward nodded. He appeared relieved, perhaps that I had not pushed the other conversation. "No one saw anything. Even Miss Morley was surprised and lacked any useful information."

"But they will keep a vigilant eye in the future?"

A half-smile graced Edward's lips. "Our minds think alike. I did ask the servants to be mindful and watchful. And I've directed the footmen to keep watch over the front door and they've been on a rotation for over a week now."

"Then that is all we can do at this point." I rose, clasping my hands in front of me. "I will not cease teaching Samuel, and I will not turn away any other children who choose to brave the criticism. I owe them more than fear and cowardice."

Edward said nothing, so I moved to leave the room.

"Wait." He reached forward and clasped my hand, causing my heart to leap. "Will you let me know the moment you feel uneasy? Or if you see anything out of place? Whoever is leaving these notes has done so with magnificent stealth."

Intaking a small breath, I said, "I did see someone, once, in fact." His hand tightened on mine, and I continued. "It was impossible to see who it was, for they were very quick and the rain altered my visibility. But I ran into the loft and a feeling of unease stayed with me."

"Why didn't you mention it?"

"Because it was little more than a rustle of leaves and a general sense of discomfort. There was nothing to share."

"It is my duty, as your husband, to protect you. Promise me that we will keep no secrets in the future. Your life is not something I wish to wager."

"I promise." I smiled at him, the concern and firm gentleness he exuded lifting me up. But I was unable to shake the first of his sentiments. He was acting out of duty. He would do the same, regardless of who his wife was. I merely fell under his care; filled a line on his list of responsibilities.

"Very good." With a concise nod, he squeezed my fingers once more before releasing them. Pausing, he lifted a hand to smooth away a tendril of hair from my forehead and my breath caught. "Now, I think Sarah is waiting to meet you in the drawing room with the Misses Robinson. Shall we?"

Did I have a choice? Sighing, I took his arm. "I suppose we must."

The Misses Robinson occupied the sofa in the drawing room and a beautiful woman with light brown hair and green eyes sat opposite them. Her similarities to Edward were striking; had I not known she was his sister, I likely would have guessed the relationship regardless.

"Sarah, please meet my wife, Lydia."

I curtsied for her and she stood, crossing the room slowly with a small, cat-like grin on her lips. Dipping her head in acknowledgement, she said, "I am delighted. Please, come and sit. Miss Abigail was just informing me that you are to have a dinner party to celebrate your union."

Following her toward the grouping of chairs, I claimed the chair near Sarah, forcing Edward to retrieve the chair from the writing desk in the corner and set it beside mine. A small part of me rejoiced that he chose me from the group of women to sit beside, but he likely chose the space because it was farthest from the *gossiping old biddies*.

"I am to have a dinner party?" I inquired.

"On Thursday next," one of the older women said. I could not tell them apart and their equally blank smiles were not comforting.

Edward's sister—I did not know yet how to think of her for Edward had always used her Christian name when speaking about her and even our introduction had been uncomfortably informal—laughed a melodious, amused sound. "May I inquire why this celebration is occurring so far past the wedding date?"

The Misses Robinsons' expressions were identical visions of irritation. "Tradition," they said in unison, before glancing between one another. They stood, as though they'd planned to do so, and dipped in equivalent curtsies. "Good day to you all. We must be off."

Edward jumped to his feet to see the women out, leaving me alone with his sister in the calm quiet of the drawing room.

"Thornville is positively ancient, but I assume you've begun to grow used to it?" Miss Thornton said.

When no horse hooves or carriage wheels sounded outside, I peered out the window to see the women walking down the lane, arm in arm. At least I could appreciate their desire to walk from place to place. I turned back to my sister-in-law. "Yes, the house is growing on me."

She narrowed in on me, smiling in a way that did not reach her eyes. "It is nothing a little redecorating can't fix."

She prepared a cup of tea as though she was the hostess and handed it to me. I said nothing. The woman *had* been mistress of Thornville for nearly her whole life, so the habit was likely difficult for her to break.

I wanted to have the courage to ask her outright if she intended to stay. Working myself up to the point, I reworded the phrasing in my mind over and over again until the drawing room door opened, and Edward stepped back inside.

He lifted a folded sheet of paper in his hand and my stomach lurched. Another one?

"We've received an invitation from Lord and Lady Cameron to dine with them tomorrow evening. Shall I write back and inform them that we have a visitor?" he asked, looking pointedly at his sister.

She brought her teacup to her lips, sipping the liquid and watching her brother over the rim of her cup. "Whatever you wish to say, Edward. I am at your disposal."

Whatever could that mean? Was she here to stay as a guest for a short while, or had she come here to live?

The latter of the two options was infinitely less pleasing. Not that I didn't like her, but I could not imagine a scenario in which I resided under the same roof as this woman and felt any sense of comfort.

"I will write to them," Edward said, crossing to the desk. "I am sure they will include you in their invitation once they know you are here."

CHAPTER 29
EDWARD

I sat on the edge of the bed while Sarah busied herself at the table in the corner of her room, her maid putting up her hair for dinner while she told me of her time in Bath.

Glancing at me through the looking glass, she said, "You have a quiet wife, Edward."

I nodded. It was not a crime to be shy. "She merely needs to know you better."

She held my gaze a moment longer before sighing. "And then what does she become?"

I shook my head. My sister was opinionated and cunning and I could not imagine her and Lydia becoming fast friends. They were too different, and Sarah wouldn't be able to see Lydia's quiet strength. She would only consider her reserved demeanor a weakness. But Sarah had been forced to grow up at a young age when our parents died and Aunt took us in.

I did not blame her for her impetuousness and occasional spitefulness. She was a survivor. If that made her too quick to judge? Well, she had other redeeming qualities. I did not, however, appreciate the slight tone of bitterness laced into her words, though even for that I could identify a cause. Sarah wished to be married above all else and was sitting closer and closer to the shelf.

Clearing my throat, I said, "Radmahl is back."

She lifted a hand to halt her maid before turning around and staring at me, a few long curls trailing down her back which had yet to be secured to the knot. "Here, in Melton?" she inquired.

"Yes. He was recently in London, but he's followed me here."

She shook her head, scoffing. "You are disturbed, Edward. He was likely just returning home."

"Imagine what you wish, but I am sure Radmahl followed me here. He's never forgiven me for chasing you down."

She turned back toward the mirror. "Well, you did what you thought was best."

"And I would do it again," I said, loud and clear. Lest she get any ideas.

The room was stuffy with irritation and untold emotions, silence sitting thick while Sarah's maid completed her toilette. Once she helped Sarah into her slippers, she walked from the room, leaving the door open for us.

"Have things not changed for you, too?" Sarah finally asked. It was a question I had feared from her.

"They have not changed that much."

"You are free from your gaming debts and married to a woman who, I am sure, brought with her enough of a dowry to refurbish this horridly outdated house. And yet, she has done nothing. It forces me to question her intellect."

"Not everyone has the same priorities as you, Sarah. I am sure Lydia does not refine too much upon the color of drapes or state of the carpets."

"Any woman worth anything would care about the incessant red drapes. They are in every room on the ground floor, Edward. *Every* room."

I couldn't help but smile at the derision on her face. They

were just drapes. "Save your judgements until you know her. And you are wrong, by the way," I said, offering her my arm to lead her down to dinner.

Lifting one eyebrow, she asked, "Wrong about what, precisely?"

"She did not bring with her an enormous dowry. It was perfectly acceptable, but we shall not be living like lords anytime soon."

"If you say so," Sarah said, placing her hand on my arm. I couldn't help her disbelief. I was not about to inform her that I had wagered this house and lost it to Lydia's father. And I certainly would never tell her that Lydia's father had traded all of my debts for Lydia's hand in marriage.

If I ever told anyone, it would only be Lydia. No one else deserved to know.

Eager to return downstairs, I did not bother responding but merely led Sarah to the corridor. I was anxious to see Lydia, and not ashamed to admit it to myself. Regardless of my sister's opinions, Lydia had captivated me. Her selflessness regarding children, as well as her sharp wit and intelligent conversation were not obvious at first sight, perhaps, but they were there. The threats to her safety only heightened my desire to keep her close. Every moment she was not in my line of sight was concerning.

Lydia

Sarah did not need to like me. Her judgements were ridiculous, but I'd heard her speaking to Edward as I walked down the hall to go downstairs for dinner.

I had overheard her say how she questioned my intellect and was sure her brother only married me for my money.

Clenching my fist, I remained at the window as I heard Sarah and Edward enter the drawing room. I had been tempted, when I heard Sarah speaking of me, to remain and listen further to their conversation. But alas, I could not bring myself to eavesdrop on my husband. However far their voices carried, it did not feel right.

"Lydia," Edward said, and I turned around to face him. His smile reached his eyes, and he led his sister to the sofa before crossing the room toward me. He looked pleasantly satisfied in a way that he had not before. Though I could not put my finger on what it was, I *knew* he was glad to see me.

It caused my heart to flutter and I cast my eyes to the floor, uncertain what I was meant to feel. I was glad to see him, as well. My heart jumped whenever he entered a room. I looked forward to the moments I knew I would be spending in his presence.

"Are you well?" he asked.

I nodded. "Yes."

Dickson announced dinner and Edward immediately offered me his arm. We would eat informally, I assumed. Ever since Edward had changed the way we dined, placing me to his right instead of at the foot of the table, dinner had become infinitely more enjoyable.

Edward led me into the dining room and sat me at his right, walking around the table to seat Sarah at his left. I glanced up and found her watching me curiously and promptly glanced away.

Perhaps dinner would not be as enjoyable now as it used to be.

Sarah cleared her throat. "Aunt has found a new friend by the name of Harold Newsbury. Do you have the pleasure of knowing him, Edward?"

"I cannot say that I do," he answered politely.

"Well, I shall inform you of his character because it is vastly diverting. The man has stark white hair, for he must be a grandfather, at least, and he wears it quite long. He also has an affinity for purple, and I vow every article of clothing he wears is some shade of purple, besides his black walking stick. He has taken a fancy to Aunt and has begun trailing us about England. Last I heard, he arrived in Bath shortly before my arrival here."

"He sounds interesting, to be sure," Edward said, shooting me a look from the corner of his eye. Was he checking on me?

"Yes, and the best part is that he has begged Aunt to marry him five times over, at least," Sarah said, chuckling. "The old bird keeps refusing. But Harold Newsbury will not give up."

"You cannot be serious," Edward said, his fork suspended mid-air. "Who would become *that* smitten with her?"

"Harold Newsbury," Sarah said simply, taking a bite of her potatoes.

Shaking his head, Edward resumed eating. I could not appreciate the anecdote, as I had not met their aunt. Silently I spent the remainder of dinner hearing about the people they both knew, in such artful and cunning ways that I could never quite appreciate the whole story, while Edward seemed to grasp the whole of it.

"And can you believe Miss Pollard and Mr. Peterson?"

I perked up. Mr. Peterson, I did know. He was also a friend of my father's and I'd had the pleasure of conversing with him on occasion. I'd heard of his recent marriage just a few months ago, but nothing about his wife.

"It shocked me, too, I daresay," Edward responded.

"Not me," Sarah said with authority. "I had them pegged as soon as I arrived at that wretched house party. The way she watched him was telling."

Edward shrugged. "But Mr. Peterson? You could not have guessed his affections, surely."

"Of course I could. I did. He was a flirt with every woman present, but he was different with Miss Pollard. Besides, did you not notice how they constantly paired off together? It was not so odd when they announced their betrothal."

Edward turned toward me. "We recently attended a house party in which four of the guests ended up betrothed."

"How fascinating," I said.

"Though one of those engagements broke," Sarah added, matter-of-factly.

Edward shot his sister a look. "Yes, but the woman did marry a different man from that party." He turned sharply toward me. "Lord and Lady Stallsbury, in fact."

"Oh," I said. It was not my business, and I was not one to pry. If her engagement broke, then she must have had a good reason, for she ended up with a marquess.

There could be worse fates to such an experience.

I rose at the completion of the meal and Sarah followed me from the dining room and into the drawing room. Settling herself beside me on the sofa, she turned toward me.

"How are you enjoying Melton society?"

"It is interesting, to be sure. The Misses Robinson have been quite welcoming. And I've enjoyed Lady Cameron's company." I could not say the same for Mrs. Whitaker, who had not spoken to me beyond bland greetings since our conversation about the Sunday school, nor Miss Gould, who had not spoken to me at all. The Melton women were fickle, but thankfully Elsie remained constant.

"I'm not familiar with Lady Cameron, but I dearly love the Misses Robinson. Quite diverting, are they not?"

I could not help but feel that Sarah was mocking me in some way, but I couldn't figure out exactly why, or how. It was merely an impression, but it still left me eager, after an hour of stilted conversation in the drawing room, to remove to my bedchamber for the evening. I had watched the door for Edward's entrance, but had been vastly disappointed. I'd grown used to seeing him after dinner.

I stood. "I am tired. I hope you will excuse me."

"Of course," Sarah said magnanimously.

Halfway up the stairs, footsteps in the foyer forced me to pause, their deliberate, quick staccato causing me alarm.

I glanced back down and began descending the steps when Edward passed the foot of the stairs with determination.

"Edward," I called, causing him to halt and glance up the steps. "What is it?"

He immediately altered course, ascending the stairs until he reached me, standing at eye level. He picked up my hand and held it securely. "You are safe," he said.

My eyebrows drew together. I could tell at once that he was frightened. "What is it?"

Glancing over his shoulder and then above mine, he leaned in. "There has been another note."

"What did it say?"

"It is not what it said, but where it was found."

Cold washed through my body at the severity of his tone and the shiftiness of his eyes, as though nothing around us was safe.

"Edward," I whispered, "you are frightening me. Where was the note found?"

His swallow was audible. He read my eyes as though gauging how I felt.

"In your bedchamber."

CHAPTER 30
EDWARD

Her voice falling to a whisper, Lydia asked again, "What did the note say?"

I tried to ignore the fear evident in her eyes, but it pierced me. I had considered not telling her of it, but if I didn't tell her then she would have found my next request odd.

"It was not very different than the rest," I explained. "Come, let us go upstairs." I began to walk, tugging at her hand so she fell into step beside me. I led her to her bedchamber and paused at the threshold before following her inside. I'd spent many hours in Sarah's bedchamber as she'd readied for events or written her letters, but this was different. It felt entirely more intimate.

Lydia paused in the center of the room, looking about her for the note I'd ripped from the window and shoved in my pocket.

"I took it down," I explained, "but it was wedged in the windowpane."

"They accessed the room from outside?" she asked.

I shook my head. "Not possible. The window was locked."

The color drained from her face, causing my throat to

constrict. Whoever was tormenting us would pay, one way or another. "I will find out who is doing this," I said.

She nodded. The door opened behind us and two servants appeared, carrying a chaise lounge from downstairs. I stepped aside to allow them entrance and was suddenly overcome with insecurity about the notion that had driven me to order the chaise upstairs in the first place.

I waited for the servants to leave before turning back to Lydia. "I will sleep in here this evening," I explained.

She turned toward me sharply and I nodded to the chaise. "I will sleep on that, so you needn't be concerned."

Nodding slowly, her delicate eyebrows remained drawn together. I stepped closer. "I will not press myself upon you, but I will not sleep if I think you are in danger, either."

"What of your sister?"

"I have instructed the footmen to stand guard outside her door."

"And you cannot do the same for me?"

"It is not enough."

She was still and quiet, regarding me closely. She took a step toward me and my breath caught, my heart galloping faster than Rebel when I give him his head.

Swallowing, I stood still, allowing her to approach me. "Do you mind terribly if I stay?"

Shaking her head, she said, "No. You may stay."

My lips tipped into a smile, the warmth from her gaze filling my chest. I couldn't help it. I wanted her to know how I felt. Stepping closer, I reached down and lifted her hand, bringing her knuckles to my lips and bestowing a light kiss on the back of her gloved hand.

"I will give you half an hour to ready yourself for bed and then I shall return. There will be a man outside your door in the meantime, should you need anything."

She nodded, and I swept from the room. I could kiss her. I

planned to, in fact. But I would not do so when I was about to sleep in her room, for I did not wish to give her cause for alarm.

Perhaps tomorrow would present an appropriate opportunity. And if it did not, then I would create one.

Lydia

My heart was beating faster than Edward's galloping runaway mare. I watched him leave, waiting for the door to click shut behind him before dropping onto the edge of my bed and wrapping my arms around my waist. The man had said it *wasn't enough* to simply post a guard outside of my door.

Instead, he had to know for a surety that I was safe. I'd never felt so cared for in my entire life. Even if he was acting from duty...but, no. He could not be. I felt it innately within my soul that Edward acted from his heart. Whether he would ever be in love with me, I couldn't know, but he did care for me.

Maybe, he cared for me as I was beginning to truly care for him.

We'd built a proper foundation of friendship, and the affection blossoming from that solid base fed the hope I'd only tentatively allowed to blossom in my heart.

A small knock at the door preceded Christine, and she swept into the room ready to prepare me for bed. I submitted to her ministrations and allowed her to brush my long, wavy hair and secure it in a long braid down my back. Climbing into bed, I blew out all of the candles except for one and waited for Edward to return.

It was dark and dim when he came back, a stack of blankets in his arms. He was in shirtsleeves and breeches, and I did my best not to stare at his state of undress. It was far more than he likely wore to bed on a typical day, but I was grateful for the respect he chose to show me.

I turned away as he climbed onto the chaise, listening to the rustle of blankets as he settled in.

"You may blow out the light, Lydia."

I raised myself in bed to reach the candle and caught his eye just before extinguishing the flame. His dark eyes were secured on me and even in the depth of night I could feel them watching me. I slowly lowered myself back onto my pillow.

"Edward?" I asked.

"Hmm?"

"Thank you."

Silence sat in the room a moment longer before he cleared his throat softly. "It is my pleasure."

Lydia

It was a miracle that I obtained any sleep at all with Edward so close, his steady, heavy breathing filling the small room with rhythm. My mind worked tirelessly all night long to determine who could be at fault and why they were targeting me, but I was no closer to discovery by daybreak.

Sitting up in bed, I pulled the blankets up to my neck and glanced about, but it was empty. Edward had already left.

Swinging my legs around the side of the bed, I pushed myself up and crossed to pull the rope and ring for Christine. The sooner I could get dressed, the better.

Half an hour later I was dressed in a yellow muslin gown, my hair thrown up in a knot on the back of my head. Listening for

Edward's voice, I was disappointed to find the breakfast room empty besides a footman, and no one about the halls.

I was positive Sarah was still abed, since a footman remained posted outside her bedchamber door.

Forgoing breakfast, I checked the downstairs rooms but came up short. Drawing on my strength, I bravely let myself out the front door and crossed to the barn. Climbing the steps to the loft, I found it empty as well and lowered myself on a bale of hay. Edward must have been in the only room I did not have the courage to enter: his own.

Blowing out a hot breath of frustrated air, I crossed to the loft door and let it swing open, my gaze running along the hedge row of Blackthorn. It was spiky and dangerous. If only we could surround the entire house in Blackthorn. We may never be able to leave it again, but we would be safe.

CHAPTER 31
LYDIA

Edward had been on edge all day. I finally found him in the drawing room after my venture to the barn, and he was crazed and frightened, watching me with wide eyes while I explained my ridiculous—to him—notion of looking for him outside.

The remainder of the day passed in Edward's company, with Sarah occasionally joining us as well. Edward was taking his responsibility to protect me quite seriously; by the end of the day, I wondered at the necessity of the extra attention.

We filed into the carriage to ride to Downing Wood for the dinner party. Sarah sat beside me and I tucked my feet underneath the bench to keep out of Edward's way. His knees brushed mine as he got himself settled and his gaze immediately sought mine.

Turning for the window, I watched the trees pass us in the waning light, concentrating on the bare branches instead of my rolling stomach.

We arrived a short time later and Edward led me into the house, his sister trailing behind us.

Lord and Lady Stallsbury sat close beside one another on the sofa, with Elsie and Lord Cameron just opposite them. I pulled up short when the man on the ladder-back chair beside the sofa turned, his serious eye catching mine.

Mr. Radmahl.

Sarah gasped behind me and Edward's hand tightened on my arm. I felt time go still as the entire room seemed to hold its breath of one accord.

Elsie finally stood, breaking the silence. "Miss Thornton, I presume? I am Lady Cameron Nichols."

Sarah stepped forward and delivered a graceful curtsy. "It's a pleasure."

Clearing his throat, Edward stepped forward and made introductions around the room. He led me to an open seat and I hardly touched down on the cushion before the butler came into the room and announced dinner.

I felt a sense of repetition when Elsie announced that the dinner would be informal and we could sit by whomever we wished.

I caught Sarah's disturbed eyes as she suddenly searched out Edward's and knew, at once, that I must do something to put myself between her and Mr. Radmahl.

Mrs. Whitaker's words from the last dinner party I attended in this same house filtered through my mind. *He did not marry Sarah. Why would he settle for anyone less?*

Edward stood as well, shooting me a sincerely apologetic look before offering his arm to his sister.

Was everyone in the room aware of the awkward tension between the Thorntons and Mr. Radmahl? He gave me a tight smile as Mr. Radmahl, the only available gentleman, offered me his elbow and I took it, following the rest of the party into the dining room.

I had only known Sarah for a very short while, but I'd never before seen such quiet meekness from her. Her gaze remained fixed on her plate for the duration of the meal, and for the first time, Radmahl did not speak much either.

The remainder of the table guests seemed to trade stilted conversations, intermixed with sidelong glances at Sarah, Edward, Mr. Radmahl, and myself. I counted the moments until the evening would come to a blessed end.

Perhaps Edward would trust me with an explanation by the end of the evening. This was absolutely ridiculous.

When Elsie stood to signify the close of the meal, Sarah shot from her seat and bolted from the room in a gracefully speedy exit. I followed behind her, but by the time I reached the drawing room she was nowhere to be seen. Elsie glanced around the room before casting a worried glance my way.

"What can I do to help?" she asked.

"I hardly know her," I said, as Lady Stallsbury approached us. "I am not aware of the situation, merely that there is one."

Lady Stallsbury looked uneasy, glancing back over her shoulder toward the dining room. She gave me a no-nonsense look. "I think it is a safe assumption that everyone who sat at that table is aware that there is a *situation*."

"Quite true," Elsie said, lifting a shoulder apologetically.

I took a fortifying breath. "I must find her."

"I will help," Elsie said. She led us from the room, pointing down the hall. "Eleanor, will you look that way? Lydia, come with me."

I followed her toward the foyer and waited as she questioned her butler. She nodded once concisely before leading me to a small parlor down the corridor and nodding toward it. "I will leave you to speak with her. You may return to the drawing room if you wish, but I will not be offended if you choose to go home."

"Thank you, Elsie," I whispered, grateful for her kindness and understanding.

I opened the door to the parlor slowly, peeking my head

inside. Quick, ragged breathing reached my ears and my heart squeezed for my sister-in-law.

"Sarah?" I asked, softly.

A slight gasp met my ears, followed by sniffles.

"It is Lydia. May I come in?"

She did not reject me, but neither did she admit me. I waited a moment longer before hearing a soft, "Very well." I stepped into the dim room, closing the door behind me.

She sat on the rug in the center of the floor, her arms folded across the seat of a small sofa and her head bent down, resting upon her arms. Sobbing, she did not attempt to stem the flow of tears at my approach. I sat on the edge of the sofa beside hers, my hand hovering over her head before I swallowed my fear of rejection and began to stroke her hair.

She stilled at once and I did as well. But, the desire to be of help overcame my awkwardness and I continued, stroking her hair with my fingertips while she sat on the floor and cried.

We must have remained that way for a quarter of an hour, at least, before her sobs shuddered to a halt and her breathing regained something of a normal rhythm.

"What can I do for you?" I asked.

"I should like to go home," she replied.

Nodding, even though she was not looking at me, I said, "I will call for the carriage if you would like to remain here. I can make our excuses and return for you when everything is ready."

She nodded against the couch and I waited a moment in the event she would like to say something more. When the silence stretched long, I got to my feet and left the room.

Elsie was leading Edward toward me as I crossed the foyer. I explained what Sarah had asked for and he agreed at once, quickly preparing to leave.

"I am quite sorry," Elsie said. "I hadn't any idea…"

"Neither did I," I told her. "You are new to the area as well. You couldn't have known."

"But Mrs. Whitaker did mention something about it. I merely forgot."

Elsie's sorrowful eyes were more than I could bear, and I pulled her in for an embrace. "Truly," I said, "everything shall be fine. Thank you for a delicious meal."

She shot me a wry smile as Edward returned for me and I pointed to the room where Sarah was hiding. He nodded, his green eyes serious and his mouth set in a firm line as he left us to retrieve his sister.

Elsie leaned in and whispered, "You will keep me informed, will you not?"

"Yes, I shall."

The ride home was silent, and Sarah escaped the carriage the moment it rolled to a stop before running into the house. I turned to Edward, the shadows cast over his face making him look more grim than the situation called for.

"What was that about?" I asked.

He watched me a long moment. "Honestly?"

I sucked in a breath. He was trusting me? "Yes, Edward. *Honestly.*"

"The last time they saw one another, they were trying to elope."

Edward

Lydia was silent on the bench opposite me. The cold from outside was beginning to seep through the open door and chilled me.

I let out a pent up breath and rubbed my eyes. "They have a

history. Radmahl convinced Sarah to elope with him. I caught them just before they reached the border."

"Why didn't you tell me before?" Lydia asked.

"Because I did not wish to spread gossip. It was well contained when it happened, and no one knew of it. I paid off Radmahl and forced him to promise to remain silent on the matter. To my surprise, he has."

"But I am not a gossiper," she said. "And it would not be *gossip* to inform your wife about the character of such a man."

"I did try to inform you," I said. "But you did not heed my advice."

"Because you did not give me a reason. You merely requested that I stay away from him. For all I knew, you did not like him because he'd once glanced at you sideways. How was I to know of the serious nature of your concerns?"

I sighed, searching for her eyes but not finding them within the darkness. "I don't think we will ever reach an understanding on this topic. I merely wished you to trust me, and you did not."

"Funny, that," she said, laughing mirthlessly. I saw the outline of her hand as she reached forward to push the door open. "I wished for the same thing."

She lifted her skirts and hopped down onto the drive before walking into the house. I watched her go, irritation evident in the set of her stride. She had wished for *me* to trust *her*? Groaning, I scrubbed a hand over my face before following her into the house.

There was so much about women I did not understand.

Lydia

If he had only told me of the horrid nature of Mr. Radmahl's misdeeds, I gladly would have given Mr. Radmahl the cut direct and ignored him at every pass.

Guilt, however, slithered through my gut. Though I was loathe to admit it, Edward was correct. I should have just trusted him.

He, however, could have just trusted me, as well.

The fact that he did, eventually, fill me in was beside the point. He should have done so when we first arrived at Thornville.

Crossing the foyer, I turned sharply on the stairs and came face to face with a man. My scream ripped through the air before I could get it under control. A moment too late I noticed the livery and powdered wig, and I stepped back, resting my hand upon my speeding heart.

"What is it?" Edward called, running toward me.

"A footman." I turned to the servant. "I apologize if I gave you a fright."

He did little more than excuse himself and walk away, but the wideness to his eyes was telling and my cheeks grew warm.

I turned to speak to Edward and nearly ran into his cravat. Why was he so close? I stepped back so I could see his face, and said, "I believe we are all a little on edge."

His serious eyes did not give way to levity. "You frightened me," he finally said.

"I was frightened myself," I defended.

He watched me a moment longer before sighing. "I will sleep on the chaise again this evening. But I will not bother you for some time. I'll be in my study if you need me."

Nodding, I turned for the stairs.

"Lydia?" he called. I glanced back and waited, my hand resting on the bannister. He took a step toward me but then halted. "I will not allow any harm to befall you."

"I know, Edward," I said. I then reminded him, "It was merely a footman."

His stone face broke into a small smile. "Yes. That it was."

I turned and ascended the stairs, feeling Edward's gaze upon my back for the duration of my climb. Emotions were high, but I could not deny the rawness of his sentiments.

If I had not been sure before, I was nearly positive now: Edward cared for me. And, silly girl that I was, I cared for him as well.

CHAPTER 32
LYDIA

The morning sunlight brought with it the promise of a new beginning. I sat up, refreshed from my full night's rest, and stretched my arms high above my head.

It was Sunday, and that meant I got to teach Samuel today. And, if his friends chose to come with him, two more pupils as well.

I readied for church with the help of Christine and went directly to Sarah's room, knocking on the door and waiting for admittance. She called to me faintly and I opened the door, stepping inside before she could think better of letting me in. I was not surprised to find the woman in bed.

Her hair was in utter disarray and her eyes puffy, red, and swollen.

"I cannot leave the house like this."

I nodded in agreement, causing her to show the first sign of humor ever since the moment we'd stepped into Elsie's drawing room the evening before. A wry smile touched her lips before sorrowful self-pity fell over her face once more.

Hesitating at the edge of the room, I closed the door before crossing to her bed. Pulling a chair beside it, I sat down without waiting for her to invite me, and clasped my hands lightly in my lap. "I know of the elopement," I said.

Her face immediately transformed into an expression of defensive irritation so I spoke before she could. "Don't be angry at Edward. He did not tell me until last night. And I vow never to speak a word of it."

She was still angry, but my words seemed to pacify her slightly.

"Did you love him?" I asked.

She stared at me for a moment before tears gathered in her glassy eyes and rolled slowly down her cheeks. The green of her eyes was vibrant against the tears. She even looked beautiful in her grief. Nodding her head, she said, "Yes. I still do."

I felt sad for my sister-in-law; loving a man she could not be with had to be difficult to bear. "And Edward forbade the union?" I guessed.

She nodded. "He does not know Mr. Radmahl as I do, though. He does not understand."

I assumed that regardless of the misunderstanding between the siblings, Edward likely had a good reason for turning away Mr. Radmahl. It was neither the time nor the place, however, to make such an observation.

Rising, I said, "I must go. But if you need anything at all, you merely need to send for me."

She looked at me. "I did not think I would like you."

I tried not to take offense at her words, but she continued. "I don't mean that unkindly. I just did not think we would suit. You were so quiet. But I can see why Edward loves you. You are clearly a very good person."

I stilled. She'd said *loved* so casually. As if it was assumed that my husband cared for me in such a way. How she could deduce Edward's supposed love or my own goodness of character in a few short days of our knowing one another was beyond me, but I smiled just the same. I thanked her for her words before turning to go.

"I mean what I said," she called softly as I reached the door. "I appreciate what you've done for me."

Looking back over my shoulder, I nodded and then left.

As the day progressed, I could not remove her words from my mind no matter how hard I tried. I sat in the pew at church, stealing surreptitious glances at Edward and wondering at Sarah's observation. I could feel that the man cared for me. But *love*?

The sermon came to a close and I stood, following Edward from the church and toward our carriage. I sought Mr. Radmahl in the congregation but came up short. Was the man home grieving like Sarah?

Elsie sent me a little smile as I passed her, and I nodded back. I would see her soon at the barn. We were equally anticipating the likelihood of more students and I'd put in a special request that morning with Nora to bake a few extra sweets for the children. I figured, if no one else showed up this afternoon, then I would send the remainder of the sweets home with Samuel once more.

Edward was silent for the ride home. I took myself directly to the kitchen to check with Nora about the tea and was pleasantly surprised by the array of treats she had baked.

That my only guaranteed pupil was her nephew was likely part of the reason she had gone to so much effort with the detail work on the cakes, but I did not blame her. Little Samuel was worth it.

I picked up extra blankets on my way out to the loft and Edward called to me as I opened the front door.

"Yes?"

"Let me carry those for you," he said, reaching for the blankets.

"You needn't—"

"I am coming to the loft, remember? I cannot let you teach there alone. Not after those notes."

I tried to read his expression but he seemed equal parts annoyed and determined. "Very well. Have we received anymore notes?"

"No," he said, shaking his head. "But I am not going to take any chances."

He followed me to the loft and set the blankets on the end of one bench. I crossed the floor to open the loft door and let in more light when a dark bundle moving in the corner caused me to jump.

Upon closer examination, I made out the small form of a person. "Samuel?"

He looked up, his nose scrunched up. "It was warm in here," he said.

"Is it not warm in your own house?" I asked softly, crouching down to his level.

"It's warm," he said, lifting a shoulder. "I just like it here better."

"In a *loft*?" Edward asked in disbelief. I shot him a look of reproach and he lifted his hands in resignation before lowering himself onto the bench.

"You are welcome here anytime, Samuel. I hope you understand that."

He watched me a moment before nodding.

Nora came up the stairs then with a platter of food, a footman behind her carrying a tea tray laden with tea and more pies.

Samuel's eyes immediately lit up and he stood. "May I?" he asked. My heart soared at the simple improvement he'd made. The last time a tray was brought out, he'd instantly ran for it, grabbing at things with no decorum or manners.

"You may."

Elsie approached then, the smile lighting her face upon

seeing Samuel both sweet and sad, simultaneously. She picked up a blanket and immediately crossed to put it around Samuel's shoulders.

Footsteps sounded on the loft stairs and I caught Lady Stallsbury's smile as she stepped into the loft. "Good day," I said. "Welcome to Sunday school."

She nodded in acknowledgement and glanced around, taking in everything from the benches and blankets, to the tea and Samuel's little satisfied smile as he stuffed his mouth full of miniature cakes and pies. I supposed we ought to work on manners a little more.

"Thank you for allowing me to come," she said as she approached. "When Elsie told me about your project, I was absolutely fascinated and wished to see it for myself."

"Did your husbands accompany you?" Edward asked.

"Yes," Elsie said. "They were hoping to steal you for a game of billiards."

Edward smiled, glancing at me.

I nodded. "With three of us, I think we shall be fine."

He agreed, apparently, for he stood and bowed before leaving. Billiards would be vastly more enjoyable for him, I knew, and with both Elsie and Lady Stallsbury, I severely doubted that any harm would befall me.

I allowed the women to get settled and took my post at the front of my makeshift classroom when small, hesitant footsteps sounded on the stairs. I shared a glance with Elsie before moving to peek down the stairs. Two small, dirty children were climbing the stairs. Their blonde hair was stringy, and their clothing ragged.

"Welcome," I said softly. "Are you Lizzie and Jacob?"

Their eyes widened in surprise and I took that for a yes.

"Well, we have a tea tray here if you would like some. And some plates if you are hungry."

They crossed to Samuel and I heard him whisper, "I *told* you they had pies."

Jacob shot him a look full of cheek and I swallowed my chuckle.

I allowed the children time to fill their plates and find their seats before beginning. I introduced Elsie and Lady Stallsbury as my assistants, which they likely found humorous if their expressions were any indication. Class flew by with a basic introduction to the new students and a refresher for Samuel. They seemed easily distracted, so we finished our lesson quickly to allow the children time to eat more.

I stood beside my friends as the children left together and said, "I did not accomplish much teaching today, but I would like to think it was a success regardless."

"You filled their bellies," Lady Stallsbury said. "The academics will come in time."

I nodded. Turning back to the tea tray I filled three more glasses, preparing the tea and delivering the cups into Elsie and Lady Stallsbury's hands.

We sat on the benches in something of a circle, each of us with a blanket draped over our shoulders.

"Did you notice how little they wore?" Elsie asked.

"Yes," Lady Stallsbury agreed. "And it is freezing outside. Surely they have warmer coats."

"I can inquire with my cook. She is Samuel's aunt."

Elsie lowered her teacup. "If they do not, then I would like to arrange an outing with all three children to get them properly attired before the snow arrives."

"I have a feeling it will come to that," I said. "Are you certain?"

"Yes," she said without hesitation. "It is the least I can do."

CHAPTER 33
EDWARD

I found Lydia coming out of the servants' stairs long after our guests left. Was it not enough that I feared every time she was not in sight? Must she constantly disappear to the most obscure places, to boot.

"Must you hide from me?" I asked.

Her eyes widened as she stopped herself from running into me. Perhaps I should have waited to speak and allowed her to collide with me. I would not have minded. I shot out my hands to steady her and she took a step back, her eyebrows raised.

"Hiding?"

"Yes. In the barn yesterday. With the servants today. What have I done to deserve this?"

I noticed the moment she caught on to my teasing. "If you must know, Edward, I was speaking to Nora. We've discovered that Samuel does not have suitable clothing for winter, and neither do our other two students, if their lack of coats today was any clue."

"Let me guess," I said, rubbing my chin. "You are going to immediately begin knitting hats and scarves for your students."

Her eyes lit up. "What a grand notion! I can give them hats to accompany their new coats."

"New coats?" I questioned.

"And boots. Elsie is afraid they will not come to school after it snows if they do not have boots." She raised her eyebrows. "I am more afraid that they will still attend, but without proper footwear."

"You think very highly of your school."

"I think very highly of my cook," she countered. "And the children's hungry bellies which draw them to the school to eat."

I had been correct in my initial assumption. Lydia was the best sort of person. I could never be as good, regardless of how dearly I tried.

"What can I do to be of assistance?" I asked.

She looked at me closely before shaking her head. "There is nothing, really. I am planning to send a footman out tomorrow to request the children's presence here on Tuesday at noon, and then we shall take them into Melton to get them measured."

I reached forward, unable to stop myself, and brushed a curl away from her forehead. She stilled under my touch and I ran my knuckles down her jaw. "If only I could be half so kindhearted as you."

"You would do the same," she whispered.

Shaking my head, I cupped her cheek in my hand. "I would not think of it. Therein lies the difference."

"You do not do yourself justice. You are a kind man. I knew that from the first time we met. And since, your consideration for me has exceeded all of my expectations for marriage."

My heart began to gallop and I noted the very secluded corridor we stood in. Bringing my other hand to the other side of her face, I said, "At the ball?" I did not clearly recall meeting her the *first* time, but I did know it was at a ball.

She stiffened and I knew at once I had said the wrong thing.

"No, I suppose I should amend my comment. I knew from

our first meeting after our betrothal. You paid me notice and consideration and I valued it at once."

My fingers traced the soft skin of her cheekbone and the sides of her neck. "But not from the ball?"

She smiled and I felt the balls of her cheeks rise under my hands. "No, Edward. I did not think you paid me much consideration when you left me stranded in the ballroom and forgot to retrieve me for our dance."

My hands fell in accordance with my mouth and I stared at her, stunned. "What are you referring to?"

"The very first time we were introduced. You requested my hand for the quadrille and then did not come for me. I saw you dancing with Miss Hannigan instead."

"Who?" I could not for the life of me recall this scenario. And who was Miss Hannigan?

"She had dark hair, like me. But otherwise I would like to think we differ greatly in appearance."

All at once, the ball came back to me and the quadrille with it. I recalled the moment I went to retrieve the brunette—Miss Hannigan, evidently—and her confusion. I'd thought it odd at the time, but she had gone along with the dance anyway and I did not refine too much upon it.

I could clearly see now, however, my mistake. "I mistook Miss Hannigan for you."

Lydia watched me a moment. "If you say so," she said. "Though that is not a compliment."

I cringed. It would *never* be a compliment to be so wholly forgotten, particularly on a dance floor. I paused, the rest of the situation fully taking root in my mind. "And then you agreed to marry me only a week later?"

She gazed at me for a minute before saying, "I did not agree to anything, Edward. The arrangement was decided upon without my approval."

My head began to spin. She was an even better person than I

realized. The situation was agreed upon, documents signed, and notice sent to the paper without her knowledge.

"But your father wrote to me that he'd apprised you of the situation."

"He informed me that he had obtained a husband for me," she said. "And that I would marry you within three weeks."

I had realized, at the time, how vastly I was uprooting this woman's life. What had not occurred to me, however, was how it might affect her. She had seemed so aware and resigned to the marriage that I did not once ask if she minded marrying me.

Staring at this woman who I now loved, I ached for the situation I'd placed her in.

"I must write to Elsie and inform her of our updated plans," she said. I could see that she needed a moment to herself. These revelations were taking something of a toll on her as well, I was sure.

Stepping back, I bowed, allowing her to leave the hallway. She did so at once, with great speed. I only hoped it was emotion she was running from, and not me.

Lydia

My hands were shaking when I went into the drawing room and lowered myself at the writing desk. So it was true. Edward really had forgotten me almost immediately upon meeting. I did not know whether that made the situation better or worse, but his evident distress soothed my pride a fraction.

Pulling a sheet of paper from the desk, I immediately addressed it to Elsie and described what I had learned from Nora and how I planned to send a footman to the children's homes the next day to request their presence. I invited her to meet me at Thornville so we might all travel together and finished the note with a postscript that Lady Stallsbury—should she still be in residence and wish to come—was invited, as well.

Sanding the paper and setting it aside, I pulled out another blank sheet of paper and dipped my pen. Addressing this letter to Mrs. Coulter, I described to her our ongoing efforts with the Sunday school and the success I'd felt in obtaining two new students. I then proceeded to request advice in regard to teaching the children when they clearly were only coming for the food, and how I could teach varying levels and skills in the same hour.

By the time I sealed and directed that letter, I felt infinitely better. I might not know what I was doing, but I was sure Mrs. Coulter or her husband could give me enough advice to help.

Hesitating, I lifted another sheet of paper from the drawer and addressed it to my father before I could lose my determination. This letter took longer to compose, but by the time I'd reached its completion, my last bit of energy waned. I had begun the missive with gratitude that he'd found me such a goodly husband, then proceeded to inquire after his health. It was not until the end that I slipped in the question: *How, exactly, did you and Edward decide upon our betrothal?*

Sealing the letter before I could fully lose my nerve, I set it aside with the others and let out a long, weary breath. Leaning back in my chair, I did not hear the butler enter until he was clearing his throat beside me.

"Mrs. Thornton?"

"Yes?" I asked, sitting up tall in my chair. Concern was etched on his face and dread immediately pooled in my stomach. "What is it?"

"We've found another note."

CHAPTER 34
LYDIA

I found Edward upstairs, coming from Sarah's room, and met him on the landing.

"How is she?" I asked. I could feel the tension between us and wished it was not there. But I would not wish the things which had passed between us earlier unsaid. And neither could I erase the feel of his hands upon my face.

He shook his head, his eyes downtrodden. "She will recover. She only needs time."

"I happen to agree with you," I said.

His lips tilted up in a self-deprecating half-smile. "Did you need me?"

"Yes." I cleared my throat. "Dickson found this."

I reached forward and handed the sheet of paper to Edward, watching his face closely as he read the revealing statement.

"Radmahl."

I nodded. "I agree, it can be no other."

"But how did he get in Thornville's gates undetected?"

I shrugged. "I don't know. It has stumped Dickson as well. The footman at the gate has not left his post, and the man stationed in the barn to watch the drive did not see anyone either."

"This does not make sense," Edward snarled. Lifting the paper, he said, "At least now I have something to take to the magistrate."

Setting my hand softly on his arm, I gently said, "But if you take that to the magistrate, you will be revealing Sarah's part in the elopement as well. It will ruin her."

He looked down at the paper again and read aloud, *"You took what I love once, and now I will take what you love. Her heartbroken gaze during that dinner was the final straw, Thornton. I will make you pay."*

"He sounds so angry," I whispered.

"Do not fear. I will not let anything happen to you."

Lydia

The next two days passed slowly. Edward did not allow me to leave his side, and Sarah did not leave her bed. She was brokenhearted, I assumed, and I did not fault her sorrow.

Edward did, however, and showed her the notes to prove Radmahl's iniquity. I had watched from the doorway as Sarah merely cried harder, clutching the notes to her bosom and pronouncing that they only proved Radmahl's undying affection even more, now.

Against his sister's wishes, Edward rode out to the magistrate—who, incidentally, happened to be Mr. Gunman—and explained the situation. He returned home frustrated, for unless we caught Radmahl performing nefarious deeds or produced the threatening notes, he could do nothing for us.

And Edward would never produce the notes, not when they would put Sarah's reputation in such jeopardy.

I waited outside the house for my students to arrive at the arranged time. Edward was in the barn while the servants readied the carriage, and I stepped out onto the drive, turning in a slow circle to take in the surrounding space.

Blackthorn surrounded the house, thick and dangerous, and would never admit a small animal, let alone a man. Beyond that was an iron gate, tall and imposing, which would keep out anything else. It was confusing, but there *had* to be a way to slip past the footmen and approach the front door.

Three small children walked through the gate and came toward me, and I shoved the unease and discomfort away. This was about them.

The carriage pulled up with Edward already seated inside and I ushered the wide-eyed children toward the open door.

"What about Miss Elsie?" Samuel asked. Edward looked taken aback by the informal address, but he did not see Elsie with Samuel as I had.

"She will meet us at the shop," I said, soothing his worry. It was the right thing to say, for Samuel climbed in immediately and Lizzie and Jacob followed him soon after.

I took a seat beside Edward and then we were off. The children were fun to watch. I was fairly certain they hadn't ridden in such a fine carriage before, and their expressions were positively adorable. I shared a look with Edward when he moved aside the drapes behind us and Lizzie gasped, taking in the world as it passed us by. It warmed my heart in ways I couldn't define.

If the carriage ride was amusing, the modiste's shop was significantly better. The children were awed by the vast amount of fabrics and ribbons, though graciously, they kept their hands to themselves.

The modiste got to work immediately measuring the children and pulling thick, heavy fabrics for them to choose between. I opted to go with the wool, but the children wanted humorously different things. Jacob was smitten with the sheep's wool, and Samuel with the fur.

Elsie came into the shop as Samuel was being measured, her husband just behind her. I caught a worried glance on Edward's face but he did not seem inclined to speak, so I turned to welcome them.

"Are you quite thrilled to be in this fancy shop?" Elsie asked, getting down to the level of the children.

I watched Lord Cameron gaze at his wife with admiration, before he looked to the children and the blood drained from his face.

"Lord Cameron?" I asked, but he did not seem to hear me.

Elsie did, however, and turned back. She stood at once, crossing to her husband and laying a hand on his arm. "What is it?" she asked in hushed tones.

He gulped. "Nothing," he said, shaking his head. "I only…it is nothing."

Elsie appeared as unconvinced as I felt. Only Edward looked between us with a grim expression on his face.

"It is just…" Lord Cameron paused, looking at the children through narrowed eyes. "It is merely a coincidence, that is all."

"*What* is a coincidence?" Elsie asked.

He looked at her and said, "You will think this is crazy. But we have a painting in our family home of Geoffrey, Tarquin, Rosalynn and me as children, and that boy there is the spitting image of Tarquin. In fact," he said, looking back at the children, "he looks very similar to Geoff as well."

Elsie smiled up at her husband and I felt the desire to leave the room and give them a moment to talk. As it was, I could not leave the children alone.

"That is Samuel," she explained. "Perhaps now you see why I have developed such a fondness for the boy."

I turned away from them but paused at the clear distress on Edward's face. "Are you unwell?" I asked.

He looked to me for help, as one might when they felt helpless or afraid. "No," he finally said. "We must finish our business and return to Sarah. I don't like leaving her long."

Something was not right, and it had nothing to do with Sarah. The very distress on Edward's face when Lord Cameron stepped into the modiste's shop was plain to see, and his helplessness was apparent. What I did not understand, was the secret he was holding, or why he could not simply explain himself.

I watched as though from afar as the children were helped and the modiste settled with Edward and Lord Cameron. Elsie helped me corral the children together and walk them to her library to choose a book which we would begin to read during our Sunday school. All the while they were choosing, I stood at the back of the room and observed.

"Have you finished *Pride and Prejudice* yet?" Elsie asked, approaching me.

"Not quite. We are very close to the end but have not found time to read recently."

"We?"

"I read to Edward," I explained. "Sometimes. In the evenings."

"How lovely," she said.

I could not help but smile. "Yes. I happen to agree."

"Tell me," she continued, "do you know much about Samuel's parentage?"

I wanted to give her the answer she sought, but I did not have it. "I am sorry, I know nothing more than what I've already shared with you."

She smiled at me, but disappointment was clear on her face. "It is nothing you must apologize for."

I glanced to the window and saw Lord Cameron and Edward speaking in the street. They seemed deep in conversation and I only hoped it would not derail this precious day for these sweet children.

CHAPTER 35
EDWARD

My heart beat rapidly as I stood beside Lord Cameron outside of the Whitakers' school while our wives were inside helping their students choose a book.

"I cannot shake it," he said, literally shaking his head. "That boy is precisely the spitting image of my brother at that same age."

"How old was Tarquin when the painting was commissioned?"

Lord Cameron cast his gaze up. "If I had to guess, he was around five."

"And Geoff?" I knew where this was headed, but I wanted Lord Cameron to discern it for himself. He was nearly there, he only needed a little prodding.

"Probably closer to eight."

"And you were a toddler, if I am doing the correct math. I suppose he looks like Tarquin because they are around the same age."

I let that piece of information dangle for a moment, gazing at the windows of the lending library and searching for Lydia's outline. She was standing so close to Lady Cameron that I could not quite determine which shadow belonged to whom.

"Thornton," Lord Cameron said, his voice low. "How old is that boy in there?"

"I'm not precisely sure, but he is around six years old."

"And his mother?"

I looked at him then. "Died in childbirth."

"Where was she from?"

"London," I said.

He paused, his eyes boring into mine. "And how did Samuel come to reside in Melton?"

"I was asked by a friend to find a home for him outside of the London slums, where he could grow up in the country, taken care of by his aunt and grandmother."

Though we were outside, the air grew thick between us. A carriage passed by us on the street and I waited for Lord Cameron to ask the question which I knew was coming.

"Who asked this of you?"

I held my tongue. "I promised I would never say."

His eyes drifted closed as he let his head drop back.

I gave him a moment to compose himself. Minutes later, he said, "I would believe Geoffrey capable of such a thing if not for the request he gave you. Geoffrey did not care for anyone but himself. He would not have *cared* about this boy enough to arrange a home for him."

I shook my head. "You are mistaken. He held Samuel, agreed to the name, and then walked away."

Lord Cameron's eyes locked on mine. "When you phrase it like that, it is very believable indeed."

The secret was revealed, though not entirely of my own doing. I comforted myself that I had not broken it outright, but that Lord Cameron had deduced it for himself. "I do believe, as odd as it sounds, that Geoff loved Samuel's mother in a way," I said. "He never would have married her, of course. But I believe he did love her."

Lord Cameron looked to the school, his eyes solemn. He nodded once and released a shuddering breath. "I don't know what this is going to do to Elsie."

"Then do not tell her."

He looked at me suddenly, shock in his eyes. "I could not keep such a secret from her. Not when part of her knew all along. She even mentioned to me once how Samuel looked like I might have as a little boy. But Elsie has never seen the painting, so she would not have made the connection on her own."

"But if it is going to bring her pain to know that Samuel is your blood nephew, then why tell her?" I did not understand. He could save her so much pain.

"Because we are partners," Lord Cameron said. "We are honest with one another, always, and work through our trials side by side. If we did not do that, we would not have so much joy and satisfaction. It is through selflessness and communication that we have built a marriage full of trust and compassion."

I was tempted to ask him if that was something he really thought, or something Lady Cameron had convinced him to believe. But I could see in his eyes that he believed his own words, and it struck me.

"Shall we?" Lord Cameron asked. "I am eager to get back to Elsie."

I indicated the stairway up to the house. "After you."

Edward

The children chose a book and we bid Lord and Lady Cameron farewell as Lydia and I loaded them into the carriage to deliver them home.

"Lord and Lady Stallsbury were sad to have missed it," Lydia said as she sat beside me in the carriage, "but they shall attend the wedding dinner on Thursday."

I grumbled low so as not to bother the children. They were distracted by the peppermints Elsie had procured for each of them, however, and were not paying attention to us. I felt distracted as well, for I was certain Lord Cameron was explaining Samuel's genealogy to his wife right now.

"How long are they planning to be in Melton?" I asked.

Lydia shook her head. "I don't know. But I like Lady Stallsbury very much. It is a shame they do not live closer."

I couldn't help but smile. "An hour's ride would not be too horrible for most people, but I can see how the prospect is unappealing to you."

She shot me a wry smile and I reached for her hand, on impulse, squeezing her fingers gently within my own.

"If I could take away your sickness from riding within a carriage, I would."

Her gaze sought mine, a solemn look about her eyes. She nodded, before glancing to the window; I knew she was doing so to stem her discomfort.

The children were delivered to their homes and we pulled into Thornville's drive. I helped Lydia out and up the steps to the house before following her into the foyer.

"I believe I would like to finish reading *Pride and Prejudice*," Lydia said. "Would you like to join me?"

"Yes," I said at once. "I have not endured the majority of the book only to *not* discover how it ends."

"Endured?" she teased, leading me to the drawing room.

"Well, if I am being honest, then that is something of a

stretch. I suppose I ought to admit that I have enjoyed it very much."

She paused, turning to me, and my heart squeezed. Would it be very inappropriate to admit that I loved her in the brightness of the drawing room with little to celebrate outside of finishing a novel together?

I supposed it beat Darcy's first proposal by yards.

"What was it that you said to Lord Cameron?" she asked, catching me off guard. "He seemed very disturbed when you came into the lending library."

She was astute. How did I ever think I could get away without telling her? I considered Lord Cameron's words and my mind traveled quickly over the course of Lydia's and my relationship. Perhaps if I had been honest from the beginning, we would have reached the point of love and harmony more quickly and avoided the trouble with Radmahl.

"Samuel is their nephew," I confessed, and felt a weight leave my shoulders.

She stared at me, stunned. "Elsie was correct. He *is* the spitting image of her husband as a boy."

"Indeed. Samuel is the son of Lord Cameron's eldest, deceased brother."

"Oh, how terrible. But how did he come to be here?"

I did not speak. I merely watched her make the connections on her own.

"You," she said.

"Yes," I confirmed. "I was acquainted with Lord Stallsbury—that was Geoffrey's title, at the time—and he felt he could trust me. He knew me from our younger years at Eton and that I had an estate in Northumberland where I would be able to find a home for Samuel far from London."

"It was kind of you to help him," she said softly. "I cannot imagine it was easy."

I shrugged. "It was not very difficult. Samuel's grandmother and aunt were willing to go, and even more willing to accept the money Lord Stallsbury had offered."

Nodding, Lydia looked up at me with admiration. "All the same, it was a good thing you did."

I smiled, enjoying her praise and basking in her esteem. Stepping closer, I trailed a finger down her cheek. "Do you think you've made a mistake, Lydia, in following your father's direction and marrying this flawed gambler?"

She looked into my eyes as though she could read my soul. I felt the draw to her lips and could not help but wrap my hands around her waist. I looked into her eyes, allowing her a moment to refuse me, when she said, "I do not regret it."

The words were like a fire beneath me and spurred me into action. Sweeping Lydia into my arms, I bent my head and pressed my lips to hers. Heat rushed through me, igniting my soul and reiterating that the woman in my arms held my heart.

A throat cleared behind us, forcing me to crash back upon the earth in an uncomfortable wave. I turned, without releasing Lydia, prepared to dismiss immediately whoever dared to interrupt us.

Mrs. Patton stood nearby, her face white and a note clutched in her hand.

"What is it?"

"I am sorry to disturb you, sir, but Miss Thornton is missing."

CHAPTER 36
LYDIA

I stood within the circle of Edward's arms, my heart reeling from that kiss—that amazing, heartstopping, glorious kiss—and blinked.

"What do you mean?" Edward asked.

Mrs. Patton reached forward with the note and Edward released me to snatch it from her hands. I read the note over his shoulder.

Meet me at noon beside the north stream. I will have the curricle ready.

"He cannot be serious!" Edward expostulated. "Drive her over the border in a *curricle*? It simply is not done."

"But it is fast," I said. "And I am sure that is their top priority."

Edward looked to me as though I'd sprouted antlers. His eyes softened momentarily, and I wondered if he was recalling the kiss like I had been.

I had been ever so close to admitting to him that I loved him, but now no longer seemed the perfect time.

"I must go after them." He turned to Mrs. Patton. "Tell Dickson to have Rebel saddled straight away."

"Edward, think this through." I tried to calm him with my voice. "You've been down this road before."

"Literally," he mumbled.

I pressed on. "If they are not hidden by a carriage, then anyone could have seen them drive away together, and when their marriage is announced, will easily deduce the scandal. What can you do to stop it now?"

"I can stop *him*," he said. He looked away before focusing on me again, gripping my shoulders tightly. "Lydia, I am not evil. I do not approve of Radmahl, and clearly he has proven his depravity with these blasted notes. But if the scoundrel wants to marry Sarah, and she clearly wants the same as well, then I will no longer stand in their way. But they must do so in a church, *properly*, and not over the anvil."

I sucked in a breath. "Then you must go."

He clutched me to him, stealing my lips with his own once more. I hardly had time to grip the back of his coat before he tore himself away, a wild look in his eyes. "Will you be safe?" he asked, hoarsely.

"The threat is on his way to Scotland," I reminded him. "I will be very safe."

With a final glance, he was off. His boots pounded up the stairs, most likely to change before the journey, and within minutes he was flying out the door. I stood at the drawing room window and watched him race out of Thornville's front gates.

Casting a prayer up for his and Sarah's safety, I lowered myself on the sofa and prepared to wait.

Lydia

The remainder of the day passed excruciatingly slowly, and the night, even more so. I felt exhausted by the following morning but forced myself out of bed to inquire with the servants about any updates. I had hoped Edward and Sarah would have returned in the night, but I was sorely disappointed.

Taking myself back upstairs, I let myself into Sarah's room to search for anything which might indicate that she was taken against her will. I needed to know, I think, that she had made this choice herself.

A minor search brought nothing forward above a small bottle of extremely expensive scent and the gowns she chose to leave behind. Which, it seemed, appeared to be most of them.

I sat on the edge of her bed and imagined how Mr. Radmahl might have gotten a note to her when she did not leave her bedchamber.

In fact, it was likely the same way he had been able to get a note into my bedchamber, and past the footmen in the front of the house. I'd examined the depth of the Blackthorn myself, and it seemed now that the answer had quite literally been staring us in the face.

Standing, I rang the bell pull and waited, pleased when Mrs. Patton, herself, entered the room instead of a lower maid. "How was the note delivered to Sarah?" I asked at once.

Surprise played on her features but she had been trained well and it was quickly masked. "I do not know."

"The note had to get past the servants. Surely someone would have noticed a tall, red-haired man who snuck into the house and up the stairs."

She watched me, silent.

"In fact," I continued, "it had to be a servant who had easy, ready access to Sarah in order to deliver the note without frightening her. Which indicates it was probably a woman."

Mrs. Patton watched me, her eyes as wide as saucers. "I don't know what you mean, ma'am."

"Actually, Mrs. Patton, I believe you do. What I am having a hard time determining is *why* you did it."

We stood in Sarah's room, the silence engulfing us. I had no secure way to prove it was Mrs. Patton, and she was not about to confess.

"Perhaps," I said, "I shall have to ask Mr. Radmahl when he returns with Edward. Or I could ask Sarah. I am sure she will be happy to explain it to me."

The color drained from Mrs. Patton's face and I knew I had won.

"Will you just tell me why?" I asked.

The silence stretched and I was convinced she would not speak, when she finally said, "Mr. Thornton. He left us here without so much as a visit in years. When the money stopped coming in and Dickson wrote about the cook leaving last year, we received no word and no extra funds to procure a cook ourselves. I've eaten that wretched stew for an entire year, and Mr. Thornton did *nothing* to stop it."

"And because of his negligence you deemed it appropriate to assist Mr. Radmahl in terrorizing us?"

She did not back down and I was disgusted by her.

"You are dismissed," I said. "It would likely be in your best interest to be gone before Edward returns."

Her gaze pierced through me but I held my ground. "My wages?" she asked.

"I will give you the wages you are owed, but nothing more."

Turning away from me, she hurried from the room and I felt drained. But my job was not over yet. I needed to go down to the study and determine what Mrs. Patton was owed so I might be able to send her on her way. I let myself into the study and sat at Edward's desk, pulling drawers out one at a time until I found the correct ledger.

Opening the book wide on the desk, I found the servants' wages and calculated what I needed to give to Mrs. Patton. I was about to shut the book when something caught my eye, and I peered closer.

A line, dated just before our wedding, declared the amount of debt Edward had accumulated. Shock reverberated through my body and I sat, stunned, as my eyes traveled to the line below, where it stated, *James paid debts.* The box beside the note indicated the balance of Edward's debts paid in full.

When Father announced that he obtained a husband for me, what he really meant is that he had sold me. All of Edward's debts, for my hand in marriage.

Given my conversation with Edward about the ball where he had mistaken me for Miss Hannigan, he had most likely made the agreement without even understanding who he was agreeing to wed.

I slumped down in Edward's desk chair and my heart fell to my feet.

I was not a woman admired or loved. I was a commodity.

After a few more moments of wallowing in shock and disbelief, I took myself upstairs and rang for Christine to help me out of my stays. Whether Edward returned in an hour or in a day, it was irrelevant to me. I had not slept the night before, and I was going to make up for that lack now.

CHAPTER 37
EDWARD

The road from Scotland felt longer than it was and as I trotted down the tree-lined lane to Thornville, my heart swelled with anticipation. Sarah and her new husband were off to the continent for a wedding trip and I was going to sleep for two days straight.

After I greeted Lydia, of course.

Approaching the iron gate, I saw Mrs. Patton hovering behind the edge of the Blackthorn hedge, clearly wishing not to be seen. I tipped my hat to her and she froze upon recognition.

"Mrs. Patton?" I called. "Are you unwell?"

She shook her head, training her gaze at the ground. Rebel was antsy, his hooves prancing uneasily on the ground. Turning for the barn, I trotted away from the housekeeper. Odd, that.

"Dickson," I said, as I stepped into the house after delivering my horse. "What has gotten into Mrs. Patton?"

He looked away uneasily. "Perhaps that is better coming from Mrs. Thornton. But I will say that I had no idea, sir."

Confusion swirled within me. "Where might I find Mrs. Thornton?"

"She is sleeping, sir."

Well, the day only grew more and more strange. In our few short months of marriage I'd never once known Lydia to sleep during the day. It was a blessing, perhaps, for it allowed me time to remove the dirt from the road and the stench of Rebel from my person.

Taking my time to prepare for dinner, I could not help but grin. My teeth were widely displayed as I dashed down the stairs. I checked the drawing room first, but it was still empty, before taking myself to my study.

The absence was only causing my eagerness to grow. The burden of caring for Sarah was officially lifted from my shoulders and placed upon Radmahl's, and regardless of how little I thought of the man, he was no pauper. Sarah would be taken care of.

The sight of the ledger open upon my desk was odd. I lowered myself in my chair, sweeping my gaze down the page for new entries.

Nothing.

Beginning at the top, I froze. This was not the most recent page, but the one prior which outlined, in embarrassing detail, my massive debts.

Had Lydia seen this? Her father told me he'd explained our situation to her, but I could not imagine him outlining exactly how deeply I was in debt. Would she think very little of me with this new information?

Or, maybe it was not Lydia at all. Perhaps it was Dickson.

I rang for Dickson and he arrived moments later. "Have you been in here?" I asked. I attempted to sound calm, but I could hear the panic in my own voice.

"No, sir. I believe Mrs. Thornton accessed this room to determine what was owed before authorizing me to settle with Mrs. Patton."

"Settle?" I could not wrap my mind around the events which

had transpired at Thornville since I left to chase after Sarah. I shook my head. "I must speak with Lydia."

"Yes?" a soft voice said from the doorway. I glanced up and my heart jumped at the lovely woman framed by the light from the open drapes. The fire roared and cracked beside me in the hearth but sound and time seemed to halt.

I stood. "I am confused," I said lamely.

"So am I," she responded, her voice low and hard. I realized in that moment that she was not smiling at me. She actually looked quite perturbed.

Oh, dear. She *had* read the ledger.

"It is in the past," I said. "I know how it makes me look, but can we not put this behind us?"

Dickson moved to leave the room and I felt my cheeks warm. I had forgotten he was there, as I only had eyes for my wife.

Lydia stepped aside to allow Dickson room to pass her and I stepped around the front of my desk, pausing when she turned serious eyes on me.

"Well?" she said. "What do you have to say for yourself?"

CHAPTER 38
LYDIA

I could see at once that Edward had no idea to what I referred. His green eyes were wide and he sat back against the edge of his desk, folding his arms over his chest.

"Perhaps we ought to step back first," he said. "What happened with Mrs. Patton?"

I remained standing on the other side of the room as I said, "She was responsible for delivering the notes."

He could not appear more comical if he'd tried and I swallowed the humor I felt. I was not ready to feel joy. I needed to understand, first.

"How?" he asked.

"She had access. I did not ask her for the particulars, but she aided Mr. Radmahl to get revenge on you for leaving her without funds, consideration, or a cook for the last year."

His grin was wry. "Yes, that is true. But I could not send funds which I didn't possess."

I sought the ledger where he left it open on the desk. Clearly, he hadn't had funds.

"She was very bitter," I said.

He sighed, running a hand down his face. "I don't blame her.

Though she could have spoken to me instead of terrorizing us. I hope you dismissed her right away."

"I did. I asked Dickson to settle the remaining amount she was owed and she has left."

He nodded.

Swallowing, I said, "And what of Sarah?"

Looking up, Edward seemed to relax, his shoulders settling back. "I was too late. They'd already married by the time I crossed the border. But it is done now and while I am disappointed and will likely despise Radmahl for the remainder of my life, he will provide well for her."

"Will you allow them to return to Thornville?"

"Eventually, if they wish to visit. But they have left for a wedding trip to the Continent, and I do not need to concern myself with that for some time. Sarah explained that they plan to remain away from London for long enough to allow the rumors to spread and then die down."

"Probably wise of them," I agreed. "I am surprised you are taking this so well."

He lifted one shoulder in a shrug. Narrowing his gaze on me, his voice deepened and he said, "I have other things on my mind. And the burden of caring for Sarah is on Radmahl now, so there is nothing more I can do. There is no sense in worrying anymore."

The room was thick with the things I had not yet had the courage to address. Judging by the unease on Edward's face, he did not want to bring those things up, either. But if we didn't, we might never reach an accord again.

Gathering courage, I drew in a steadying breath and took a step forward. It would be better to know the truth than replay the scenario I had created in my mind. "How did you and my father decide upon our engagement?"

He stared at me, stunned. Clearly this was not the question

he had anticipated. Clearing his throat, he straightened himself. "Did he not tell you?"

Shaking my head, I waited for him to continue.

"He told me he had informed you." He waited, but so did I. I would not speak until I understood. Running a hand through his hair, he huffed out a frustrated breath. "It is all very unsavory. Are you certain you wish to know?"

"Yes."

"Very well. We wagered Thornville in a game of cards. Your father won."

"What has that to do with me?" I asked.

"He offered to allow me to keep my house and pay off my gaming debts if I agreed to marry you."

I felt the blow to my stomach like a hammer. It was *worse* than I'd imagined. Father had offered Edward a deal he could not refuse. I moved toward the sitting area and lowered myself into a chair, waiting for my feelings to catch up with me.

He continued, though his voice sounded strained. "I took the deal and married you right away. I was pleased with the woman I'd agreed to wed, and grateful for your kindness and thoughtfulness. I believed we could form a friendship. But what I did not count on was falling in love with you, Lydia."

I sucked in a breath. "And have you?"

He crossed the room and knelt before my chair. "Our origin was not ordinary, perhaps, and I was slow to appreciate you. It took me time to value honesty and realize the importance of communication. But I have righted my errors and I am completely and irrevocably in love with you. Lydia, you hold my heart."

I gazed down into his sincere, green eyes and my heart soared. I loved him too, but I couldn't convince my mouth to open and say as much. He reached forward and clasped both of my hands, holding them above my knees as he remained kneeling.

"I do not regret my decision. Many people in arranged marriages are not so fortunate as I, and I thank the heavens above that I was blessed with you. Please forgive me for not being honest in the beginning. Had I known that the agreement was unknown to you, I would have insisted your father inform you."

"It is in the past," I heard myself say. "And I cannot refine too much upon it if I wish to move forward. It was wrong of me not to trust your judgment, and I think we can safely agree that we both have improved greatly through our short marriage."

Nodding, he said, "I must ask you again. Do you regret marrying me?"

I gazed at him for a long moment. I knew the answer, but I wanted him to know that it was sincere. Pulling my hands from his tight grasp, I framed his face, cupping his cheeks. "Edward, I could never regret that choice. Not when it led me to you."

His smile was brilliant as he stood up quickly and I leaned back in surprise. Pulling me to my feet, he wrapped me in an embrace, burying his face in my hair.

"Thank you, Lydia."

"What for?"

He pulled back, smiling at me with the smitten expression of a lovesick fool. I would be lying if I said that I didn't love it. "For being mine."

CHAPTER 39
LYDIA

We stepped out of the carriage and onto the gravel drive lined with torches. The Robinson sisters had written to us and expressly begged us to arrive early so we might be there to greet our guests, and we obediently arrived a quarter of an hour early.

The Robinson house was larger than I had anticipated. I had assumed the sisters were not wealthy, but judging by the house they lived in, I was sorely mistaken. Edward placed my hand within the fold of his elbow, and I grinned at him before squeezing his arm.

"Are you prepared to face Melton society?" he asked.

"Now that I know they are merely perturbed by my school and not threatening me because of it, I am no longer afraid of their selfish snubs. If they cannot find value in teaching young, poor children, then I need not count them among my friends."

"Well said."

We entered the stately home and the butler took our coats before leading us into a parlor. It was snug, but well decorated, and the Robinson sisters pounced on us right away.

Miss Abigail craned her neck to see around us. "Miss Thornton did not come with you?"

"No," I said. "As I wrote to you, she will not be able to make it this evening."

Miss Robinson tsked. "What a shame."

Edward shot them a smile. "I must thank you ladies for the thoughtful gesture."

Both of the older women smiled coyly, dipping their heads in pleasure. "It was the least we could do for a Thornton man."

I did my best to keep my gaze from Edward's face, for fear that if I caught his eye, I would lose my calm reserve and chuckle. Miss Abigail led us to the sofa and sat close beside me while Edward took my other side. She inquired about the Sunday school, which surprised me, and I informed her of my three students and how they were progressing.

I was proud of Samuel's efforts. He was doing far better than my maid, who struggled with the concepts of sounding words out. Of course, we hadn't had much time recently to devote to our lessons, but that was a fault I intended to rectify.

The door opened to admit Mr. and Mrs. Stockman, with the vicar, Mr. Cartwright, close behind them. They were all cordial, though they did pay more attention to Edward than they did me. I tried not to be offended by it. I stood by my earlier words: I would not quit teaching those children for all the friends in the world.

The butler stepped inside once more and announced, "Lord and Lady Cameron; Lord and Lady Stallsbury."

Comfort settled over my shoulders at once. The people who would not think less of me for my work with the Sunday school were here. Both women in the party looked radiant, carrying themselves with poise and elegance. Lady Stallsbury's gown was particularly stunning, light pink silk with an embroidered sheer overlay which flowed as she walked, causing her to look like an angel.

I remained seated beside Miss Abigail, for I did not wish to be rude, but I sent Elsie and Lady Stallsbury a smile which they both returned immediately.

"Do you play the pianoforte?" Miss Abigail asked beside me.

"I do not," I said at once. "I have a very rudimentary knowledge of how to play but I never quite took to it."

"For shame," Miss Abigail said. "I should have loved to be entertained this evening."

I caught Lord Stallsbury glancing at his wife with his eyebrows raised as they took their seats on a vacant sofa beside the fire. He seemed to receive an answer to his unspoken question, for he said, "I am sure my wife would be glad to play for you."

Lady Stallsbury said, "Yes, I do quite enjoy it."

A few more people trickled in and it did not take long to discern that the Misses Robinson did not do anything by halves. Anyone with any claim to fortune or title was present in this room, as far as I could tell.

We were directed into dinner and it was a lavish affair with more courses than Edward and I usually bothered with. It was with blessed relief that the women were excused, and I was able to find a comfortable corner of the room to stand beside Elsie and Lady Stallsbury.

"Dare I ask?" I said to Elsie the moment we were separated from the other women. It was an organic split and I did not feel the least as though I was hiding away from the older Melton society ladies—even though that was precisely what I was doing.

Elsie seemed to sense the purpose behind my question and her eyes widened slightly as she nodded. "I can clearly see the resemblance, as I've told you before, but the knowledge of Samuel's lineage was a right shock to both Cameron and myself."

"And Tarquin, as well," Lady Stallsbury added. "I never knew the former Lord Stallsbury, but I'd heard of his reputation."

Elsie nodded knowingly. "Cameron and Tarquin would like to properly meet the boy. In fact," she said, glancing away as if for listening ears, "I would like to speak to Mrs. Morley about taking him on."

Drawing a sharp intake of air, I gasped. "I've met his grandmother, Elsie. I don't think she'll be amenable to the idea."

"I hope she will. It seems as though she hardly pays Samuel any notice as it is. One would only think we were doing her a favor by taking the boy off her hands."

"Yes, but he is the only piece left of her deceased daughter."

"And he is the only piece left of Cameron's deceased brother. I think we have a chance."

The determination in her eyes was something to behold. I almost believed she *did* have a chance, solely because of how firmly she believed it to be true.

Lady Stallsbury stepped closer, lowering her voice. "Tarquin and Cameron would like to approach her tomorrow, but I told them it was probably better for Elsie to go alone. What do you think?"

I hadn't been asked such an important question before, and I fumbled for an answer. The woman was old and bothered and didn't care about running her own daughter ragged as long as she was bringing in money—at least, that was how it felt when she permitted Nora to be our cook as long as she could keep up her mending.

"I wonder," I said slowly, "if your mother heart does not sway her, if money will."

The women stared at me and my cheeks blushed pink. It sounded horrible the moment it left my mouth, but I did stand by it.

"That is a thought I hadn't considered," Lady Stallsbury said. "It is sad, but it does have merit."

"Hmmm," was all Elsie replied, her mind clearly working.

"What of little Samuel, though?" I asked, my voice gentle. "Will he have any say on the matter?"

"Certainly," Elsie said. "But I am confident he will not be opposed to coming to live with me."

I reached forward to squeeze her hand. "He would be lucky to have you for a mother."

She gave me a small smile and I pulled back, afraid of raising her hopes, only for them to be dashed on the morrow.

The men came in the room then and my heart leapt at the sight of Edward, walking beside Lord Stallsbury. Would my heart do that every time Edward entered a room for the rest of my life? I sure hoped it would.

"Lady Stallsbury," Miss Robinson called. "Will you be willing to play for us now?"

"Certainly."

We took seats upon the sofas and chairs surrounding the room as Lady Stallsbury readied herself at the pianoforte. I noticed that she did not use sheet music and when she opened her mouth to sing, I was struck by her glorious soprano. Her voice was positively breathtaking, and her playing well done.

I relaxed in my chair and imagined my own children playing with Elsie's as we sat by and watched.

Glancing at Edward, I caught his eye and smiled comfortably. He was the best sort of man, and I was grateful he was mine.

EPILOGUE
LYDIA

Three Months Later

I paced the drawing room, tempted to peel back the curtains and glance outside to the front garden. I paused on the carpet, debating the merit, when my shoulders slumped and I resumed my pacing. I could not do that to Edward. He'd planned this surprise for weeks now, he told me, and he would be heartbroken if I ruined it now.

My hand came to rest on my belly and I smiled. There was no mistaking it now, I was certainly with child. Little did Edward know, I had a wonderful surprise to share with him as well.

The drawing room door opened and Dickson stepped inside, proffering a platter. I took the letter sitting there and dismissed Dickson. It was from Father.

We'd written back and forth over the last few months and he'd done nothing but avoid answering my initial question. It led me to believe that he knew his actions were questionable, so

I chose, in my last letter, to explain that I was well aware of the origin of my own betrothal and that my darling husband had explained the whole of it to me.

Clutching the letter tightly, I stared at Father's familiar scrawl. Would he avoid the answer now?

There was only one way to find out. I broke the seal, unfolding the thick paper and read without delay.

Lydia-

You were always too intelligent for your own good. I should have known I wouldn't be able to avoid this forever. Perhaps I ought to have asked Thornton to promise secrecy.

Alas, I suppose I owe you an explanation. That is what you believe, is it not? I have two good reasons for my actions. The first: without my assistance, you would have eventually become an old maid. It was not lost on me that you chose to avoid men who posed a particular threat to your unmarried state. And while I love you, I do wish to have grandchildren someday.

The second: Thornton is a good man. Yes, he was not wise in wagering his house, but he was desperate. And I was of the opinion that he saw the error of his ways when he lost the house and it was likely the push he needed to correct his behavior. In every other regard, I could not have wished for a better man for you, Lydia, and I hope you can see my good intentions with the match.

I am glad you are happy. Perhaps you will come for the Season and enjoy yourself this time?

Father

Folding the letter, I had to chuckle to myself. When he laid his intentions out so plainly, I was surprised I hadn't deduced them for myself already. It was so very like him to decide that I was avoiding marriage and take it upon himself to rectify the situation.

Crossing to the writing desk, I tucked the note inside for later and glanced at the door as it creaked open once more. Edward came inside, a decided lightness to his step. I could not help but smile lovingly at him; I was sure I looked silly in my devotion.

"Are you ready?" he asked.

"Absolutely."

He grinned, grasping my hand and leading me from the drawing room, through the foyer and to the front door. He spun to face me and said, "I shall carry you from this point, but don't be alarmed. I want you to close your eyes."

I shut them obediently and squealed when Edward's arm came under my knees and swept me into the air. I threw my arms around his neck and held tightly. "Do you feel safe?" he inquired, his voice hardly above a whisper.

"Yes," I replied.

I heard the front door open and felt the sunlight on my face when we stepped outside and walked down the steps. We crossed a good deal of earth before Edward paused.

"We are here."

"May I open my eyes?"

He drew in a breath and then said, "Yes."

Still held in Edward's arms, I opened my eyes and gasped. The entire hedgerow of Blackthorn was no longer spiky and dangerous, but covered in beautiful white blossoms. It was lovely and pure and wreathed Thornville in an ethereal halo.

"It's beautiful," I said reverently.

"This was why my mother chose this particular plant."

Nodding, I said, "I can see why now." Peeling my gaze from the lovely image of our home, I looked at Edward, my face mere inches from his. "I have a surprise for you as well."

He frowned. I tightened my hands around his neck.

"What is it?" he asked.

I waited a moment, unsure of how to tell him. I'd imagined multiple scenarios which were all equally acceptable, but when it came to saying the words, I faltered.

"You're beginning to worry me," he said softly.

Quickly, I put his mind at ease. "It is nothing concerning. It is quite good news, actually."

His eyes snapped to mine and he gazed at me a moment until the pieces clicked together and he knew. "You are going to have a baby?"

"I am," I said, unable to soften my grin even the slightest bit.

He appeared stunned. "I am going to be a father?" he reiterated.

I nodded. "And you will be a wonderful father."

Suddenly he spun me around and I clutched him tighter, laughing at the motion.

"What in heaven's name is going on here?" a voice called from the gate. Edward turned me and the world still spun a little, my stomach growing queasier than the action necessitated. Elsie stood in the road, framed by the iron gate. Her hands were clasped before her and Lord Cameron approached behind her.

"We are dancing," Edward explained. "You couldn't tell?"

Elsie's smile was brief. "I did not mean to interrupt. I merely stopped to admire your flowers."

I wanted to ask if she was coming from a visit to see Samuel but held my tongue. His grandmother had denied Elsie's claim to him and every other tactic she'd used to convince Mrs. Morley to let Samuel go.

I was of the opinion that the woman's pride stood in her way. But perhaps I did not guess her character correctly and she truly loved her grandson.

"I also," Elsie said, approaching us, "was hoping to see you. I have something to share."

"As do we," Edward said quickly. He set me on the ground and I could have groaned aloud were Elsie and Lord Cameron not so close. It was not a good time to tell our friends of our growing family when they'd left the boy they wished could be their son only minutes before.

Elsie paused, looking to me. There was nothing I could say at this point to put it off. She was so astute, she'd likely already caught on. Surely it was Edward's glowing countenance which did us in.

"Yes, it is true. I am expecting." I lifted a hand. "Though it is early, still."

Elsie's radiant smile was quite the opposite thing I had expected to see from her. She crossed the distance and pulled me into an embrace. "I am so thrilled for you," she said, pulling back.

"You have news as well?" I prompted, glancing between her and her husband.

"You shall *never* credit it," she said, "but Mrs. Morley has finally agreed."

I gasped. "You mean it? She will let you adopt Samuel?"

She nodded, tears forming in her eyes. "We have agreed to pay her a sum for her troubles, but it is nothing compared to the joy he will bring to our home."

"Where is he?" I asked.

"Morley cottage," Lord Cameron said. "We must return with the funds and then he can come home with us."

Edward clapped Lord Cameron on the back. "Good news, man."

"Indeed," Elsie said with feeling. "I only wished we'd had the foresight to drive the carriage instead of walking today so we might be done with this transaction sooner." Her face pulled into a frown. "It feels odd, like Samuel has become a commodity."

Edward and I shared a look. "You are a good person, Elsie. It does not matter how Samuel becomes a part of your family. The wonderful thing is that he will be."

"I suppose there is truth to that," she said. "Now if you'll forgive me, I am eager to be on my way."

"I shall see you at Sunday school tomorrow?" I asked. Our class had grown to fourteen pupils and I did not think I could handle them on my own.

"Absolutely," Elsie called as she turned to go. I'd never seen her walk so fast in the length of time I'd known her, and it did not surprise me one bit.

We moved to return to the house and Edward paused just before the door, spinning me around to face him.

"Thank you," he said.

"What for?"

He smiled, moving a curl away from my forehead. "For being mine."

"I believe, Mr. Thornton," I said, reaching up on tiptoe to kiss his nose, "that the pleasure is all mine."

Air was sucked from my lungs as Edward swooped down and lifted me against his chest once more, his face a breath away from my own.

"I love you," he said simply.

"And I love—" Edward cut me off, his mouth crashing down on mine. I tightened my arms around his neck and kissed him with all of the joy I possessed. When he backed away and let me catch my breath, I chuckled at his unapologetic grin.

"You were saying?" he asked.

"You, Edward. I was saying that I love *you*."

AUTHOR'S NOTE

While Thomas Coulter and his wife, Mrs. Coulter, were fictional characters, they were inspired by a real man by the name of Thomas Cranfield and his wife. I came across his name while down the rabbit hole of research, where I went on to read about him in his memoir (written by his son) and was struck by his story. A pioneer in free education for the poor, Thomas Cranfield worked tirelessly to start Sunday schools across the slums in early Regency and Victorian London. One particularly touching story was a time when he realized that a large portion of children had quit coming to school because they did not have sufficient shoes for the snow, so Thomas Cranfield's wife took it upon herself to make the necessary items for each child who needed them in order to attend school. I decided that a selfless man who cared so deeply for such a worthy cause needed a place in this story and chose to have him inspire Lydia as he inspired me.

SNEAK PEEK
LOVE IN THE BALLROOM

Chapter One

My hammock rocked and swayed with the boat and I sucked in a deep, stale breath of damp air. In a week's time when I finally stepped foot in London, the very first thing I planned to do was soak in a hot bath. The second: to eat a large, hearty meal until I became deliriously full.

A smile formed on my face of its own accord and I used my boot to push away from the wall, swinging my hammock even more.

"John, you've got a stomach of steel," Dyer called from his bed on the other side of the narrow lodging hall below deck. "I get queasy just watching you swing."

"The motion has never bothered me," I reminded him.

Dyer groaned, shutting his eyes and shaking his head. "I will kiss the ground the moment we land and never touch a boat again for the remainder of my days."

I chuckled.

"Distract me," Dyer said, and I wanted to curse. I'd only created the blasted game to keep him from casting up his accounts in a particularly angry storm a few days back. Now he wouldn't let me quit.

"Please?" he begged.

"Fine. What do you want to know?"

"The letter. Read the letter again."

Casting my gaze to the low ceiling, I sighed. "Very well." I fished the note from my sack of belongings which hung on the wall beside me. "Mr. John Wilkins," I began. Stating my own name had felt funny the first time, but now I'd grown used to it. "I have written to inform you that Noah Clarke has died, leaving me as executor of his will. Within said will he states that you, a John Wilkins, are named guardian of his younger sister, Charlotte Clarke.

"Miss Clarke, aged seventeen, remains in the care of her elder sister, Mrs. Eleanor Wheeler, with myself as controller over her funds until we receive word from you regarding how you would like to proceed. She is in possession of four thousand pounds at the present time.

"I understand you have business in Barbados and I await your further direction. Until that time, I will act in accordance to Mr. Clarke's will however I see fit. Sincerely, Mr. Lynch."

Dyer laughed and I could have swat him. "You have all the luck," he said. "Imagine being placed guardian over a beautiful, rich young woman. Do you think she's lovely?"

"I haven't the faintest idea if she's beautiful or rich, and neither do I care. She might be horse-faced or snub-nosed. It hardly matters to me."

He laughed, and I could see that the repetitive conversation we'd had multiple times already was doing its job and distracting him from his sickness. "You realize that you must care for this young woman when you return. She has become your ward."

"I do," I said. "And I have a plan."

Dyer watched me. This variation on our conversation was new to him. I had yet to inform him of my plan.

"Well?" he asked.

I couldn't help but smile at his lack of social graces. Barbados would do that to a man. "I shall marry her off as quick as I'm able—if she has not married already—and be done with it. You know..." I paused, unsure if I should reveal this to him.

"What do I know?"

"Well...this is all by accident."

"What do you mean?" Dyer asked.

Shoving the letter back into my sack, I closed my eyes and leaned back in my hammock. "This relation. I am not Noah Clarke's cousin, though I am aware it is what he was led to believe."

I peeked over the rim of my hammock to catch Dyer's face screwing up in confusion. "I don't follow."

I leaned back again and watched the ceiling. "I am not even related to this family by blood. I was taken in as a small child and my mother reared me as her own. But I never met this branch of the family. When Noah Clarke named me the guardian of his younger sister, he must have been quite desperate, for I do not know them at all."

Dyer tsked. "What shall you do?"

"What I've already mentioned. Marry this woman off to the first man who glances her way."

About the Author

Kasey Stockton is a staunch lover of all things romantic. She doesn't discriminate between genres and enjoys a wide variety of happily ever afters. Drawn to the Regency period at a young age when gifted a copy of *Sense and Sensibility* by her grandmother, Kasey initially began writing Regency romances. She has since written in a variety of genres, but all of her titles fall under clean romance. A native of northern California, she now resides in Texas with her own prince charming and their three children. When not reading, writing, or binge-watching chick flicks, she enjoys running, cutting hair, and anything chocolate.

Made in United States
North Haven, CT
29 December 2025